W9-BUK-642

W

Shelton, Gene
  Brazos dreamer

DATE DUE		
AUG 1 3 1993		
SEP 1 4 1993		
SEP 2 9 1993		
OCT 1 9 1993		
NOV 1 9 1993		
JAN 1 1 1994		
JAN 2 5 1994		
AUG 1 7 1994		

TEXAS LEGENDS ★ BOOK 5

Brazos Dreamer

The Story of Major Robert S. Neighbors

GENE SHELTON

A DOUBLE D WESTERN
DOUBLEDAY
New York London Toronto Sydney Auckland

A Double D Western
PUBLISHED BY DOUBLEDAY
a division of Bantam Doubleday Dell Publishing Group, Inc.
1540 Broadway, New York, New York 10036

Double D Western, Doubleday,
and the portrayal of the letters DD
are trademarks of Doubleday, a division of
Bantam Doubleday Dell Publishing Group, Inc.

Library of Congress Cataloging-in-Publication Data

Shelton, Gene.
Brazos dreamer: the story of Major Robert S. Neighbors
Gene Shelton.—1st ed.
    p.   cm.—(A Double D western) (Texas legends; bk. 5)
1. Neighbors, Robert Simpson, 1815–1849—Fiction. 2. Indian agents—Texas—
Fiction. 3. Comanche Indians—Fiction. 4. Texas—History—Fiction. I. Title.
II. Series: Shelton, Gene. Texas legends; bk. 5.
PS3569.H39364B73   1993
813'.54—dc20   93-16243
CIP

ISBN 0-385-42491-4

To Greg—

Author, editor, publisher and longtime friend of Western writers, who developed the concept of this series and offered it to me at a time when I desperately needed a morale and career boost, this work is dedicated with gratitude.

—Gene Shelton

FOREWORD

This is a work of fiction based on the life of Major Robert Simpson Neighbors, Texas Indian agent in the turbulent years of westward frontier expansion—a man who was a respected friend of the native Texas tribes and who spent his adult life in the crossfire of prejudice and politics while attempting to help the Indians find a permanent home, peace and a place in the sun.

Many of the individuals portrayed in this work actually existed, but the reader should draw no conclusions as to their actual characters, motivations and actions on the basis of this story.

Every effort has been made, within the framework of the fiction novel, to portray as accurately as possible the actual dates, locations and sequence of events that shaped the life of Major Robert Neighbors and his role in the history of the State of Texas.

ACKNOWLEDGMENTS

The author wishes to express his gratitude to the staff of the Archives Department of the East Texas State University Library in Commerce, Texas, who were never too busy to help research the life and times of a man about whom little has been written.

Thanks also to the staff of the Dallas Public Library and the Sulphur Springs Public Library for their help in tracking down many details crucial to the development of the novel.

Among the many scholarly works made available by the librarians and private historians, Kenneth Franklin Neighbors's book, *Robert Simpson Neighbors and the American Frontier,* proved to be an invaluable source.

Other works which provided substantial information and detail included Rupert Norval Richardson's *The Comanche Barrier to South Plains Settlement;* Robert A. Trennert, Jr.'s *Alternative to Extinction;* Walter Prescott Webb's *The Texas Rangers;* W. W. Newcomb, Jr.'s *The Indians of Texas;* and literally dozens of monographs and scholarly studies by writers from several states.

And finally, a special thanks to fellow members of the Western Writers of America, Inc., for their individual help, encouragement and comradeship.

TEXAS LEGENDS ★ BOOK 5

ONE

Texas Frontier
April 1849

Robert Simpson Neighbors pulled his big bay gelding to a halt on a rock-studded knoll and stared at the buzzards circling above the Colorado River a quarter mile beyond the ridge.

The birds meant only one thing this deep in Comanche country. Indians. The big birds always followed roving Comanche bands. They fed on camp carrion and often on human flesh when the Indians were on a raiding expedition.

And this sky was full of buzzards.

The birds rode the currents above the Colorado for almost a mile, the more distant ones mere specks in the clear spring air.

Robert Neighbors twisted his six-foot-two frame in the saddle and glanced at the smaller man alongside. The sunbrowned face of veteran Texas Ranger and Indian-fighter John S. "Rip" Ford was drawn into a deep scowl as he stared at the circling birds.

"Looks like we've got company, Rip," Neighbors said casually.

Ford shifted the chew of tobacco to the other cheek, turned his head and spat. "Company, hell," Ford said, "there's a regular damned redskinned regiment out there." Ford's right hand dropped to the scarred stock of the rifle slung in the saddle boot at his stirrup. "What's your pleasure, Major? If it comes to a fight, eight men might be in a touch of trouble if there's a Comanche under every buzzard up ahead."

Robert Neighbors hadn't worn a uniform or held military rank since his days as acting quartermaster of the Texas Army during the Mexican War, but the tag "Major" had stuck. No one called him Robert or Bob, just "Major." He gazed back toward the Colorado, then nodded at a distant figure on horseback. The warrior seemed to simply materialize at the top of the ridge overlooking the river. "We've been spotted, Rip. Might as well ride on in and bluff it out."

Rip Ford glanced at the burly man at his side. "Major," he said, "I think that time you spent in the Mexican lockup scrambled your head. Or maybe you've just got too much sun here lately." He sighed. "What the hell. I've been studying for years to get scalped. Might as well get it over with before my hair all falls out on its own. I reckon the eight of us can surround them easy enough."

Robert Neighbors grinned to himself. There was no fear in Rip Ford's tone. The Major had known Ford long enough to realize the wiry soldier-frontiersman feared no man or beast. A man didn't ride through Santa Anna's army and fight Indians in his spare time if he spooked at shadows. Or Comanches.

Neighbors glanced over his shoulder at the other men in the small exploration team, two white frontiersmen and four Indian guides. They were a little more cautious than Rip Ford. The Major heard the murmur of worried voices from the group. "Nothing to fret about, men," he said. "I know that Indian up ahead. Rides with Sanaco's band of the Panetekas. I've known Sanaco for years. He's not likely to try to lift anybody's hair without a reason, so just keep your hands away from your guns and don't do anything foolish."

Rip Ford glanced at Robert Neighbors and snorted in mock disgust. "Dammit, Major, is there one savage in Texas you don't know on a first-name basis?"

The Major shrugged. "A few. But a man doesn't serve as Indian agent more than four years without meeting up with most of them. We might as well find out if Sanaco's in a good mood today." He touched heels to the big bay and took the lead as the small troop neared the solitary mounted warrior on the ridge.

The Major raised a hand in greeting. "Little Elk," he said in the Comanche tongue, "it is good to see you again. I grieve with you for the loss of your brother." He pointedly did not use the dead man's name. To do so might call forth the ghost of the departed. Comanches had less fear of ghosts than other tribes, but they still tended to the cautious side where spirits were concerned.

The Comanche stared into the Major's eyes. Open contempt and anger showed in the warrior's gaze. "The white man killed my brother. He brought the disease among us."

The Major nodded. Smallpox had not been one of the finer gifts the white man gave the Indian. "It is a sad thing. The loss of a fine young warrior . . ." His voice trailed away for a moment, the silence a sign of respect for the bereaved. "Is Sanaco in the camp? I would speak with him, Little Elk."

The Comanche turned his horse about without reply. The Major followed, letting the warrior lead the way. Neighbors heard Rip Ford's low whistle of surprise as they topped the bank overlooking the Colorado. "Damn," Ford said, "there must be ten thousand Comanches down there."

"Maybe not quite that many," the Major said as his gaze swept the sprawling camp, "but it's one of the biggest gatherings I've seen outside of treaty councils." The scene was similar to many others the Major had witnessed in his previous visits among the Comanches. It differed only in scope. This camp was huge. Lodges dotted the banks of the Colorado as far as the eye could follow. The north end of the Indian encampment lay out of sight beyond a bend in the river. Shields and lances decorated for war leaned against buffalo hide lodges. A smattering of the men carried rifles; most still used the lance, war axe, bow and arrow. The warriors lounged about, sharpening knives, smoking, talking or resting with the day's hunt done.

None of the women idled away the time. Some sat before lodges, plaiting ropes of rawhide or horse hair. Others tended cooking pots, carried water and nursed babies. Still others plucked fruit from berry thickets that grew wild along the river. A few knelt over fresh hides, scraping away the remnants of flesh and fat in preparation for tanning. Several were busy butchering deer and other game downed by their hunter husbands, cutting strips of meat to dry in the sun or smoke on racks of tree limbs placed over slow fires in pits. Young girls sat beside their mothers, helping if they were old enough or watching and learning if they were too small to lend a hand.

Throughout the camp young boys played at games designed to teach and test skills that would be needed as they grew to manhood. Scores of yelping dogs charged from the camp toward the approaching riders. In the days before the horse, dogs had been the beasts of burden of the Comanches. Now they were less useful except in times of extreme hunger. Then they went into the cooking pots.

One cur dashed out to nip at the heels of Rip Ford's sorrel and caught a hoof alongside the ear for his troubles. The dog fled with its tail between its legs, high-pitched yelps marking the sudden switch from brash bravery to wounded cowardice.

Across the river and downstream a vast herd of Indian ponies grazed on the rich green grass of the western slopes or stood knee-deep in water to escape the bothersome heel flies. The herd was under the watchful eye of a few braves and a number of boys on the verge of manhood. The Major knew that many of the horses likely had been stolen—from Mexican ranchers, Texas settlers or the so-called "tame" Indian tribes—but he also knew he wouldn't raise the issue during this visit. There was a time and place for all things. This was not a time to go hunting trouble.

Little Elk led the small column through a growing throng of curious children and yapping dogs as warriors edged toward their weapons and watched the procession, suspicion reflected in clenched jaws and dark eyes. Little Elk stopped before the largest lodge. A buffalo hide shield outside the lodge boasted decorations of bear teeth, scalps and horse tails. The teeth told the world the shield's owner was a great hunter; the scalps that he was a great warrior; and the horse's tails that he was a great raider.

Little Elk called out. A moment later the flap of the lodge opened. The man who stepped out was medium height, heavy of chest and leg, and his bare torso carried several scars. His cheeks and chin were painted red, with ocher and black stripes along the eyes and across the broad forehead. *Sanaco's painted for war*, the Major thought. *Somebody is due for some serious trouble.*

Sanaco wore the traditional leather leggings and breechclout of the southern Comanches, disdaining the cotton shirts and trousers that many others of his band had adopted from the Texans. His only white man's accouterments were a battered flat-crowned black beaver hat and a Colt pistol in a U.S. Army holster at his hip. He stood for a moment and stared without expression at the big man on the bay, then casually lifted a hand.

The Major stepped from the saddle and nodded a greeting. "Sanaco, it is good to see you," he said. "It is long since we sat in council. How goes the hunt?"

"It goes well," Sanaco said, his tone flat and without expression. The Comanche's painted face showed no emotion as he gazed past Neighbors at the other members of the party.

The Major made the introductions. Sanaco had heard the stories about Rip Ford; the expression that flickered in the Comanche's obsidian eyes told Neighbors the chief was not overwhelmed with joy at the former Texas Ranger's presence. Sanaco showed little interest in the other two white men. But the chief frowned in open contempt at the presence of the Indian guides, a Delaware, two Shawnees and a Choctaw. The Major sensed that the "white man's Indians" would wind up spitted over a slow fire if Sanaco had his way.

"You are far from the white man's country," Sanaco said. It was a question as much as a statement. "We will talk of this later. You and your friends are welcome in Sanaco's camp, Bear-Who-Walks-Like-Man. You may set up your camp where you wish."

The Major touched fingers to his hat brim in salute as Sanaco turned away, flipped the skin flap of his tepee aside and disappeared into his lodge. Before the entry flap fell, the Major caught a glimpse of a young woman lounging on a blanket with her skirts awry. *Can't think of a better reason to delay a parley,* he thought. *Sanaco must have added a fourth wife since our last meeting.*

The Major turned back to the men in the scouting party. The two Shawnees looked wary. Sanaco had little patience with former allies turned enemies, and they knew it. The Delaware and Choctaw sat outwardly impassive. One of the whites, a slightly built man named Alpheus Neal, looked even more jumpy than the Shawnees.

"Relax, Alpheus," the Major said. "We're guests here. A Comanche can lie, cheat and steal with the best of white men, but he'll never harm a guest—as long as the guest behaves himself. That would cost him status in the tribe."

The comment didn't seem to reassure Neal. The slender frontiersman's face had gone a few shades paler than normal.

The Major strode toward the river, looking for a good camping spot not already occupied. Rip Ford walked alongside. "Bear-Who-Walks-Like-Man," Ford said with a chuckle. "Damn me for a chicken-eatin' Methodist preacher if the name doesn't fit. Any part of that pelt you call a skin would make a top scalp for a brave to brag on. It would make big medicine hanging from a lance or war shield."

The Major had to grin himself. His Comanche name was not widely known outside the Paneteka band, but he had to admit it was descriptive enough. Robert Simpson Neighbors was as hairy as he was big. His thick forearms were covered with hair and a patch of wiry fur showed at the throat of his sun-faded blue cotton shirt. Reddish-brown hair covered the tops of his ears and tumbled past his collar. He wore a beard that extended from sideburns down square jaws and covered his chin. He kept his lips, cheekbones and neck shaved. The hair framed blue eyes in a broad face that, for some reason he could never quite understand, the ladies considered handsome.

The Major found an unoccupied stretch of sand only a few steps from the water's edge and gestured to his companions. "This will do. We'll set up camp here."

The Major laid the foundation for a small cooking fire as Rip Ford squatted on his heels at his side. "Major," Ford said, "this bunch is painted up for a fight. Are you sure this Sanaco can be trusted?"

"I'd bet my life on it."

Ford snorted. "Wish you wouldn't be so damn free to bet mine too."

Neighbors scratched a sulphur match against his boot sole and fired the shavings at his feet. A wisp of smoke drifted upward. "Sanaco's a man of his word." Neighbors removed his hat and fanned the flames. "Of course, we've got a little ace in the hole that Sanaco's not sure about." He glanced toward the chief's lodge almost two hundred yards away. "He probably thinks we'd be crazy to come into his country with such a small group. I expect he's wondering where our Army escort is."

Ford sighed. "He's not the only one who thinks we're crazy, Major. I'm not all that damn sure about us myself."

Twilight had fallen on the banks of the Colorado as Major Robert Neighbors sat cross-legged in Sanaco's lodge and dragged at the Comanche chief's pipe. The tobacco tasted sharp and bitter against his tongue. The smoking ritual told the Major that this would be a serious if somewhat informal talk, short of council status but more than a friendly chat. *Sanaco's got a bee in his breechclout for sure,* he thought as he handed the pipe back to the Paneteka chief. The Comanche lowered the pipe onto its sacred pouch and sat staring into the small fire laid in the center of his lodge. The Major respected the silence that stretched into minutes. Sanaco would open the talk when he wished; for a guest in his lodge to speak first would be an affront bordering on insult.

At length Sanaco lifted his gaze from the fire to study the face of the big man. "Major Neighbors, you are one of the few white men trusted as a friend of the Human Beings," the Comanche said solemnly. "You are the first peace chief to ride among us, to talk with us in our own lodges instead of summoning us like women to travel to some distant place. We have faced each other across the council fire, and many years ago on the field of battle. I find you to be an honest man. It is something that cannot be said of all whose skin is white." The chief shifted his weight on his haunches. "What brings the peace chief of the white man to our hunting grounds?"

"Sanaco, the Great Father in Washington seeks a path across southern Texas to California. He would open trade routes from the Gulf Coast to the great sea to the west. I have been instructed to locate such a road, one well watered and smooth enough that wagons may travel upon it."

Sanaco stiffened as if slapped. "And you wish to make this road through the hunting grounds of the Human Beings?"

"Yes." The Major paused, studying the Paneteka's face. Anger flashed in the black eyes, emphasized by the war paint on the hairless face. *This is not going well,* Neighbors thought. "I asked for this assignment, Sanaco, that I might be able to keep my friends among the Human Beings advised as to the movements and intentions of United States citizens and soldiers. A misunderstanding about this matter could lead to the unnecessary shedding of the blood of brave men on both sides."

For a long moment, Sanaco merely sat and stared at the Major. "Then it is true, what I have been told," he finally said.

"What have you been told?"

"That the Great Father plans to put soldier forts and white villages along this road and that the iron rails will follow. That this will be the first step in driving the Human Beings from their rightful hunting grounds." Sanaco's words were sharp and angry. "We will fight." The Comanche's hand drifted to the haft of the knife at his belt. The move was not a threat but a reflex, an unconscious but telling gesture.

"What you have been told is not true, Sanaco," the Major said, trying to keep his tone even. One did not plead for understanding; that was a sign of weakness in the eyes of the Comanches. "The Great Father has given his word, spoken through me, his agent."

Sanaco sniffed in indignation. "The Great Father has broken his word before. He promises us a line beyond which the white man will not pass, then he allows the Texans to cross that line—but not the Indian. The line in the dirt holds back the red man, but lets a river of white men flow through. We are promised peace, but our camps are raided, our women and children killed by the white man. No. This new road will not be permitted."

The Major masked his growing apprehension behind a placid face. What he had told Alpheus Neal was true, up to a point. A Comanche would never harm a guest. What the Major hadn't added was that once the talks ended and the visitors were a few miles from camp they were no longer guests. At that point all bets were off. And the Comanches had some decidedly unpleasant ways of dealing with adult white captives. "What you say is true, Sanaco," the Major said. "There have been mistakes made and promises broken by both our people." He fixed a steady gaze on the Comanche's face. "Before you reach for the war lance, why not call a council of the other major chiefs? I have seen the symbols on lodges. Yellow Wolf's band is here. So are Buffalo Hump's people. Should we not hear them out?"

Sanaco sat silent for several heartbeats, staring into the distance. The angry set of the chief's jaw slowly relaxed. Finally he turned to Neighbors. "You know us well, Bear-Who-Walks-Like-Man. I cannot speak for other bands. I will call a council." Sanaco stood, the signal that today's meeting was at an end. "Tomorrow when the sun stands overhead we shall hear your words."

The Major nodded his thanks and rose to his feet. "It is as it should be." He started to turn toward the lodge opening, then stopped. "Sanaco," he said, "you wear war paint." It was a question, and the chief knew it.

"We ride for Mexico," Sanaco said. Neighbors heard the open challenge in the chief's reply.

For an instant the Major paused, considering his options. Under the Treaty of Guadalupe Hidalgo, the United States Army and the volunteer militia forces of Texas were supposed to stop Comanche raids into Mexico. But he could not stop generations of tradition with only seven men at his side. To even hint at an attempt to interfere would not only jeopardize the current mission, it might also get eight men scalped and spitted, and he was not here to fight. It wasn't worth the gamble.

"Until tomorrow, then, my friend," Neighbors said. He stepped through the tent flap into the late evening and drew a deep breath. The air held the heavy scent of woodsmoke from hundreds of campfires along the banks of the Colorado.

"Well, Major," he muttered to himself as he strode toward his own camp, "the next day or so won't be just a whole lot of fun—"

• • • •

Major Robert Neighbors strolled along the bank of the Colorado in the morning sun, stretching his legs before the council reconvened for a second day of long-winded deliberations. Rip Ford strode alongside, his gaze sweeping the Indian campsites, impatience plain on his stubbled face.

The Major understood Ford's twitchiness. Waiting was not one of Rip's strong points. It showed in his military record and in his other accomplishments as well. Ford had served as adjutant to Captain Jack Hays's regiment of Texas Mounted Volunteers in the campaign from Vera Cruz to Mexico City during the Mexican War. It was there he picked up the nickname Rip. As adjutant it was his duty to inform relatives and friends of the death of a member of the regiment. He tried to add a personal touch to the grim news by writing "Rest In Peace" above his signature. As casualties mounted during the campaign and Ford found himself sorely pressed for time, he started abbreviating the condolence to a simple "R.I.P." A Ranger soon tabbed him "Old Rip," and the nickname stuck. After the war Ford fought in Indian campaigns on the Texas frontier, practiced medicine and wrote for several influential newspapers. Ford was something of a paradox, the Major mused; he had a command of profanity that raised cursing to an art form, but he confined his outbursts to incidents afield. In contrast, his writing style was smooth, fluid, almost poetic. Ford still wasn't overly fond of Indians—or Mexicans for that matter—but he tempered his earned dislike for the races with a dose of realism and common sense. Most of the time he kept a tight rein on the temper that often boiled just below the surface of the normally jocular face.

Ford came to an abrupt stop and barked a bitter curse.

"What is it, Rip?"

Ford's face flushed with rage as he stabbed a finger toward a lodge a few yards away. A woman sat before the lodge. A white woman. Her red hair was hacked off short in the Comanche style, her face lanced by angry red scars. She stared at the two white men with vacant and unseeing blue eyes. The tip of her nose and part of an ear had been burned away and her once-fair skin was marred by ridged masses of scar tissue. A warrior stood nearby, a tree limb almost the size of a man's wrist gripped in his fist. The Comanche raised the stick and whacked the captive hard across the shoulders.

"That son of a—!" Rip Ford's hand dropped to the Colt New

Army revolver at his belt. The Major stabbed out a big hand and clamped Ford's gun arm against his side.

"No, Rip!" The Major's tone was quiet but sharp. "Let it go. There's nothing we can do about her now."

"Dammit, Major, I won't stand by and see a white captive abused by some damn savage! Look at her! What kind of animal would do that to a woman?"

Neighbors kept his grip firm on Ford's arm. "I'm not saying I like it either, Rip," he said, "but if you kill that man, there's a better than fine chance the Comanches will gut and skin us all. Dammit, man, we're guests here! If you meddle in their affairs now we won't live to see sundown."

The tension of rage slowly drained from Rip Ford's solid muscles. "All right, Major. But one of these days I hope to meet that red son on different terms and make him pay for what he's done to that woman."

The Major let his hand drop. "I understand how you feel, Rip. I'll find out before council if she's for sale. Maybe we can ransom her." He turned on a heel and strode back toward the scouting party's camp, his own belly churning in disgust. It was the hardest part of his job, accepting the fact that Comanche warriors looked upon their women as working livestock, particularly where captives were concerned. They were oxen, to be worked, whipped, and counted like horses as part of a man's wealth. It was part of their culture, as ingrained as the need for war and raiding. *Nothing says I have to like it,* Neighbors thought, *but for now I have to tolerate it.*

He heard Rip Ford's angry strides behind him and glanced over his shoulder. Ford's face was twisted in a scowl, dark with unreleased rage. The Major slowed his pace until Rip was alongside.

"Rip, I'm going to ask for your word you'll do nothing about that captive," the Major said. "The council is more important—at least where the greatest number of people are concerned—and I'd sort of like to leave here with my hair. I've grown somewhat attached to it over the years."

Rip Ford spat in disgust. "You have my word, Major." The expressive eyes still glittered. "I won't kill him. At least not in this camp."

"That's all I ask, Rip. Maybe someday, when the Comanches realize the old days are gone, they'll change. I wouldn't count on that happening any time soon."

The Major stopped on the riverbank a few yards from Sanaco's lodge. The council would be starting within the hour. Comanches made a show of arriving late for everything formal, especially when a white man was involved. It added to their status within the tribe, a sign of independence and pride. When a Comanche chief called a tribal council, being a few minutes late was sufficient. When a white man sought talks with the Indians days might pass before all the head men showed up. Major Robert Neighbors had played the game many times. The delays didn't even bother him that much. An impatient man would never make a good Indian agent.

"I'll be stopping off here, Rip," the Major said with a glance toward the late morning sun. "I want you and the rest of the men to stay close to camp today."

"We'll be there, primed and powdered," the still disgruntled Ford said. "If you have any problems, yell. As the Sioux would say, what the hell—it's a good day to die."

The Major turned away and strode toward Sanaco's lodge. In a way, he admitted, he rather enjoyed these parleys. The Comanches might be hellers on the warpath, but they were courteous and considerate in council. There was no bickering. Not like the shouting matches that went on in the white man's council lodges in Austin and Washington. Each chief or medicine man spoke his piece, then the senior warriors, and finally any younger men invited to the session. Each man listened with patience and intensity and never interrupted another man's turn before the audience. They asked no questions of the speaker and tolerated no quarrels. And most Comanches had a command of oratory that would shame the white man's best politicians. Robert Neighbors possessed something of a gift of oratory himself, but he freely admitted he was no match for the Plains tribes when it came to making speeches.

The Major paused outside the lodge and drew a final breath of the woodsmoke-tinted breeze. Inside, the air would soon grow heavy with the smell of the council fire, the traditional pipe, and the scent of bear grease from the bodies of the Comanches. There was always a pot of food on the fire to ease the hunger of anyone attending council. All in all, there were worse ways to spend a day.

He called out to announce his presence, then flipped the lodge flap open and stepped inside. It seemed that every chief and senior warrior in the Paneteka nation had gathered for the council.

The Major took his place, seated with his legs crossed, and waited. Soon the last Comanches would arrive, the pipe would make the rounds and the talks would pick up where they left off the day before.

At midmorning of the council's third day, the Major breathed a silent sigh of relief. The persuasive oratory of Yellow Wolf and Buffalo Hump had backed Sanaco into a tribal corner. He might be the most powerful of the chiefs, but no holder of Comanche office went against the wishes of the majority. It was a sure way to lose one's position of leadership.

What had ultimately turned Yellow Wolf and Buffalo Hump to the Major's side was not the white man's golden-tongued oration or even thinly veiled threats that the Army would send troops to force the road through anyway. What swayed the chiefs was his promise that the Great Father would send presents—calico, mirrors and combs, powder and lead—to the Comanche bands at the next general council. It was a small price to pay for the sorely needed road through the southern lands of the Comanches. All he had to do now, Neighbors reminded himself grimly, was to convince the Great Father and his bean-counting bureaucrats that a handful of trinkets might save a sea of blood. It helped considerably that most of the warriors were anxious to open their raid into Mexico where scalps, women and children captives, many horses and mules and other riches waited for the taking. The size of this raiding party, the Major thought, would make a number of Comanches wealthy men almost overnight.

The deal was sealed with another round of Sanaco's ceremonial pipe. The explorers would be permitted to mark their road, but any attempts to build soldier forts along the trail would meet resistance. For now, it was enough. The Major thanked Sanaco for his hospitality, noting the suspicion that still remained in the war chief's eyes.

He waited respectfully until the major chiefs and senior warriors had left the lodge, then privately made a present of a sack of fine Virginia burley tobacco, a pound of lead and a quarter pound of powder, to Sanaco. The war chief accepted the gifts but the distrust remained in the black eyes.

Major Robert Neighbors stepped outside, took a deep breath to release the remnants of tension and strode toward the explorers' camp.

Rip Ford and the others were waiting, passing the time smoking and thumbing a greasy deck of dog-eared cards. Ford glanced up. "Well, Major? How much longer does this parley last?"

The Major let a slight grin crease his lips. "It's over. We're even getting a guide—Guadalupe, chief of one of the smaller bands—to see us through to El Paso del Norte." He saw the sense of relief flood the faces of his companions. Being in an enemy camp for several days was not a pleasant way to pass the time. And talk or not, personal friendship or none, the Comanche and the white man were still enemies. The name Comanche literally meant "enemy," a corruption of the Ute word *Komantcia*. The Utes and the Comanches had despised each other for centuries.

Rip Ford raised an eyebrow in an unspoken question.

"Sorry, Rip," the Major said, "I couldn't ransom the woman."

Ford's brows dropped into a clump above eyes that still simmered in anger. "There'll come a day," he muttered.

The Major glanced at the sun overhead. "Let's break camp, gentlemen," he said. "I'd like to be a few miles away from here by sunset. We've a trail to find."

TWO

San Antonio
June 1849

Major Robert Neighbors signed his eight-page report with a flour-ish, leaned back in the chair at the small table which served as a desk in his rented San Antonio home, and tried to shrug the ache from his thick shoulders.

He was satisfied with the terse account of the expedition to find a passable wagon route from San Antonio and Fredericksburg to El Paso del Norte on the Rio Grande. From El Paso travelers could follow the established southern trails to California.

The trip out had yielded nothing of promise, but the party's return route was adequately watered most of the year and the ter-rain as hospitable as could be hoped.

The Major's report did not mention the hardships of the expedi-tion. The days of heat, wind, thirst, hunger, bugs, exhaustion and guts twisted by bad water and inadequate food—especially on the outward journey—had nothing to do with the objective. It was enough that the eight pages told the authorities a route had been found.

The inbound passage, which the Major called the Upper Trail, passed by the old Spanish fort on the San Saba, crossed a tributary of the Colorado and followed the Middle Concho, known to the Indians as Blue Water, to Horsehead Crossing on the Pecos. There the trail turned north to Hueco Tanks before veering southwest to El Paso del Norte. The Major calculated the distance from Austin to El Paso at 598 miles. Mule miles, he called them. He based his estimates on the distance traveled in a day by mule. The long-eared beasts had averaged three and a third miles an hour on the route back home.

He sprinkled sand on the final page to absorb any excess ink, cleaned his pen staff as the grainy blotter did its work, then brushed the sand away. *We may run short of pen and ink out here,* he thought, *but Texas will always have plenty of sand to blot with.* He bound the finished report with a pair of cloth strips. The government would have its road. Already the winding path was becoming known in San Antonio as the Ford-Neighbors Trail, an honor not lost on the two men who had made the trek.

The Major tucked the report into a dispatch case for delivery to military authorities. He hefted his almost empty coffee cup, stood and strode to a window overlooking a busy thoroughfare. The street was crowded, pedestrians and vehicles elbowing each other for space along the narrow road. Already hundreds of immigrants were flooding into San Antonio, eager to reach the gold fields of California and the promise of great riches to be found there.

Robert Neighbors stared at the hubbub for several moments. On the one hand he wished the gold-seekers well. Perhaps they would find the dreams and homes they sought. At the same time he resented their presence. The steady flow of settlers into and across Texas spelled trouble for—and probably with—the Indians.

It was a story often repeated during the early days, even before Texas became a republic. It continued during the war for independence and intensified after annexation. The settlers kept coming, drawn by the promise of land and riches free for the taking. That the land was already occupied meant little to them.

It meant a lot to the red men.

It meant the loss of still more of their homelands, their hunting ranges, their entire way of life. The stronger bands, the Comanches in particular, would fight to save those lands.

In the years he had served as Indian agent in Texas the Major had come to know the red men well. Most of them he respected. A great many of the individuals he personally liked. He knew that among Texans he was in the minority. Most Texans saw the Indian as something less than human. They wanted the bronze-skinned people dead or chased from the state. Eventually, the Major reluctantly admitted, it could come to that. There was one alternative, if he could get anyone to listen. The Indians had to be guaranteed their own part of Texas. Each tribal group would have to have land suitable for farming and stock raising, away from other tribes who were traditional enemies. It wasn't a simple proposition and it certainly wasn't a popular notion at the moment.

The Major turned away from the window. The sun had slid half-way down the western sky. The meeting of the San Antonio Democratic Party Plan Committee would begin in an hour at the cafe on the downtown square.

He downed the last swig of coffee, content. The report was done and his belly was full of the thick, rich stew that had gained the Major considerable fame on the trail and in town. He knew he was a good cook. Rip Ford called him "as good as any woman at the skillet but too damn ugly to marry." The muted tink of dishes from the kitchen reminded him of the cup in his hand.

He wandered into the small but well-equipped kitchen. A Mexican boy in his early teens stood over a tub of steaming water, washing the plates and cookware from the noon meal. Sweat beaded the scarred forehead over eyes so dark as to be almost black. The young man's short but sturdy frame hinted at the rapid growth of muscles beginning to flesh out. The scars were the legacy of a Comanche raid on his village in Chihuahua. They had saved his life. The boy, armed only with a hoe staff, had put up such a determined scrap against two grown warriors that the Comanches had spared him to honor his bravery. They even gave him the Paneteka name "Little Badger" for his courage and tenacity.

The Major had ransomed him from Yellow Wolf's band almost two years ago. A hundred dollars was a substantial sum, but it had been money well spent, the Major mused. For both of them.

Ignacio Serna glanced up from the soapy water and smiled. "More coffee, Major?" The youth's voice was surprisingly deep for his age. A boy grew into manhood fast in a couple of years in a Comanche camp.

The Major shook his head. "I slosh when I walk now, Ignacio." He handed the cup to the youth. Ignacio had become like a son since he had ridden away from Yellow Wolf's camp with the Major. He had shaken off the last of the Comanche influence a few weeks later, cutting his hair at collar length in the fashion of the Texans. Among the Comanches, the men prided themselves in the length of their locks, kept them greased and plaited, the braids falling to near waist length and tied off in bright colored ribbon or leather thongs.

The boy was a big help to the Major, keeping watch on the house during the Major's frequent trips afield. Ignacio was a good hand with the Navy thirty-six revolver the Major had given him. The place was safe in his hands. The boy was a hard worker, too. The house was always neat, the horses and stables well tended, saddles and weapons cleaned and ready for quick use if needed. *Anybody who thinks all Mexicans are lazy never met Ignacio,* the Major thought.

"I'll not be here for supper," the Major said. "Democrats never get anything decided in less than five hours. I'll eat at the cafe on the plaza. Do you have something here for your own meal?"

Ignacio scrubbed the Major's cup and dropped it into a tub of rinse water. "There's plenty of stew left," he said. "I'll warm that up."

The Major reached for a dish towel and dried the utensils Ignacio had washed. Some men he knew would never touch anything that resembled domestic chores. But as far as the Major was concerned it was no lack of manliness to do a job that needed to be done. Besides, a single man had no choice. The truth be known, he admitted to himself, he enjoyed the chance to share even mundane chores with Ignacio. The boy seemed wise beyond his years. He spoke four languages including two Indian tongues. He knew the cultures of the Mexican, the Comanche and the white man, and when the Major was "thinking out loud" in Ignacio's presence the boy sometimes pointed out a flaw in his reasoning or made a sensible suggestion.

The Major finished drying the dishes, nodded a good-bye to Ignacio and started for the door.

"Major," Ignacio called, "don't forget to take the *pistole* along."

The Major chuckled and shook his head. He reached for the gun belt. "You're right, Ignacio. Walking the San Antonio streets can be more chancy than riding into a Kiowa war party." *A lot of those folks out there live fairly expensive lives and never work,* the Major thought as he buckled the heavy belt that carried the forty-four-caliber percussion Colt high at his waist, *unless you considered stealing livestock and lifting another man's wallet as work. Makes a man wonder just who the real savages are—the Indians or the white men.* He pulled on his hat and stepped into the street.

The late afternoon sun filtered through dust raised by the wheels of carts and wagons and the hooves of horses. Woodsmoke from cooking fires spilled from chimneys or the open pits in front of hovels of the poor, doing its part to obscure the sun. For an instant he thought he caught a whiff of fresh, clean air from the hills beyond the Balcones Escarpment to the northwest. The swirl of breeze that poked a hole in the dust vanished as quickly as it had appeared.

He stepped from the narrow boardwalk to let a woman pass,

lifted his fingers to his hat brim, and in the process put his boot heel into a pile of fresh horse manure.

"Civilization," the Major grumbled to himself as he scrubbed the heel against the sand, "isn't all that it's cracked up to be. At least it was just horse droppings. I've stepped in worse in my time."

He let the flow of the crowd carry him toward the plaza and the hotel where he and a handful of others who made up the core of the Democratic Party were to meet. He strode past the building where he and others attending a district court session had been captured by the invading Mexican army. Jack Hays's Rangers and the Texas militia had stopped General Adrian Woll's advance and chased him back into Mexico. That day in September had been seven years back, but it seemed like only yesterday. The year and a half in the Mexican prison remained painfully sharp in the Major's mind. He had spent most of those eighteen months trying not to hate all Mexicans.

"Hey, you! Big man with the whiskers!"

The call jarred the Major back to the present. He turned toward a lean man with a pinched face standing in a doorway a couple of yards away. "Are you addressing me, sir?" he asked, his tone pleasant.

"Yeah. You that damn Injun-lover, ain't you?" The thin man's pale eyes glittered in hate. He held an axe handle in one hand. He had the stooped shoulders and scarred, oversized hands of a farmer.

"I'm the Indian agent, if that's what you mean." The Major checked the quick flare of irritation that warmed his gut. He had been called by the "Injun-lover" epithet many times. It went with the territory.

"Your damn pet savages kilt my folks a couple years back." The thin man tapped the axe handle against an open palm. "Kilt 'em slow. Raped my ma and my sister before they scalped and gutted 'em." The glitter in the man's eyes bordered on madness. "I reckon you're feedin' them red killers right now, Mister Injun-lover. Probably beddin' one of them fat, ugly squaws, too."

Robert Neighbors fixed an even gaze on the lean farmer's face and ignored the personal slur. "I'm sorry to hear of your loss, friend. If you can tell me which Indians were responsible, they'll be brought to justice."

"Damn right they will be. The whole lice-bit bunch of 'em,

hacked up in them dirty blankets before I'm done. But I reckon I'll start with you, Injun Agent." The man took a step forward.

The Major raised his left hand. He kept his right near the holstered Colt at his belt. "Mister," he said, "I'm not looking for any trouble. Don't do anything foolish."

A crowd had begun to gather, drawn by the thin man's loud accusations. "Better back off, friend," someone said from the edge of the crowd. "That's Major Neighbors there. He ain't a man to mess with."

"Go ahead," another voice called out. "Beat the hell out of the Injun-lover!"

A twisted grin lifted the corners of the thin man's mouth. "I reckon I might just do that, by God." He took another step forward.

The Major lifted the flap of the holster and wrapped a hand around the walnut grips of the pistol. "I'm asking you to let it drop, mister," he said.

The thin man raised the axe handle to shoulder height, gripped in both hands. The Major pulled his Colt. "That's enough, dammit!" he snapped. "Put the stick down!"

The farmer barked a curse and swung the hard hickory handle. The Major flexed his knees, ducked as the wood whipped past the crown of his hat, then cocked the Colt and pulled the trigger. The slug hammered against the farmer's hip. The man's eyes went wide; he grunted in surprise and pain, dropped the axe handle, staggered back against a building and slid down the coarse wall. Blood stained the fingers pressed against his hip.

The heavy muzzle blast of the Colt momentarily shocked the crowd into silence. A couple of heartbeats later, the Major heard the ratchet sound of a pistol hammer drawn to full cock behind him. He spun and eared back the hammer of his own Colt. Then he relaxed and lowered the weapon. Rip Ford stood at the edge of the crowd, the muzzle of his own Colt stuffed into a scruffy man's ear deep enough to draw a bit of blood.

"Put the smokepole down slow, fellow, or I'll give this trigger a little tug," Ford said. The scruffy man, bloodshot eyes wide in sudden fear, crouched and placed an ancient flintlock shotgun in the street. The former Ranger glanced around the half circle of onlookers. "Anybody else want to dance, we've got two fiddles warmed up," Ford said casually. "Always wondered how far a man's brains would splatter from a slug fired in his ear."

Several men in the crowd started to back away, hands held away from their weapons. Others turned and all but ran from the scene. A couple stayed behind, still curious.

Ford pulled the muzzle of the revolver from the scruffy man's ear. The would-be shotgunner fell to his knees, his fingers trembling. "You, there," Ford said, motioning with the Colt's barrel toward a man standing a few feet away, "go fetch a constable."

"You need a doc, too?"

"I don't." Ford nodded toward the whimpering farmer at the base of the wall. "But I reckon that fellow might."

Ford waited until the man scurried away, then holstered his pistol and grinned at Neighbors. "Been keeping an eye on this man, Major. He was making whiskey talk about whopping a certain Indian agent between the ears with a stick." He knelt beside the wounded man. "I think his appetite for the chore just faded somewhat."

Twenty minutes later the injured man lay on a makeshift litter awaiting the trip to the physician's office down the street. The San Antonio constable tucked a stub of pencil into his pocket. "I suppose you had no choice, Major Neighbors," the constable said. "I could fine you for firing a gun in public, but we'll let it slide this time. Try not to get in the habit of shooting people in my district, though." He turned and walked away.

The Major extended a hand to Ford. "Thanks, Rip," he said. "That could have been a bit sticky."

Ford returned the handshake and shrugged. *"De nada.* Pull a Comanche off me sometime and we'll call it even." He grinned and flashed a wink at Neighbors. "Major, have you *really* got a squaw stashed somewhere?"

The Major felt his skin flush. "Now, Rip, you know better than that."

Ford clucked his tongue in mock reproach. "That's the problem with you, Major. Too damn many morals. You'll never amount to much."

Neighbors glanced toward the man he had shot, now being carried toward the doctor's office. "Is he hit bad?"

"Bad enough to get his attention for a while," Ford said. "Maybe he'll live. If he does he can consider himself lucky." Ford cocked an eyebrow at Neighbors. "You don't look so good, my hairy friend. Got a problem?"

"I was just thinking. I don't remember the last time I shot a man."

"I do," Ford said with a chuckle. "It was just a few minutes ago. You still handle a *pistole* pretty good." Ford clapped the big man on the shoulder. "We best get on to the meeting. I don't think the boys would start without us, but you can never trust a Democrat."

Major Robert Neighbors leaned back in his chair and once again scanned the message from Washington. He had been ordered to report to the nation's capital to help work out a "satisfactory policy" for the handling of the Texas Indian problem.

The message brought a smile to the Major's bearded face. Someone had finally listened to his pleas on behalf of the red man. Now he would have the chance to outline his ideas in person to those in authority. The seeds of the plan had been planted during his years of service to the various Indian bureaus of the Republic and the early days of Texas statehood. It had been fertilized by personal observation and watered by common sense. In a way, he mused, it even dated back to the feud between Republic presidents Lamar and Houston. Lamar favored annihilation of the Indian. Houston leaned toward pacification and absorption of the red man into the white culture. The Major was a Houston man where Indians were concerned.

He tucked the message into his shirt pocket, called for Ignacio, and pulled the leather traveling case from beneath his bed. "I'll be gone for a while," he said in response to the question in the youth's brown eyes. "Keep a close watch, Ignacio. That farmer with the axe handle might have some friends. If they do come, just slip out the back door and let them have the place."

"If they come, I fight," Ignacio said, his beardless young jaw set.

"Don't take the risk, son," the Major said. "The only thing here that can't be replaced is you." He finished packing and fastened the final strap on the travel bag. "That big bay of mine needs new shoes. No need to fight the beast yourself, Ignacio. Take him to the blacksmith."

The Major reached into a bureau drawer and hefted the money bag he kept there. He counted out what he thought he might need for the trip to Washington, then handed the pouch to Ignacio. "There should be enough cash here to hold you until I get back. If you run short, see Rip Ford or Sam Maverick." The Major grinned at the Mexican youth. "The three of us have loaned each other money so often we've forgotten who owes who what. Go to either of them if you have any trouble here."

He returned Ignacio's handshake. It wasn't quite enough. The Major wanted to pull the youth into his arms and give him a solid hug. But Ignacio was almost a man now. Such a show of emotion might embarrass him.

The Major released the boy's hand and strode to his gun belt on its peg by the door. *Better wear the darn thing until we cross the Mississippi,* he thought. *When we hit civilization I'll put it in the travel bag. As the man said, anything can happen and it's a long way from here to the headwaters of the American river of government.*

Washington
July 1849

Major Robert Neighbors sat in the slat-backed chair in the cluttered office of the Undersecretary of Indian Affairs and stared in growing disgust at the small, stooped man in the rumpled suit behind the big mahogany desk. *The fool hasn't listened to a word I've said,* the Major grumbled inwardly.

The undersecretary had stared out the window, fiddled with his pen, thumbed through the papers on his desk, picked up and then put down the Major's outline of his plan for the conduct of Texas Indian affairs. The rumpled man had looked at everything, it seemed, except Robert Neighbors. The Major had little use for a white man who wouldn't look another in the eye. Among some Indian tribes, avoiding eye contact was a sign of respect. In the white man's tribe it was at worst an insult and at best a show of disinterest. It was obvious the man behind the desk had no Indian blood in his veins. The almost chinless face was the color of fly ash, untouched by sun or wind. The Major doubted if the man had been outside in the daylight since the ark landed.

The Major breathed a silent sigh. "Sir," he said, "my plan should be workable. And it's fair to the Indians. God knows we haven't been to date." He shifted his weight, trying to ease the numbness in his backside. "It's time we started treating the red man as a human being. We've taken his land, his culture, his dignity. We've rewarded the tribes who helped us with cholera, smallpox and poverty."

The hell with it, the Major thought; *my butt won't take much more of this sitting around.* He rose and began to pace the small office. "The only way we can hope for peace between the races is to give back some of what we've taken from the Indian. We must give him a home and a future."

The undersecretary drummed nervous fingertips on the top of the desk and stared at a spot somewhere over the carved marble bust of President Zachary Taylor on a small table near the door. "Your plan seems to have some, uh, merit, Major Neighbors. I will —that is, the entire commission will—study your proposals in more, uh, depth at a later date."

The Major stopped pacing before the desk. *Maybe if I try one more time I'll get through to this little rat-faced bureaucrat,* he thought. "The plan may need some minor refinements, but in theory it's simple enough—five basic points." He raised a hand and ticked off the highlights of his proposal on his fingers. "First, the federal government should set aside enough land for the immediate use of Texans. There's plenty of room beyond the current frontier to expand the state and still leave enough land for the Indians."

The undersecretary glanced at the Major, then quickly turned his head away. "It is, uh, possible, I suppose. But I must admit to some doubt that you Texans would agree to that."

The Major ignored the condescending tone of the statement. "Second, the federal government should acquire from the state as much territory as would be needed for a permanent settlement for the Indians. Third, we must extend the trade and intercourse laws of the United States to the tribes, as if each were a separate and distinct nation. In point of fact, they are precisely that. No two tribes are alike. Each has its own religion, its own culture, its own form of government." The Major paused for a moment and shook his head as the undersecretary cast a furtive glance at the ticking clock on the mantelpiece. He tried to fight back the feeling he was wasting his time.

"Fourth, we must establish a general Indian agency, with sub-agents and interpreters who would live among the Indians, not in some distant city. That is the only way to see their true needs and hear their wants. And finally"—the Major tucked down the remaining finger—"we must establish military posts where needed to help the agents see that all laws and treaties regarding the tribes be carried out to the letter."

The Major turned away from the desk and resumed his pacing.

"There are other things Washington could do to help the Indians become self-sufficient. Tools, teachers, subsistence supplies until they master the techniques of agriculture and stock raising. I've mentioned a few such items in the report."

The Major returned to his seat. The chair seemed less hard now. He sat with his arms folded across his chest, determined to wait until the little man behind the desk said something. Anything. Since the Major had walked in that door more than an hour ago he had done most of the talking, and he was getting tired of it. Especially when he was being ignored. The tick of the mantel clock seemed to grow louder in the silence.

Finally the undersecretary cleared his throat. "Mister Neighbors, there have been certain, uh, developments in the War Department's Indian Affairs Bureau since you were first summoned to Washington." The bureaucrat ran shaky fingers through thinning gray hair. His gaze flickered from the open window to a point somewhere beyond the Major's left shoulder. "It is my duty to inform you that you, uh, have been removed from your post as Indian agent of Texas."

Robert Neighbors sat for a moment in stunned disbelief. His gut churned in growing outrage as the full impact of the news soaked in. He leveled a cold, hard stare at the undersecretary. "What did you just say?" The Major heard the icy tone of his own words. The rumpled man's gaze caught the Major's eye for a split second and quickly darted away as he picked up a pen and fingered it nervously.

"The commissioner has stressed to me that he, uh, finds no fault in your work. It has been decided that Judge John H. Rollins could perhaps carry out the duties more, uh, efficiently, shall we say?"

"Rollins." The word was an epithet on the Major's tongue. "The man's old. He's ill. He knows nothing about Indians in general and less than that about the Texas tribes. But I understand now why I'm being fired and replaced with an incompetent." The Major became aware that his hands had balled into fists. The nails of his right hand dug into his palm. He willed his muscles to relax.

"Judge Rollins's only qualification for this job," he said scornfully, "is that he's a Whig. And I'm a Democrat."

The rumpled man fidgeted behind the desk. He kept glancing toward the closed office door. The Major suspected the undersecretary had asked for guards to be placed outside. *Afraid to face a big, bad Texan alone, no doubt,* he thought. *The little runt's within an ace of being thrashed and he knows it.*

"Mister Neighbors, this is not my decision." The undersecretary's reedy voice quavered. "I'm only the, uh, messenger. My orders come from higher up."

The Major abruptly stood. He leaned on the forward edge of the desk, his knuckles white. "And the commissioner didn't have the courage to look me in the eye and fire me himself, correct?"

The rumpled man instinctively drew back. His prominent Adam's apple bobbed as fear flickered in bloodshot hazel eyes. "Major, I warn you to control yourself. I have guards outside."

"And I'll wager they're good Whig Party loyalists, too," the Major said. He snorted in disgust, stepped away from the desk and picked up his hat. "Don't worry, mister undersecretary." He heard the bitterness in his own voice. "I'll not break your nose for you, even though the idea does have its appeal at the moment. I'll let myself out."

He turned toward the door.

"Uh, Mister Neighbors? What will you do now?"

The Major glanced over his shoulder at the wrinkled little man. "Go back to Texas," he snapped, "and do my damnedest to make sure a Democrat gets elected next time."

Virginia

Major Robert Neighbors clung to a window brace of the Baker & Burleson Company coach as it lurched and jolted through the mud of the Shenandoah Valley Road.

He heard the labored breathing of animals and the oaths of the driver as the four-horse hitch strained against the traces to drag the vehicle through the heavy, sucking muck. The storm had brought a measure of relief from the stifling afternoon heat to the four passengers in the coach, but it hadn't made life easier for the big draft animals up front.

The Major had given up trying to start any meaningful conversation with the other passengers. One was a middle-aged and paunchy drummer who knew nothing but the peddling of pots and pans. Another was a Virginia delegate to Congress, an incorrigible Whig; the Major could find no common ground for a discussion with him. The third was an aging spinster whose upper lip was drawn into a constant frump of displeasure, bound for Georgia to organize another chapter of some temperance union whose name and purpose held no particular interest to the Major. If a man wanted to drink, that was his option. The Major himself enjoyed a glass of good wine on special occasions, though he seldom touched hard liquor.

He stared out the window at the lush green valley with its farms and mills, its orchards showing the blush of ripening fruit. Just beyond the low blue mountains to the northwest lay his boyhood home. He felt no compulsion to interrupt the trip back to Texas for a visit to the place of his youth. There was little for him there now.

Orphaned as a young child, the Major had been raised by friends of the family on a fair-sized and prosperous farm in a valley opening into the Shenandoah watershed. They had been good to him, raised him as one of their own, saw that he got the best education available and didn't ask more work of him than he could handle. They were gone now, at rest in the small family cemetery behind the farmhouse. The Major supposed the land was still in the family. There had been several sons, but he felt no strong ties to them.

He had learned many lessons on that farm. One of those lessons was that Robert Neighbors did not particularly care for the feel of a hoe handle. At age nineteen he had said his good-byes and headed west to make his own name. A couple of years later in the spring of 1836 he had crossed the Sabine River into Texas. In a matter of days he knew he was home. In the Republic a man's future was limited only by his abilities and ambitions. Within a year he considered himself not a Virginian but a Texan.

The Major stared out the window, lost in his own world and oblivious to the mutterings of his fellow passengers. His abrupt dismissal as Indian agent still rankled, but the outrage and anger had begun to fade. He wouldn't miss the small salary that went with the post. The Major had money and there were almost unlimited ways to make more in Texas.

What worried him most was the uncertain future of the Texas tribes. The Anadarkos, Lipans, Apaches, Tonkawas and remnants of the once-powerful Caddos and other bands led a precarious existence at best, trapped between the white man on the east and the Comanches on the west. It would be the height of the growing season along the Brazos where many of the smaller tribes had settled, the time of year that meant food for the winter or hungry bellies for his former charges. He directed a mental message to the wiry little leader of one small band, hoping the words would reach across the miles: *May the gods smile on your harvest, Charlie Two Blankets. There is still hope to find your place in the sun . . .*

THREE

Brazos River
August 1849

Charlie Two Blankets leaned against his hoe handle and let his gaze sweep the fields along the bank of the river.

He was pleased with what he saw.

Men and women worked side-by-side among the rows of vines and the blooms that would soon bear pumpkins. Already the sweet early summer squash and beans had been harvested, dried and stored. Later-blooming varieties planted in their stead now flourished under the bright sun. The rains had been kind this year. They had come at the right times and in the right amounts. The tall stalks of flour corn were heavy with young ears. By the next full moon the ears would be ready for the harvest. This would be the first good season in the three summers since their move to the Clear Creek of the Brazos. The first year's planting withered under a blazing sun when no rains came. The second year's crops vanished beneath swarms of grasshoppers.

This year the Caddos would not know hunger during the coming time of the snows. Their granaries would be full with enough left for trade with the white men and other tribes. *When we get the cattle the agency promised us,* Charlie thought with a sigh of satisfaction, *there will be much feasting in celebration.*

The cattle would supply most of the band's meat requirements for the winter. In days past the Caddos had supplied their own meat. But the wild game was almost gone now, forced upriver by the long rifles of the white hunters. The Caddos, who once feared no tribe, now did not dare hunt the buffalo which roamed the plains to the west. That hunting land belonged to the Comanches, mortal enemies of the Caddos.

For an instant Charlie Two Blankets felt the urge to mount his horse and defy the odds in the buffalo range. His small band would need but a few buffalo to provide meat for the winter. The urge passed as quickly as it had come. His bones had grown brittle in almost sixty winters. He knew he could not afford the chance. The danger to himself meant nothing, but his people needed a live *xinesi*. The irony of the thought brought a wry smile to Charlie's lips. The *xinesi*—supreme governor—once had been all-powerful among the Caddo Confederacies; thousands of people looked to him for guidance. Charlie Two Blankets held the title, but he now was supreme governor of less than two hundred people. It was, perhaps, a bigger responsibility than the Old Ones had faced. The Old Ones had but to govern. Charlie Two Blankets had to keep the remnants of his people alive.

It was not a simple task.

His band had been fortunate to find this place, where the water was good and flowed year-round from many springs. Wood for the cooking fires was abundant where Clear Creek flowed into the Brazos. The soil was adequate, if not as fertile as in the tribal homelands to the east. The tall pines and rich soil of his youth remained rooted in Charlie's memory. He sensed he would never see those thick trees with their squirrels and birds and deer again in this life. The white man owned them now.

At least here the Caddos were beyond the white man's settlements. That was the good part of the liver, Charlie mused; the bile was that they were now closer than ever to the Comanches, the devils of the Plains.

Charlie strode to the shade of a live oak tree and reached for a file among a pile of tools. The cutting edge of his hoe had dulled. The white man had brought many things of value to the Caddos. They brought tools of steel and metal, more efficient than the bone and stone his grandfather's grandfather had used, and guns to replace the bow and arrow and lance. A hunter with a good rifle could kill a deer at three times the distance than with the bow—if he could find a deer to kill.

Charlie tested the edge of the hoe with a callused thumb and began to stroke the file across the beveled side of the blade. Tools like the hoe cut with more than one edge, Charlie mused. He doubted that anyone else in the band still knew how to shape the shoulder blade of the deer into an instrument of agriculture. Even the crafts of the women were lost. Women now had pots and pans and even water jugs of metal. Charlie could barely remember the last time he had seen a Caddo woman fashion a basket from reeds or pull from the fire the elegant handmade pottery of his grand-mother's day. *We are losing more than our ability with our hands,* he thought with a touch of bitterness, *we are losing touch with our past, and so with ourselves.*

"Grandfather?"

Charlie looked up from his work and smiled at the young boy who stood before him. The boy was not a relative, but all Caddo children addressed adult men as "Father," or "Grandfather," depending upon the age and presumed wisdom of the adult.

"Yes, son?"

"Tell me again of the old days."

Charlie put the file aside, swept a few twigs from the ground before him and motioned for the boy to sit. "In the old days—when my grandfather's father was *xinesi* of all the clans—the Caddos were many, and proud, and strong. Our lands stretched from what is now called the Red River to the sea known to the white man as the Gulf of Mexico. Other tribes traveled for many moons to trade with us. We had great storehouses of food. We were a wealthy people. Our warriors were brave. No tribe dared go to war against us." Charlie reached for his battered pipe and tobacco pouch.

"And the white man made us poor?"

Charlie tamped the tobacco, harvested from his own field and cured in his lodge, and fired it with a sulphur-tipped match—another of the white man's gifts, a quick fire without flint and steel. "This is what my grandfather told me," he said between puffs. "The Caddos welcomed the white man"—he shook the match to extinguish the flame and pulled a deep drag of rich tobacco smoke into his lungs—"and taught him our ways of growing things, shared our food with him, fought mutual enemies at his side. He brought us new tools and weapons."

Charlie paused for a moment, his gaze locked on a distant hill to the east. The vision of tall, cool pines would not leave his mind. *That is the sadness,* Charlie thought, *that this young boy will never know the true land of his people, never know the joy of the kill in the buffalo hunt. At least he will have a home somewhere; Major Neighbors has promised us. The Great White Father will listen to Major Neighbors, for he is a wise man.*

Charlie finally dropped his gaze. The boy sat patiently, waiting. It was not polite to hurry one's elders, and the child had manners. Charlie sighed. "The white man brought more than tools and guns. He also brought sickness among us, and when disease had thinned our numbers until we were too few to fight back, the white man took the land where the Caddos had lived for hundreds of summers too many to count."

"Then, Grandfather, why do you tell us not to hate the white man?"

Charlie smiled around the toothmarked pipe stem. "Because, my son, it disturbs the soul to hate. Hate brings nothing in return but blood and grief. You know how it is when salt is placed at the base of a corn stalk?"

The boy nodded, his young brow furrowed in thought. "The corn withers and dies."

"It is so," Charlie said. "The corn is poisoned by the salt. We must not poison our souls with hate. We must accept that the white man is the more powerful tribe. Not all white men are bad—which is something you cannot say about Comanches." Charlie chuckled at his own small joke, even though it was too close to the truth to be all that amusing. He let smoke trickle from his nostrils. "The Caddos must change with the times, my son, or there will be none of us left. When the wind blows hard the willow bends but does not break; the cottonwood and the oak fight the wind and are broken. So it is with the white man. The white man is the wind, we are the trees. We cannot change that. We must work with him."

Charlie glanced toward the lowering sun, then toward the fields. His people were gathering tools and babies, the day's work done. It was time to wash away the sweat and soil from the body in the pools of cool water of the creek, then return to the lodge for food and rest. He rose to his feet and beckoned to the boy.

"Grandfather," the boy said as he strode alongside, "why are you called Charlie Two Blankets?"

Charlie chuckled softly at the question. "A few of the old ways remain among the Caddos, son. My wife's brother was killed in a buffalo hunt many years ago. I took his widow as my wife, as is our custom, that she would have someone to provide for her. Thus two wives, two different blankets. Thus, Charlie Two Blankets."

The boy walked in silence for a few moments at Charlie's side. "Grandfather, is it not hard? Having two wives, I mean?"

Charlie laughed aloud. "Not as long as the women are Caddo. They work in harmony, seldom quarrel, and divide the chores among them." He took the pipe from his mouth and gestured toward the dome-shaped sod and grass lodges of the village. "At first there was no problem in my lodge. But now both my wives have been converted to the white man's Christianity. Thus it is two times two times four harder than having but one wife, my son."

Charlie shook his head in mock despair. "Your grown brother has taken a Christian Caddo as wife. You should begin soon to make medicine that your brother lives a long and prosperous life. Now, let us put such thoughts aside, wash ourselves and watch the sun put itself to bed."

"Charlie Two Blankets!"

The call from outside the lodge jolted Charlie from his light doze. The hairs on his forearms prickled in alarm. It was the voice of a white man. He instinctively reached for the old percussion musket at the side of the lodge. Just as abruptly he checked the impulse. Not all visits from the white man posed danger. Perhaps this one was bringing the promised cattle. Besides, to appear armed would be to invite trouble. The death of a white man at Indian hands was not taken lightly in these days.

Charlie pushed aside the woven reed flap of the lodge and stepped into the cool air of early morning. The sun had not yet cleared the horizon. The light that fell over the clearing was gray.

Three men sat on big horses outside Charlie's lodge. One was broad of shoulder, powerful, and the beard on his face would glow red when the sun rose. The second was younger but also big. He had the same hard, pale eyes and red beard as the older man. The third, slender and clean-shaven, wore the uniform of a lieutenant in the United States Army. All three carried rifles and pistols.

Charlie stood for a moment, studying the horsemen. He became aware that other lodge doors had swung open. A few men and women drifted toward the visitors. A couple of the younger men were armed. Charlie frowned a warning toward the two rifle-bearers and hoped they caught his meaning.

He lifted a hand in greeting. "Welcome to the village of Charlie Two Blankets. I will ask my wives to prepare something to eat. Did you bring the cattle we were promised?"

The big man scowled at Charlie. "Cattle? I don't know what the hell you're talking about, old man." The scowl faded and the bearded one suddenly grinned. The grin was more frightening than the scowl. "Lieutenant, you want to tell the old man why we're here?"

The uniformed man cleared his throat. He looked too young to be an officer, Charlie thought, and he seemed to be nervous. Char-

lie wondered why. This village was Caddo. Not Comanche or even
Kickapoo.

The officer touched the tips of his gauntleted fingers to his hat
brim. "Chief Two Blankets, I am Lieutenant Richard Scarborough
of the United States Army. I bring greetings from the Great Father.
This man"—he gestured toward the older one—"is Hiram Oldham. The other is his son, Harris."

Charlie nodded a greeting. "Come inside my lodge. We will
smoke and talk of what brings you here."

"No time for that, old man," Hiram Oldham said, his voice terse
and disrespectful. "We come to tell you to get off this land."

Charlie stood for a moment, stunned. He heard the angry mut-
tering from the younger men in the band.

"Chief Two Blankets," the lieutenant said, "I must warn you and
your men against any hostile move. I have a company of soldiers
just beyond the ridge."

Charlie ignored the officer. He glared at the big man with the
beard. "What do you mean, get off this land? It is our home. Major
Neighbors led us to this place. He said we could live here."

Hiram Oldham snorted in disgust. "Neighbors ain't the stud hoss
around here no more, old man. You got a new agent. And this land
is mine, bought and paid for."

"How can this be? We were told the white man would not come
this far west. We signed a paper. It said there would be a line the
white man would not cross."

"The treaty was never ratified by the Senate," the lieutenant said.
Charlie thought he heard a note of apology in the officer's voice.

"I know little of this white man's Senate," Charlie said. His tone
reflected his growing bitterness. "I know only that we were promised that we could live here in peace."

The lieutenant cleared his throat. "Mister Oldham bought the
rights to this land from the State of Texas. His papers give him
legal title. I'm sorry, Charlie Two Blankets, but your people will
have to move."

Charlie's shoulders slumped. He had been through this conversation before. Only the places and the faces were different. At the
corner of his vision he saw one of the young men take a step forward, rifle in hand. He caught the man's eye and shook his head.
The warrior lowered his rifle and stepped back.

"When our crops are gathered—"

"No, old man." The bearded man's eyes glittered in the growing dawn. "You get off this land now. Today."

Charlie squared his shoulders in defiance. "My people need the crops to feed them during the winter, to provide seed for the next growing season. At the end of the harvest we will move."

"I ain't waiting that long, old man. You got two choices." Hiram Oldham leaned forward in the saddle and stared directly into Charlie's face. "One, you move out on your own. Two, I come back here with a troop of Texas Rangers and a squad of U.S. Army soldiers and move you out. I got people on the way right now to settle this land. And that's all there is to it. It's your pick."

The big man and his son wheeled their horses about. The lieutenant hesitated. "I'm sorry I can't help you," he said.

"What happened to Major Neighbors?"

"He was dismissed from the Indian service."

"And his promise was dismissed along with him?"

"It was never made into law."

"Law," Charlie snorted in disgust. "White man's law. It is like a river. It flows but one way."

The officer's face flushed but he made no reply. He reined his horse about and left the camp. He did not look back.

"Charlie Two Blankets," one of the younger men said, "what do we do now?"

Charlie stared toward the retreating soldier and shrugged in despair. "What can we do but move? We cannot fight them. They would kill us all, men, women and children. We must go west again, upriver. To the very edge of Comanche country." He turned to his people. "But if we must go and face the hunger of the time of snows, we will leave none of our work for the white man to harvest. We will burn our fields."

San Antonio
September 1850

Major Robert Neighbors slouched in his favorite chair, an oversized, overstuffed and pleasantly ugly thing covered in soft cowhide, and waved at Ignacio to refill Rip Ford's coffee cup.

Ford nodded his thanks to the houseboy and grinned at the Major. "Nice place," he said in a wryly deliberate understatement.

The Major grinned back. "Thanks. I like it."

The new house on the banks of Salado Creek six miles from San Antonio had quite a few more creature comforts than the rented house in town. It had five rooms, a crystal chandelier in the dining hall, a pump in the kitchen, a solidly built barn out back, and it sat in the center of two hundred and sixty acres of prime grazing land. Sleek mares and foals of Kentucky and Tennessee breeding stock grazed on part of the farm. A hand-picked herd of mother cows lazed under pecan and oak groves, chewing their cuds as one of their group took her turn at watching over the new calves.

"Yes, sir, mighty impressive little spread," Ford said. "You turning into a man of leisure on me, Major?"

The Major sighed in contentment. "As much as possible. Gentleman farmer, that's me."

Ford grunted in mock derision. "Gentleman, my saddle-sore butt. I know you better than that, Major." He sipped at his coffee and nodded his approval. "Boy makes a fine cup." The former Ranger leaned back in his seat on a sofa as obscenely soft as the Major's chair. "Well, what's next on your calendar? You've organized two new counties, bought into a railroad and built yourself a farm since you got fired from the Indian service."

A hint of a frown flickered across the Major's brow. "The latter still rankles a bit, Rip," he said. "As far as plans, I've a few." He cocked an eyebrow at Ford. "And if I know you, my sly friend, you've something in mind or you wouldn't ask."

Ford shrugged. "Just thought you might be interested in making a run at a seat in the state legislature," he said casually. "Way I've got it figured, you and old Sam Maverick just might be able to save Texas from the damn Whigs in the House. With a little help from one Senator Rip Ford after the votes are counted. You interested?"

"Do pigs make pork?" The Major finished his coffee and put the cup on a sturdy mahogany side table. "When I walked out of that undersecretary's office in Washington, Rip, I promised myself that if the Whigs wanted to play politics, by God I'd oblige them. But I work best behind the scenes."

"Horse apples." Ford waved a hand in dismissal. "I've seen you work a crowd. You're better than good at it."

The Major shrugged. "Maybe. But I've got a political liability in Texas. Remember that fellow who jumped me in San Antonio, called me an Indian-lover? There's a lot more like him out there."

Ford fished a pipe from a pocket, stuffed and lit it, then squinted through the smoke at the Major. "Can't say that might not be a problem. But I reckon you've got more friends than enemies, Major. Even on the Indian question. Been reading the papers?"

"Now and then."

Ford puffed at the pipe for a moment. "Then you know some pretty powerful people are raising old billy hell about the Whigs cutting you loose from the Indian service. Sam Houston's been scorching every newspaper in the country over that. People listen to old Sam. Even some of the Whig papers have come down on your side. And Rollins hasn't even made a token appearance at the Texas Indian Agency." Ford stared at the pipe in his hand. "The smaller tribes are hurting, Major. The Caddos and others on the Brazos are damn near starving. Now, if you get to say your piece at the statehouse, you might be able to help them. You know Sam Maverick's on your side. Hell, you might even get a kind word or two from this old Indian-fighter. We've got a smidgeon of pull with the Democratic Party. You game to give it a shot?"

Robert Neighbors chuckled. "I don't see why not," he said. "It shouldn't take anything more than a little time and a little money. I've got enough of both."

Seguin
July 1851

Senator-elect John S. Ford stood in the shade of a stately oak tree outside the Mays home, a cup of heavily spiked punch in hand, and watched as Major Robert Neighbors and his new bride greeted guests in the receiving line.

The wedding had been brief. The courtship hadn't been just a hell of a lot longer, Ford mused, but the Major knew quality when he saw it. Elizabeth Ann Mays Neighbors was quality.

The wedding hadn't been the "small affair" the Major had promised. Friends of the bride and groom filled the parlor of her parents' modest home, spilled outside, peered in windows to catch a glimpse of the ceremony, and now waited patiently in line to offer personal congratulations.

The two made an unlikely couple, Ford thought. The girl was eighteen, half the Major's age—and less than half his size. Elizabeth Ann Neighbors stood barely five foot tall with her shoes on, with a thin, trim body that looked like it might break in a heavy gust of wind. She was as shy and quiet as the Major was outgoing and garrulous. Her skin was smooth and pale where his was darkened and lined from sun and wind. Her dark brown hair was pulled into a tight bun at the back of her neck. She wasn't exactly a beauty, but she wasn't plain either, Ford decided. Her most remarkable feature was her eyes. They were big, brown and expressive, a mirror into a gentle soul.

Sam Maverick stepped to Ford's side, a portion of his brood in tow. The Maverick clan included not only the natural sons and daughters of the Mavericks, but a number of adopted orphans, mostly children rescued or ransomed from Indian camps. It was said that Mary Maverick never turned away a soul in need. She was expecting again, her sturdy body beginning to swell. Rip Ford smiled to himself. He had heard that Mary Maverick was more vibrant and attractive when she was pregnant than when she wasn't. Ford couldn't say. He couldn't recall having seen her when she wasn't.

Sam slipped a small flask from beneath his jacket and topped off Ford's punch cup. "Well, Rip," Sam said, "there goes another good man led off with a ring in his nose." The twinkle in Sam's eye belied the solemn pronouncement. "Said your howdys to the new bride yet?"

"Waiting for the crowd to thin out a bit, Sam." Ford sipped at the cup and savored the fine flavor of the expensive Kentucky bourbon. "Sure hope that girl hasn't stepped into something she can't handle."

Sam Maverick cast a cautious glance at his drinking companion. "You know something I don't, Rip?"

Rip Ford sighed. "We got Indian troubles brewing. Comanches painted up and on the prowl again. Word is they've already raided a bunch of homesteads out west. Killed maybe a half dozen white folks. And the tame Indians—the Caddos, Anadarkos, Lipans, Tonks and the others—haven't got a half dozen wagon loads of supplies since that damn Whig took the Major's place. I don't know how much longer they're going to stand for it. They won't let their women and kids starve. They may be farmers and tame Indians, but I'd just as soon not have a mad Caddo on my trail."

Sam muttered a soft curse. "The last thing we need now is an Indian war, my friend."

Ford drained the cup in two swallows. "And the one man who could maybe head it off is stuck out in the pasture."

Sam Maverick sighed. "Maybe the Major can get something done in the state legislature, with our help. At least we fought off the Whigs in Austin."

"Yeah," Ford said. "The problem is, who's in charge where the Indians are concerned? Annexation muddied the water. Texas owns the land but Washington's supposed to take care of the Indians. It seems to me that's a combination that won't mix."

"We've got a different sort of badger in this hole, true enough. I wish I had the answer." Maverick shook the flask. "Want me to sweeten that cup for you, Rip?"

"No, thanks. I'd best go pay my respects before the newlyweds get away, Sam." He touched fingers to his hat brim in salute to Mary Maverick and made his way to the porch where Robert and Elizabeth Neighbors waited.

FOUR

Austin
February 1852

State Representative Robert Neighbors leaned back in his chair in the House chamber and breathed a silent sigh of relief as the final votes on the joint resolution were tallied. *At least we've won one and lost one now,* he thought. *Half a biscuit isn't much, but it beats the devil out of going hungry.*

The Major felt no lingering animosity toward his colleagues in the House who had defeated his bill to reserve most of North Texas from Gainesville west to the New Mexico border for use by the Indians. The proposal had gone over like a coyote in a hen house with the delegates from North Texas and the Rio Grande areas.

The Major couldn't blame them. The representatives from North Texas saw the open plains beyond Gainesville, the westernmost settlement in the region, as fertile ground for expansion. In the southern and western counties an outbreak of Comanche raids in recent weeks had cost the lives of a dozen settlers. The Comanches also had taken several prisoners and stolen scores of horses and mules. The representatives from the stricken areas had a right to be upset. They, along with many others in the Texas Legislature, were not kindly disposed toward Indians of any stripe at the moment.

The Major knew the raids were likely to get worse in the coming months. With no laws to restrain them the Texans would keep pushing the frontier to the west. The great buffalo herds that once had roamed the lands beyond the Balcones Escarpment had disappeared, shoved toward the setting sun by settlers, white hide-hunters and the steadily increasing river of California-bound immigrants traveling roads that cut through Indian lands.

The westward movement of the frontier had to stop. There could never be peace with the Indians otherwise. And until this point the Major had seen his pleas fall on ears that did not hear. Then, when he had all but given up hope of gaining any sort of foothold for his overall plan, Senator Rip Ford had called on the Major.

"Lord knows I'm not crazy about the damn red sons," Ford had grumbled. "I don't think your idea's going to work, Major, but by God you deserve a chance to prove whether you're right or wrong. Let's get to work."

The document that grew from that meeting was the joint resolution that now had narrowly passed both houses. Stripped to the bone, the resolution granted the governor authority to negotiate an arrangement with the federal government to settle the Indians on lands set aside somewhere in North Texas. *At least*, the Major thought, *this gives us a start.*

A smattering of applause mixed with catcalls heralded the speaker's announcement of the official vote total and bang of gavel declaring the joint resolution passed.

The Major rose to exchange handshakes with his supporters. A few members of the opposition took the results in good form. Most remained in their seats. Others glowered in open disgust at the Major. *They'd like to say it if they had the nerve*, he thought. *The Indian-lover tag's a hard one to shake.*

"Well, Major," Representative Sam Maverick said as he offered a hand, "it looks like we've made us some enemies. Congratulations, anyway."

"Thanks, Sam. We should be congratulating Rip. He's the one who put the votes together to get this wagon out of the ditch and back on the road."

"Cost him some friends, too, I expect," Maverick said, his brow furrowed. He waved toward a delegate whose dark scowl and angry puffs on a foul-smelling pipe clouded a goodly portion of the House chamber. "Old Silas's hackles have never been that high. You'd think from looking at him that this resolution is the only thing we've done here."

"The rest of it didn't involve Indians, Sam," the Major said. "I'll be glad to see it end. Lizzie and I are anxious to get back to the farm on the Salado. That hotel room's not quite as comfortable as our little dugout back home. And we want the baby to be born there."

A broad grin flashed across Maverick's face. "Baby? By God, Major, there may be hope for you yet, you old horse thief." He extended a hand again. "Congratulations. How's Lizzie feeling?"

"Good at the moment, thanks," the Major said, "but we're still six months away from the big day, if the doctors are right."

Maverick released the Major's hand, chuckled and scratched at a chin that looked stubbled even when freshly shaved. "Nothing like a young one or six to brighten up a house, my friend. Just don't get too comfortable back home. You've still got some work to do. We're counting on you to help run the damn Whigs out of Washington. You've got one hammer up on the rest of us. You get a direct say as a member of the electoral panel." Maverick reached for his own pipe. "You still think Franklin Pierce is our best chance to beat Taylor?"

"That's how I see it, Sam," the Major said. "At least that's how I plan to vote. It won't be easy getting Taylor out of office. People like to vote for war heroes."

Maverick puffed furiously at his pipe. "War hero my butt," he groused. "Zachary Taylor came within a gnat's mustache of losing the Mexican War. Hell, he'd still be in Matamoros trying to figure out where the outhouse was if Ben McCulloch's Rangers and the First Texas hadn't yanked him off his duff."

The banging of the speaker's gavel interrupted the conversation. "Well, back to work, Major," Maverick said with a wink. "With luck, we'll get you out of here in time for the baby's arrival."

Brazos River
August 1852

Charlie Two Blankets awakened from a fitful sleep, his light doze broken by the weak cries of a child in the neighboring lodge.

The baby's faint wail cut through Charlie like the knife edge of a winter blizzard despite the muggy heat in his lodge. It was an almost constant keening now, the cries of hungry young ones. Twice in the last moon the whimpers of the children had been joined by the wails of mothers mourning the loss of a baby. It should have been a good time, this Season of Growing Corn. His people should be looking toward the celebration of a harvest, not singing the death songs of the Starving Time.

But the seasons had changed for the Caddos. In the stifling heat of summer, Charlie's soul was cold.

The spring crops had failed. Now the flour corn stalks and

pumpkin vines withered and died under the blazing sun and rainless skies. Half the seed corn for next year's planting was gone, sacrificed to empty bellies. The mules had gone into the cooking pots along with all but a handful of rail-thin ponies as near starvation as were their owners. Food, clothing and other supplies promised by the Great Father's new agents had never arrived. Comanche and Kickapoo raiders had stolen all but a few meager possessions of worth that remained to the Caddos.

Charlie felt his eldest wife stir in her blankets at his side. She had taken the Christian name of Mary.

"What is it, husband?" Mary's voice was soft in the thick air of the lodge.

"Corn Flower's child," Charlie replied. "It is dying. Corn Flower's milk has dried up. There are no other women whose breasts might nurse the baby. We cannot even feed the child the milk of the cow as the white man does. The one cow that was making milk has dried up as did Corn Flower."

Mary climbed from her blanket. "I will go to Corn Flower."

"There is nothing you can do, woman," Charlie said. "You have no food for the child."

"I can be with Corn Flower when the child dies. I can share her grief." Mary swung the lodge door open, her broad frame faintly outlined in the growing gray of pre-dawn light as she left the lodge. Charlie listened as her bare feet crunched on the parched, sandy soil. *Perhaps it is best that neither of my wives have given me sons,* Charlie thought. *Perhaps that has spared us the pain that so many others have felt.* He stared toward the lodge door. The reed flap had fallen askew. It showed as a gray triangle against the darkness inside the lodge.

Charlie rose, his joints stiff and protesting. Anger born of helplessness fueled the pain in his empty belly. *Sunrise comes soon,* he thought, *but the night is near for the Caddos—*

"Charlie!"

Mary's anxious cry from outside jolted the pain from Charlie's joints. "What is it, Mary?"

The lodge flap tore from its bindings as Mary scuttled inside. "Comanches—on the ridge to the north." Her voice was ragged, her breathing irregular from alarm and exertion. "I saw three of them—on horseback. Watching. It could be—another raiding party."

Charlie muttered a sharp oath. He reached for his old percussion rifle, felt to see that the nipple was in place and handed it to Mary.

He strode quickly to the blanket where his second wife, Catherine, still snored. He shook her awake none too gently. "Comanches come, Catherine. Run to the other lodges. Tell the men to arm themselves. Tell them to form a half circle on the north side of the camp. *Move, woman!*"

Catherine came fully awake. She scrambled from her blanket and scurried for the doorway. She was five years younger and fifty pounds lighter than her sister Mary, quick of foot and agile. It would take her but a few moments to spread the word to all the lodges.

"Stay here, Mary," Charlie said, his words cold and hard. "If the Comanches break through, use the rifle on the first one who steps foot in our lodge."

"What will you do, husband?"

Charlie reached for his bois d'arc bow and quiver. "The Comanches have stolen from us enough, woman." He heard the tight rage in his own words. "In the past I have stood and watched and wrung my hands as a grandmother, not as a warrior and leader of my people. This time I fight." Charlie started toward the door, then paused to place a hand on Mary's shoulder. "I have no brother," he said.

Mary's hand closed atop Charlie's and squeezed. "It is no matter, my husband. I want no other man. I never have. In my eyes you have always been a strong warrior. You make me proud this day."

Charlie pulled his hand away, tucked a butcher knife beneath the frayed rope that served as his belt and reached for his buffalo hide war shield and lance at the lodge door. He glanced back once before he stepped outside. Mary sat in the back of the lodge, her bulk a dark shadow in the growing light, the rifle across her knees. Charlie knew he was seeing her for the last time. He stepped into the new dawn.

Five warriors sat astride their horses on the ridge to the north. The first rays of the rising sun fell upon them. They were armed with rifles, bows and lances. Their war paint and the markings on their ponies told Charlie they were of the Paneteka band of the great Staked Plains. *It is good,* Charlie thought; *if a warrior is to die, it should be against a powerful enemy.*

Charlie ignored the shouts and commotion now sweeping the Caddo camp as he walked, his strides long and firm, back straight, past the shallow trench from which his men would fight. They could put up little resistance. No man had more than a few ounces of powder and lead. Charlie could only hope the Comanches did not know that.

He stopped fifty yards beyond the defensive perimeter and glared toward the warriors on the hilltop. Then he leaned his bow against a stunted bush at his side. He raised his lance high overhead and shook the weapon toward the Comanches.

"No more, you thieving sons of she-dogs!" Charlie yelled in the Comanche tongue. "It is enough! You take no more from the Caddos! We are not sheep! Come and fight!"

The years seemed to drain from Charlie's muscles. Once again he felt strong and young. The blood of a warrior pumped through his veins. For a moment the horsemen milled about on the ridge, confused at the unexpected challenge. A thought flashed through Charlie's mind. *There will be no one to lead your people, Charlie Two Blankets.* The thought vanished as quickly as it had formed. It did not matter. If the Comanches were not stopped there soon would be no people to lead. He thrust the lance into the ground before him and picked up his bow.

"Come!" he shouted toward the horsemen. "Do you fight like men? Or do you slink about in the night like the Kickapoos?"

A Comanche yelped an enraged curse and quirted his horse down the rocky hillside. Others followed, yelling and whooping. Charlie calmly pulled an iron-tipped cedar arrow from his quiver and nocked it. He counted a dozen raiders in the party. They were almost within bow range now. He pulled the stiff, strong bow to its full draw and waited. The Comanche on the right turned his head to yell to his comrades. Charlie loosed the arrow.

The Comanche never saw the shaft coming. It buried itself into his breast. Charlie thought he heard the thunk as the arrow hammered home. The raider sagged and fell from his mount.

Charlie heard the buzz of a rifle ball past his ear. He nocked another arrow, pulled and loosed the bowstring. The shaft took a Comanche's horse in the chest. The animal staggered and went down. Charlie knew he would have no time for another arrow. The yelping raiders were almost upon him. Another rifle belched smoke and Charlie felt the jar of the ball against his shoulder. There was no pain.

He yanked his lance from the ground. The lead horseman bore down on Charlie, the feathers on the shank of his lance fluttering in the rush of wind. Charlie stood his ground until the last moment, then ducked aside. The Comanche tried to correct his aim but his lance thrust went wide. Charlie drove his own lance toward the warrior's side and grunted in disgust as the tip missed its mark and sliced across the skin of the rider's ribs instead of driving deep between them.

A heavy fist hit Charlie in the hip as a rifle boomed only yards away. He staggered but kept his feet. Another blow struck him in the back; he staggered, almost went down, but regained his footing.

He heard no firing from his own camp. He realized then that the raiders had wheeled their mounts to face him once more. *It is a fair trade,* Charlie thought, *one old Caddo warrior for a whole village.* He stabbed the tip of his lance into the ground, the universal sign there would be no retreat or surrender.

Charlie saw the puff of smoke from the rifle, felt the ball drive deep into his gut. Still he stood, his hand on the lance. A Comanche whose face was painted red and black dismounted, knelt and raised his rifle. Charlie's head was still held high when the ball ripped into his chest. He stumbled and dropped to his knees. He struggled back to his feet, using the shaft of his lance for support, and squared his shoulders.

Five rifles thundered. The impact of lead balls lifted Charlie Two Blankets from his feet and tumbled him onto his back. He stared for a moment at the pale blue sky overhead. Tall pines appeared, shimmering in the mist of a cool rain, and Charlie Two Blankets saw himself once again standing amid the forests of his youth before the darkness fell.

The remaining Comanche warriors cautiously approached the crumpled form in the dirt. One man strode to the body, knife in hand, and reached for Charlie's head.

"No!"

The knife-wielding man stopped at the single word from the leader of the raiding party.

"This one is not to be scalped," the leader said. "He was a brave man and a fine warrior. As he said, this Caddo was no sheep. We leave him as he fell."

The man on foot snorted in disgust. "And let him be reborn to kill more of us? Already he has killed one man and wounded another. His arrow claimed my best war pony. Has the wind stolen your mind, Little Elk?"

Little Elk squared his shoulders and stared a challenge at the man on the ground. "We will spare this village in honor of the old man's bravery and his strong medicine."

"His medicine was stronger than yours, Little Elk. There will be much wailing when we return to our camp." The man on foot spat, but sheathed his knife. "I follow you on the war trail no more."

"That is your right." Little Elk waited until another warrior caught a loose horse and led the animal to the man on the ground. Then he kneed his mount forward. At the top of the ridge Little Elk stopped to look back. A crowd had gathered around the body of the old chief. A smaller gathering clumped around the dead Comanche horse. Little Elk saw sunlight glint on a knife blade. *Hunger must be great here,* he thought; *the old warrior's people butcher the horse before they care for his body. Perhaps that is the way he would want it to be. In death he serves his tribe as he did in life. It is a noble end.*

Little Elk reined his horse about. The fight on the Brazos, one old man against a dozen young Comanche warriors, was the seed of which legends were born. The defeat would cost Little Elk status among his own people. A Comanche warrior had died under his leadership. The success of the other raids would be forgotten. It would be a long time before he regained the trust of the fighting men of Yellow Wolf's band enough to again lead a war party.

"Old man," he muttered to the spirit of the dead warrior, "in death you win your battles. Mine have just begun. When the time comes, I hope that I die as well as you did."

Red River Trading Post
November 1852

Emil Washburn sat cross-legged on the blanket spread before the adobe building and stared into the black eyes of the Comanche chief seated across from him, tin cup in hand.

"It was a good raid, Yellow Wolf. You punished the Mexicans well," Washburn said.

Yellow Wolf grunted and sipped at the cup. Washburn knew it would be only a matter of minutes until the cheap whiskey did its work on the Paneteka war chief. Then he would drive his bargain. His gaze drifted over the Comanche camp a hundred yards away. He estimated there were fifty warriors in the party. Washburn did not fear attack. Yellow Wolf needed the trader and his goods. But five men, all heavily armed, were stationed at windows and shooting ports of the building just in case. Comanches were a touchy bunch. One never knew, so one took precautions.

"Many horses and mules, cattle," Yellow Wolf said after a lengthy pause. His words were a bit slurred from the whiskey. "Fifteen captives."

Washburn leaned forward and refilled the chief's cup from the heavy white crockery jug, then pointedly replaced the stopper. The stopper in the jug told Yellow Wolf there would be no more whiskey until a deal was struck. It was time to begin some serious talk. Washburn gestured toward the building and the wagon parked alongside.

"For each twelve Mexican mules, one fine new percussion musket," the trader said.

"Ten. Good mules."

Washburn flashed a quick, easy smile. "Yellow Wolf is no fool," he said. "The great chief of the Panetekas will leave me a poor man. Very well. For eleven mules I will give a rifle, a pound of powder, a pound of lead, and fifty percussion caps."

Yellow Wolf glanced at the stoppered jug and licked his lips. "Agreed."

"Good, my friend," Washburn said. "For four good Mexican ponies, a bolt of cloth, two pounds of sugar and a knife of finest steel and a bullet mold."

The chief nodded his acceptance. "And for the Texan horses?"

Washburn forced a frown. "That is a problem, old friend," he said, his tone solemn. "Horses taken from Texans are a gamble for me. If their owners come I will be forced to return them." He ran a hand across his bearded chin as if in deep thought. He sighed. "For one Texas horse, a mirror, comb, a half pound of fine beads, a pound of coffee and a strong steel hatchet."

The chief shook his head. "It is not enough. I take them somewhere else."

Washburn held the Comanche's stare until the chief blinked. Yellow Wolf's eyes were watery from the effects of the whiskey. The trader raised his hands, palm upward. "Yellow Wolf would have my children starve. He would leave me penniless, to go begging for scraps among the Wacos." Washburn waited for several heartbeats, then lifted his shoulders in a shrug of resignation. "Very well. I have once again been bested in the trade. I will add two warm blankets and one metal cooking pot."

"And whiskey."

"All for one scraggly horse?"

Yellow Wolf glanced at the jug at Washburn's side. "They are fine horses," he said. "Big, strong mounts."

"All right. For *two* Texas horses, the items I have spoken. Plus one crock jug of good whiskey."

"Done." Triumph flickered in the Comanche's eyes.

The fool doesn't realize he's just traded me a horse for one jug of Old Gutbuster, Washburn thought. He struggled to keep his expression downcast, as if he had just lost his last dollar.

"The cattle," Yellow Wolf said.

"All but worthless, Yellow Wolf. They are skinny, no meat. Some are near death."

"They will grow fat when the grass greens."

Washburn let his shoulders droop as if he were a beaten man. "Perhaps enough will live that I can at least break even on them. For ten head, two pounds of tobacco, a bolt of cloth, a sack of salt, a pound of powder and lead." He sighed heavily. "And a bottle of whiskey."

Yellow Wolf paused as if considering the offer. Finally he nodded. "Agreed. And for the captives?"

Washburn shrugged. He knew there were two white women and three children among the prisoners taken in the Comanche raid on South Texas and northern Mexico. But he could see no profit in the white captives. The price would likely be more than their families had. He couldn't care less about the Mexicans. "I have no use for women and children, Yellow Wolf. I pay no ransom."

Yellow Wolf shrugged. "It is no matter. We keep them. Some make good Comanche. We find buyers for others."

Washburn reached for the jug at his side and pulled the stopper. "It is good, Yellow Wolf. You best me at the trading blanket again, but we remain good friends." He filled the chief's tin cup to the brim. "My men will bring your goods and take over the livestock. Now we drink and smoke to our trade."

Three hours later Emil Washburn watched the Comanche band grow small in the distance. Some of the warriors already were having trouble staying in the saddle. They would be back, probably once more before winter, with other stolen goods to trade.

Washburn clawed at an itch on his backside. *Like finding a bird nest on the ground,* he thought. *The thieving redskins are making me a rich man.* He turned and strode to the trading post, ignoring the north wind and its slight nip that hinted of the coming winter.

Nathan Colley, Washburn's brother-in-law and part owner of the trading post, sat at a table and sipped at the neck of a bottle of whiskey. It wasn't trade liquor, watered down and colored with tobacco twists. It was prime sour mash. Colley glanced up and grinned.

"Another good day, Emil," he said. "We'll show a hefty profit on those Texas horses in Saint Louis."

Emil Washburn reached for a glass and poured himself a double shot from Nat's bottle. He downed the whiskey at a single swallow and chuckled aloud. "We won't do bad on the cattle, either. There's some good breeding stock that'll bring top dollar back in East Texas and Louisiana. Cull the skinny and sick ones, deliver them to the tame Indians, and let the government pay us for prime beef stock."

Colley took another swig from the neck of the bottle. "Yeah. The Indian agents don't know the difference and don't care. Hell, Emil, we're going to be as rich as the Bents and Torreys one of these days."

Washburn poured himself another drink and raised the glass in a toast. "Richer, Nat. The Bents and Torreys may have made a fortune trading with the Indians, but they did it the slow way. They played fair. We'll own them one of these days." Washburn downed the whiskey and savored the fire it stoked in his belly. He nodded toward the door. "Better give the boys a hand, Nat," he said. "I'll be along directly."

Nat Colley took a final swig from the bottle and reached for his hat. Washburn waited until the door closed behind his brother-in-law, then settled into a chair and stoked his pipe. *Emil, you sly cuss,* he congratulated himself, *you found the key to wealth. Whiskey, trinkets and stolen livestock. And the beauty is, it doesn't matter who steals the stock.* Hiram Oldham and his boy down on the lower Brazos were good for a hundred head of horses a year, and the thefts could be blamed on the Indians. *And now that old Charlie Two Blankets is gone, the Caddos and their friends are a brand-new whiskey market.*

Washburn fired his pipe, leaned back in his chair and stared through the whorls of smoke at the rafters and sod overhead. *A damn bird nest on the ground sure enough. And we've got old Zack Taylor to thank for it. He fired the only man who might have got in the way.*

The thought momentarily sobered Washburn. What the government gave, it could also take away. He wondered how the election had gone. If the Whigs lost out, things might change. He shrugged the thought away. Chances were Major Robert Simpson Neighbors would never be in the Indian service again. And if he started making trouble, he could be taken care of. One way or another.

San Antonio
May 1853

Mary Beatrice Neighbors smiled a toothless grin of joy as she did her nine-month-old best to pull her father's rust-colored beard from his face. The Major smiled back and let her tug. The baby was plump, happy and healthy, bubbly and easily amused except when she was hungry. Then the girl could rattle the rafters. Mary Beatrice had her mother's delicate features and the Major's reddish-brown hair. It was even more red than his own, he noted.

Lizzie had begun to lose the extra weight she had picked up during her pregnancy. Her labor had been long and difficult, but neither mother nor child was ever in danger, the doctor had said. *Seems like the Creator could have come up with a better design for building babies,* the Major thought idly. *Puts a lot of strain and pain on a woman; you'd think He would have made it a little easier—*

"Major, are you spoiling that child again?" Lizzie half-scolded from the kitchen. "I hear all that giggling going on out there."

"We're just having a little talk, Lizzie," the Major said with a chuckle. "The way this girl's growing, she'll have a full set of teeth and be needing a corset soon."

"Major Neighbors! For shame, talking that way! Bring the little one in, dear. Her bath water's ready."

The Major rose from the chair, careful not to drop the baby. After a couple of steps he decided he needn't have worried about it; with the grip she had on his beard, he would have to pry her fingers loose by force before he could drop her. He carried Mary to the kitchen, where Lizzie waited by a small porcelain tub of warm water on a counter top. He carefully untangled the small fingers from his whiskers and handed the child to Lizzie.

"Now, sir, begone with you," Lizzie said with a smile. "Go play with your horses or some such while we girls tend our toilettes."

The Major patted Lizzie playfully on the rump, saw the color flush her cheeks, and whistled an off-key tune as he walked onto the front porch. He stood for a moment, breathing in the sweet, clean air of springtime, and surveyed his growing domain.

Splashes of color from thousands of wildflowers blazed against the green of the meadows flanking Salado Creek. The light breeze was heady with the scent of honeysuckle and the red roses beside the porch. A mockingbird continued her serenade from the blackberry vines at the side of the barn. The bird was one of the Major's favorite animals on the place. She worked hard. She raised a pair of nestlings each year in the berry vines, but she seldom stopped singing. It was a happy sound outside a happy home. *Most men would kill for half of what I have,* the Major thought in contentment.

The only fly in the gravy, the Major mused, was that the situation had gotten worse on the Indian question. The Comanche raids on Texas farms and ranches had increased. One of his last acts as a member of the Fourth Texas Legislature had been to introduce a bill to fund the raising of three Ranger companies to protect the frontier. And the settled Indians along the Brazos were under constant harassment from both white men and hostile tribes. That meant unfinished business. The Major didn't like work undone.

He still felt a twinge of loss over the death of the Caddo chief Charlie Two Blankets. Charlie had been a good man. He had also been a friend. And his influence had been felt beyond his own tribe. He would be missed. *At least he died the way a warrior should,* the Major thought.

The Major watched as a distant speck on the road to San Antonio took shape. Ignacio Serna rode at an easy trot aboard a sleek young sorrel gelding he was breaking to saddle. The boy had fleshed out in the last four years. He had become a man. He had also developed into one of the best handlers of young horses the Major had ever seen.

Ignacio reined the horse toward the barn, then changed directions when he spotted the Major leaning against a porch post. He eased the sorrel to a stop, dismounted and handed a packet to the Major.

"Special dispatch," Ignacio said. "It bears the seal of the United States."

"Thank you, Ignacio." The Major broke the wax seal, slipped the message from the envelope and scanned it. He felt a wide grin spread across his face.

"Good news, Major?" Ignacio pulled at the reins, lifting the sorrel's nose from the rosebush where it was contemplating a nip at a large bloom.

"Yes, Ignacio. Very good news." The Major refolded the one-page letter and tapped it against his palm. "The Democrats and President Pierce have made the nation safe from the Whigs once more." He chucked softly. "But even more important, Ignacio, is that I am once again the Indian agent for the State of Texas. I take office in August."

Ignacio offered a handshake of congratulations. "I am happy for you. This is what you wished, is it not?"

The Major gripped the Mexican youth's hand. "I didn't campaign for the job, Ignacio. I never asked for it as a political favor or reward for my services to my party, my state or my nation. But I won't lie to you—I couldn't be more pleased at the moment." He released Ignacio's hand, impressed with the strength it had acquired. "I must tell Lizzie the news. Would you join me in a glass of wine to celebrate the good tidings?"

Ignacio shook his head. "I have two more horses to ride today," he said with a wry smile, "and one of them, the *grulla,* is hard enough to stay on without drink making the head dizzy." The smile faded. "You will leave soon?"

"Yes. There's a lot of work to do, Ignacio. I'll be splitting my time between the smaller tribes on the Brazos, the Lipans and Tonkawas at Fort Inge, in council with the Comanches on the Plains, and probably some trips to Austin and maybe even Washington. I'll make this my headquarters and be home as often as possible."

"Will you take me with you this time?"

The Major put a hand on Ignacio's shoulder. "No, son. I'll need you here, to watch over the family and the farm when I'm gone."

FIVE

Brazos River
August 1853

Major Robert Neighbors made no attempt to hide the rage and disgust that tore at his gut as he rode into the small cluster of Caddo lodges along the bank of the Brazos.

The scene before him was even worse than it had been in the villages of the Anadarkos, Ionis and other farming tribes who had agreed to treaties and settled along the upper Brazos under the Whig administration.

The Major had expected signs of neglect among the Indians; he had heard rumors of the incompetence of the agents he had inherited. But he wasn't prepared for the pathetic scenes that unfolded on his first inspection trip among the Brazos settlements.

The Caddo village was a third smaller than when he had last visited the band before his dismissal from the Indian service. Cholera, smallpox and other disease had hit the remnants of the tribe hard.

And now, able-bodied men sat in the shade of trees or their lodges, their faces slack and eyes glazed, crock jugs and bottles at their sides. Half the village, it seemed, was stone drunk. A handful of women labored in the fields, grubbing without enthusiasm at a few rows of scraggly plants. Less than a quarter of the available land was in cultivation. Even that showed neglect. Weeds flourished among the few listless flour corn stalks and heat-baked pumpkin vines.

Throughout the village children stared as the two men on horse-back passed. It was the appearance of the children that cut the Major deepest and fueled his rage.

They wore little more than rags. The children were dirty, un-washed, a condition so foreign to Caddo culture as to be almost beyond belief. Small arms and legs were little more than skin and bones. Bellies had begun to swell as starvation neared. None played at the hoop-and-stick game or other amusements of youth. They simply sat or stood and stared. It was the look in their eyes that hurt the worst. There was no sparkle of the mischief that was the normal state of Caddo youth, only blank and lifeless stares.

The Major stopped his horse and leveled a cold glare at the man riding at his side. "What the hell's been going on here, Agent Stemm?" he snapped.

Jesse Stemm shifted his lean frame in the saddle and squirmed under the Major's gaze. "I did my best, Major Neighbors," Stemm said lamely, "but there isn't much a man can do with a bunch of drunken Indians."

"Where did they get the whiskey?"

Stemm's Adam's apple bobbed. "I don't know."

"Dammit, man! It's your job to know!" The Major realized his voice was like the roar of a bull and carried throughout the camp. At the moment he didn't care. He gripped the saddle horn hard, fighting back the urge to hammer the lanky agent square in the face with a fist. "Where are the supplies promised the Caddos? The food, clothing, tools, cattle?"

Stemm shrugged. "When the Indians came to me, I requisitioned supplies according to procedure," he said. "I guess they just never got here."

The Major reined his horse around to face Stemm. "And just exactly how many times have you personally been to this village to check on conditions?"

Stemm tried to hold the Major's stare and failed. He dropped his gaze. "I—well, sir, this is the first time I've actually been afield, in an Indian camp—"

"The first time?"

"Well, I've made myself available to the Indians. At the agency station in Fort Belknap. That's all I'm required to do under government regulations." Stemm squirmed in the saddle. "There was nothing I could do about it—about the problems."

Robert Neighbors glared at the agent for a long moment. Finally, he sighed. "There's damn well something I can do about it, Stemm. You're fired."

"You can't—"

"Like hell I can't," the Major barked. "I've just done it. I want your resignation by sundown today. You've got two days to clear out of that agency office, Stemm. If you can't do the job, by God, I'll get someone in here who can."

"Look, Neighbors, I—"

"You're wasting time, Stemm. Get out of my sight. Now. Before I lose my temper."

Indignation flickered in the agent's eyes. "You can't just waltz in here and fire me like a hired hand, Neighbors. I've been duly appointed by the government. I have friends in high places—"

"I don't give a tinker's damn if you're on a first-name basis with Jesus Christ," the Major snapped. "Get out now, before I yank you off that horse and rap you over the ears with a pistol."

The faint spark of defiance faded from Jesse Stemm's eyes. He had heard that when Robert Neighbors got mad enough to curse the big man was near the breaking point. A sudden stab of fear pushed against Stemm's bladder. Stemm quickly reined his horse about and flicked the reins against the animal's rump.

The Major watched until Stemm's horse disappeared around a bend in the river, waiting until his rage subsided. As he regained control of his emotions he became aware that he was being watched. He glanced around and spotted Mary Two Blankets leaning on her hoe in a field a few yards away, staring in his direction.

The Major kneed his horse into motion. He stepped from the saddle and touched fingers to hat brim in greeting. "Mary, it is good to see you," he said.

The woman's broad, weathered face split into a wide grin. "So it is truly you," she said, her tone warm. "My old eyes sometimes fail me, but I thought when you rode into the village that our Major had finally come back to us as I had prayed he would." She offered her hand. The Major took the work-hardened fingers, careful not to squeeze in case Mary's arthritis had flared again.

"My heart weeps with you for your husband, Mary," the Major said solemnly. "He was a good man, a good friend, and I miss him greatly." The Major pointedly avoided mentioning Charlie by name. He suspected that despite her conversion to Christianity Mary would still be uncomfortable at breaking such an ingrained tribal taboo.

"His people miss him, too," Mary said. "My husband was a fine leader, a hard worker. He died as a warrior, and I am proud to have been his woman." A hint of moisture glinted in Mary's lower lids.

The Major gestured toward the cluster of lodges. "The Caddos suffer greatly, Mary. It is a knife in my heart to see such hunger and want amid the people. I promise you I will do my best to see that it ends."

"Then I will no longer fear the cold and pain of the Starving Time," she replied.

"Mary, I understand Albert Fox is *xinesi*. Will you point out his lodge? I must speak with him."

Mary shrugged her thick shoulders. "We have no *xinesi*. No governor. Only a *caddi*, and as even a lesser leader Albert Fox is *caddi* in name only." Her tone was a mixture of disgust and disappointment. "Albert Fox is probably drunk by now. He begins with the bottle when the sun rises." She waved an arm toward a grass and reed hut at the edge of the camp. "His lodge is the one with the foxtail by the door."

The Major nodded and started to turn away, then hesitated. The big woman probably knew more about what went on here than anyone in the village. "Mary, I must know something from someone whose words I trust. Can you spare a moment from your work to talk?"

Mary grimaced and glanced over the ill-tended field. "There is little use in working these fields, Major," she said. "It is something I do to pass the time. I will tell you such things as a mere woman knows." She glanced at the ground in embarrassment. "I apologize for not being able to invite you to my lodge for food. I have none to offer."

The Major nodded. "Had I known of your want, Mary, I would have brought food. I will see that some is sent as soon as I get back to Fort Belknap. Tell me when the whiskey began to appear. The Caddos I knew a few years ago had no use for the white man's liquor."

Mary sighed. "It came to our people a short time after my husband's death." The sadness in her tone was almost a living thing. The Major knew her pain was more for her people than for the death of Charlie Two Blankets. "As *xinesi*, my husband forbade the use of whiskey. When he was gone and Albert Fox became *caddi*, Albert was the first to turn to drink. He did nothing to stop others. It is a terrible thing, Major."

"Where does the whiskey come from?"

Mary's lips turned down in a scowl. "The trader called Emil Washburn. He has a post on the Red River. His wagons come here often." She snorted in disgust. "Our men trade their last bags of seed corn, their guns, everything and anything of value, for this Washburn's whiskey. Bellies go empty and crops unplanted so that minds may be numbed."

The Major nodded. "It is true. I make no excuse for those who hide in whiskey. But where there is no pride, a man—red or white —will seek escape in the bottle. I will see that this whiskey trade stops. I should have suspected Washburn was behind it. He tried to move in here while I was agent before. I stopped him then. I will stop him now." He lifted the reins. "Thank you for telling me this, Mary Two Blankets. I must call on Albert Fox now."

A few minutes later Major Robert Neighbors sat on a faded, ragged blanket inside Albert Fox's lodge. He glanced around. The lodge floor was cluttered with refuse and the interior stank of cheap whiskey and urine. It bore the unmistakable stamp of poverty. There were no woven mats of dried pumpkin hanging overhead, no sacks of smoked corn, no jars of beans or jerked meat to be seen. The one buffalo robe that remained was worn thin and showed bare spots; its warmth would be little comfort in the dead of winter.

Albert Fox sat across the dead ashes of the cooking fire from the Major, an open crockery jug between his knees. The Caddo's face was thin and drawn, his eyes watery and unable to focus on any one thing for more than a few seconds at a time. As Mary had predicted, the *caddi* was drunk. Not blind drunk yet, but well on his way. Albert Fox squinted toward the Major as if trying to identify the big object that had entered his lodge.

The Major wondered if he should make some attempt at formality and decided against it. Albert Fox was in no condition to go through any greeting ceremony.

"What has happened here, *Caddi?* Why do the men not hunt and work in the fields? I have never known the Caddos to be anything but hard workers."

Albert Fox shrugged indifferently. "What is the use? When we plant, the Texans come and tell us to move from the land before we can harvest. For two years straight they took our fields." He paused to take a swig from the jug, a serious breach of protocol. The Major ignored the affront. "Our livestock is gone, taken by thieves of both skins, red and white. There is nothing left to take. The game is gone. No more deer, not even rabbits. Only the river gives us meat, a few fish now and then."

"Did you go to the agent and explain your problems to him?"

The Major had to wait for a reply as Albert Fox again lifted the jug and swallowed twice. The Indian wiped a dirty hand across his lips. Albert Fox shrugged again. "We went." His words were beginning to slur. "We asked. We begged. All for nothing. The white agent does not care."

"This agent cares, Albert Fox," the Major said. "When was the last time you received food and livestock?"

"Six, seven months ago." Albert Fox's eyes had glazed. "The cattle were poor. No meat on their bones. The Kickapoos stole them anyway. Wacos took the last of our horses and mules." He paused for another swallow of whiskey. "The flour the agents gave us was full of bugs. We ate it . . ." The Caddo's voice trailed away. His chin sagged onto his chest. A moment later he toppled onto his side. Liquor dribbled from the jug into the soiled dirt floor of the lodge.

Major Robert Neighbors sat for a moment and stared at the crumpled form. He couldn't decide whether he was more disgusted or angry. After a time he rose and stepped from the foul air of the lodge into the heat of the scorching summer sun.

The Major stood for a moment and again let his gaze sweep over the squalor of the Caddo village. The coals of rage in his gut flared to life again. *Nobody has lifted a hand for these people since I left,* he thought. *That, by God, is going to change. And there's one problem I can take care of right now.* He reached for the reins. It was time to call on a whiskey peddler.

Major Robert Neighbors stepped through the open door of Emil Washburn's trading post on the Red River and blinked a couple of times until his vision adjusted to the half light of the interior.

Washburn stood with his back to the door, arranging a row of liquor bottles on a shelf. There was only one other man in the post, a squat, burly man seated on a flour keg, bottle in hand. The smell in the room marked the stocky man as a wolfer. The Major could identify that scent from a hundred yards downwind.

The Major strode silently to the rough plank counter. "Washburn," he said softly.

The trader turned. "Something I can do for you—" Washburn's voice trailed off for a moment as he recognized the big man standing before him. "What the hell are you doing here, Neighbors?"

"You're selling whiskey to the Indians."

Washburn shrugged. "They want it, I got it. I sell or trade with anybody I please."

"Not any longer. You just went out of the whiskey business where Indians are concerned, Washburn." The Major glanced at the wolfer and dismissed the man as a potential threat. The stocky one was watching with interest, but showed no inclination to deal himself a hand in somebody else's poker game.

The trader bristled, his face flushed in anger. "You got a lot of balls, Neighbors. You've got about three seconds to get out of my place."

The Major stabbed out his left hand, grabbed a handful of Washburn's shirtfront and yanked the trader halfway across the pine counter. Washburn squawked in outrage and tried to reach for the pistol on his hip. His fingers had barely touched the grips before the steel of the Major's Colt barrel nudged against his upper lip.

"Go ahead, damn you." The Major cocked the Colt. "Draw it. And I'll solve two problems. One of them will be what you're going to do tomorrow."

Washburn swallowed hard and tried to pull his head back. He wasn't a small or weak man, but he couldn't gain a fraction of an inch against the powerful fingers bunched at his throat.

"Put that pistol on the counter—slow and easy." The Major waited until Washburn's revolver thumped onto the wood, then released his grip on the trader's shirt. Washburn almost fell as he stumbled away from the counter. His flushed face twisted in rage as he regained his balance.

The Major lifted Washburn's pistol and holstered his own weapon.

"Damn you," Washburn croaked as he rubbed at his bruised throat, "nobody manhandles Emil Washburn like that."

"And nobody pulls a pistol on me, Washburn. You made the right choice putting that thing down. Keep your hands where I can see them."

Washburn stepped back to the counter and spread his hands, palm down. He glared at the Major. "I should have shot you years ago, Neighbors. You and your Indian-lovin' ways, highroadin' it over everybody else." Washburn's courage trickled back as his fury heated to full boil. "You can't come bargin' in here and tell me where and what to trade—"

"The hell I can't, Washburn. It's against the law now to supply whiskey to the Indians."

"There ain't no damn such law, Neighbors. It ain't on the books."

"There is one as of now. My law. And it's going to be official soon."

"You can't do this, dammit." Washburn's hand on the counter flexed into a fist. "You don't have the authority."

"That's where you're wrong, Washburn," the Major said calmly. "It may not be spelled out in legal detail what I can and can't do where traders are concerned. But I can have the government yank your trade permit. I'll do just that if I find one more Brazos Indian with a jug or bottle of your whiskey in his hands. Keep your wagons away from the Brazos, Washburn, or I'll make life more than just difficult for you."

"What do you mean by that?"

The Major pulled a big knife from his belt and hoisted Washburn's pistol. He turned the cylinder and pried the percussion caps from the nipples with the knife point, then dropped the now-useless handgun back onto the counter.

"I mean, Washburn, that I'll come after you. And I won't bring a Ranger company or Army escort. I'll do it myself. I'll be dropping by from time to time. If I find one stolen horse or cow in your corral, or one more scrap of evidence you're cheating on your contract to supply beef to the Indians, I'll tack your hide to that drying rack out front. In short, Mister Washburn, if you so much as break wind without permission in my jurisdiction, I will kill you. Is that understood?"

"Damn you," Washburn sputtered, "you can't do this!"

"Try me. That's one sure way to find out." The Major turned his back and strode toward the door.

"You ain't heard the last of this, Neighbors," Washburn yelled. "I've got friends—"

The Major paused at the door and looked back. "Seems to me I've heard that tune before, Washburn. It just scares me half to death."

Major Robert Neighbors stepped onto the hard-packed soil outside the trading post and swung aboard the big bay. He glanced at the sun. It was halfway down the western horizon. He snorted the lingering scent of the wolfer from his nostrils. The confrontation with Emil Washburn had taken a bit of the edge off his temper. He wondered idly if Washburn would fight back or if the bluff would work.

Technically, the trader was right. There was no literal law against selling liquor to the Indians, at least not yet. But the Major had already started to push for a ban on liquor trade with the Indians. The idea had solid backing in Washington as well as in Austin. In the meantime, Washburn could be big trouble. *Might be a good idea to watch my back for a spell,* the Major thought. *But if stepping on the hazy side of the law cuts down on the whiskey trade with the Indians it's worth the gamble.*

The Major knew it wouldn't stop the Indians from drinking. Once they had experienced the numbing effects of liquor they would find it somewhere. At least now they might have to work harder to get it.

As he rode, he mentally reviewed the results of his week-long horseback survey along the Brazos. The abysmal condition of the small tribes wasn't the only fly buzzing in his head. He had found only one Comanche camp along the Brazos. It held less than thirty people. He *had* seen signs of Kickapoos, Delawares, Shawnees and other eastern tribes. The Indians from outside the state were not supposed to be in Texas. The eastern tribes preyed on the smaller and weaker bands like the Caddos and Wacos, and on any white settlers they felt could be overpowered without too much risk. The eastern bands had to go. The Major nudged the big bay into a steady trot. He could be back in Fort Belknap by sunset. There was much to do there.

Fort Belknap

Major Robert Neighbors signed his third official report in as many weeks to the Commissioner of Indian Affairs and leaned back in the creaky cane-bottomed chair in the cramped quarters assigned to the Texas Indian agent in the small clump of post buildings.

He flexed his right hand. It was trying to cramp from long hours of writing. At least he had accomplished some things without pen and paper. Stemm was gone, back on his farm a few miles away—a farm which, the Major suspected, had been stocked by cattle and horses which should have gone to the Indians. George Hill was on his way to the Brazos to take Stemm's place. Hill was a good man, sympathetic to the Indians and as honest as any man in Texas.

The Anadarkos, Caddos and other small tribes along the river at least had subsistence rations for a time. The Major had pleaded, wheedled and threatened until a handful of sutlers, farmers and the U.S. Army supplied enough beef and flour to keep the Indians alive.

The Major stood, stretched and strode to the window. The officer in command of Fort Belknap had to go. The man had done nothing to help the Indians, made no effort to see that supplies were delivered or those who stole from the tribes were pursued and punished. The latest dispatch from the War Department said a new commanding officer would be arriving within the month. *I hope they send a good man,* the Major thought, *but whoever they send couldn't be worse than what we have now.*

The Major stared for several moments toward the southwest. If things were in as big a mess at Fort Inge as they were here, he groused inwardly, the southwestern tribes would be in bad shape, too. *If that's the case I'll fire George Howard just as quick as I fired Stemm,* he promised himself. *The Lipans, Mescaleros and Tonks have shorter fuses than the tribes here. It won't take much to set them off, and the southwest frontier would be one big bloodbath.*

He turned away from the window and sighed, trying to blink the exhaustion from his eyes. The eighteen-hour days were beginning to take a toll. And they weren't over yet. When George Hill arrived at the Brazos agency, it was back in the saddle for one Robert Simpson Neighbors. He still had to meet with the Comanche bands along the Colorado, check on the status of the southwestern tribes under Howard's jurisdiction and spend still more time writing reports and arguing with the legislature in Austin for a permanent home for the Indians.

It was going to be a busy few months. But at least he could spend some time with his family. Reports and proposals could be written just as easily from the farm on the Salado as from some outpost in the middle of nowhere.

The Major could only hope Mary Beatrice would still recognize her daddy.

SIX

San Antonio
May 1854

Major Robert Neighbors scooped the red-haired toddler into his arms just before she pounced on the hound that slept blissfully unaware of the impending ambush on the porch of the Salado Creek farm.

"Mustn't bother a sleeping dog, Mary," the Major half-whispered in the girl's ear. "It scares them and they might bite." Even as he gently admonished the child, the Major wondered idly how many more sleeping dogs he could kick himself without getting bitten. That they needed a brisk application of boot to backside didn't matter. The Major had made some dangerous enemies, red and white, in the last few months.

He jostled the girl in the crook of a big arm and listened to the delighted giggles in his ear. Mary Beatrice Neighbors was getting to be a handful, both literally and figuratively. She was a healthy, happy and active youngster whose knees and elbows were almost constantly scabbed from her attempts to get from one point to another at a dead run when her stubby legs could hardly manage a steady walk. Her fingers locked into the Major's beard just below the sideburns. He made no effort to pry her grip loose.

The aroma of pot roast and fresh-baked bread wafted from the interior of the house. The tantalizing scent mingled with the clean spring air, the heady fragrance of flowering plants and tree blossoms and the faint soap smell of freshly bathed child in his arms.

This was the hardest part, these days before leaving the comforts of home and the ones he loved most on yet another trip afield. And it seemed to the Major that he could count on one hand the days he had spent at home since his appointment as supervising Indian agent for Texas. It seemed that as soon as he settled in, comfortable and content, there was a knock on the door and a problem to tackle somewhere. *The wages not of sin but of happiness,* the Major thought. *The more content a man is the more he realizes how much he can lose.*

His efforts in the last few months had brought a mixed bag of results. The meeting with the Comanche bands of Buffalo Hump, Yellow Wolf, Sanaco and Ketumse on the Colorado had not gone well.

Yellow Wolf was openly suspicious. Buffalo Hump was less surly, but he was not to be trusted. The chief had talked from both sides of his mouth on many occasions. Ketumse was a whiner and on occasion an outright liar. The Major figured Ketumse had been around the white man too long; he had picked up some of the pale eyes' less honorable habits. Sanaco's dark eyes glittered in tightly controlled anger throughout the council. But it was a senior warrior yet to earn a chief's title who worried the Major the most. Little Elk seldom spoke, but his jaw was set and his eyes gleamed in disgust when he glared at the Indian agent. Little Elk's anger was such that he had even scorned the Major's presents. That was unheard of in a Comanche.

They had a reason to be upset, the Major granted. The United States Army had manned new garrisons along the southern border. The outposts disrupted the Indians' raids into Mexico. Game was scarce. The ranks of the people of the Plains had been thinned by disease. The Major had never known the Comanche people to drink, but now liquor flowed freely in their camps.

The situation on the northern and western frontier was near the flash point. The Major had pointedly made no promises or threats during those ten days on the Colorado. It had been a visit to probe the attitudes of the major southern Comanche bands.

That attitude was not good.

He shifted his daughter's weight and firmed his gentle grip on the child's waist. She still had an impulse to ambush the sleeping hound.

In Austin the Major had scored his biggest victory to date. The reservation proposal he had nursed from seed had finally sprouted. Rip Ford's joint resolution of 1852 provided the roots, and the Texas Legislature had—somewhat reluctantly, the Major had to admit—deeded to the federal government twelve leagues of land for the establishment of Indian reservations in North Texas. In a few days he would gather his handful of picked guides and head for Fort Belknap. There he and Army Captain Randolph Barnes Marcy would survey and select the reservation lands. But the Major's dream came with a price. The survey would take him from Lizzie and little Mary for weeks, perhaps months.

Mary Beatrice squirmed in his lap and yanked at his beard. He chucked the child under the chin with a finger and listened to the happy gurgle. "Mary Beatrice," he said, "one day you'll be old enough to help your old daddy solve the philosophical problem of whether a man's neglect of his own family for the benefit of many others is justified."

Mary Beatrice stuck a finger in the Major's ear.

"So much for debating philosophy with a two-year-old," he muttered with a grin as he removed the offending digit.

The Major's exhilaration at the passage of the reservation bill had been quickly tempered by an outbreak of violence among the southwestern tribes, the Tonkawas in particular. Agent Howard wasn't doing his job. He was frequently absent from his post among the Indians. He had an excuse for everything that went wrong, including a series of outrages that threatened to set off open warfare between the Tonkawas and the whites.

A band of white men had tried to steal horses from the Tonks and even gone so far as to attack a Tonkawa village. That triggered a rampage of Tonkawa braves along the Bosque Valley. They raided farms, killed a settler, and then hit an Anadarko village. Tonkawa and Lipan outlaws struck homesteads along the Leona, Sabinal and Rio Seco; the Major and a company of Texas Rangers had been afield for several days trying to run down the culprits, with only modest success. White settlers all along the southwest frontier were clamoring for Ranger companies to be formed for protection. The whole situation was a constant source of worry for the Major. If the settlers got together with revenge in mind, innocent and peaceful Indians would die. Most of the settlers didn't know which Indians were guilty of the depredations. They didn't care. To them one redskin was the same as another.

Matters along the Brazos were also a mix of good news and bad. The Caddos and other small tribes settled there would survive at least for a time. The Major and the new Brazos agent George Hill had managed to requisition enough stores to keep the Indians from starving to death until an equitable supply system could be established.

The sound of footsteps on the hardwood floor inside broke the Major's reverie.

"Dinner's ready, Major," Lizzie announced from the doorway, "if you can quit indulging that child long enough to come and eat." The Major rose, shifted Mary Beatrice to a hip, and hugged his wife with his free arm. Lizzie was already beginning to waddle. She was four months into her second pregnancy. She was pale and drawn, and even though she tried not to show it the Major knew she was miserable. He heard her soft moans of pain and discomfort in the night. And the morning sickness had lasted much longer this time.

"Are you sure you're all right, dear?" the Major asked as he released her and followed her inside.

Lizzie's smile was wan and weak. "I'm all right, Major. Don't worry about me."

"I do worry, Lizzie. I wish there was some way I could postpone this trip until the baby comes."

"Hush that talk, Major," Lizzie said. "You've worked long and hard on your dream for the Indians. Don't let them down now. As long as I have Anna with me I'll be fine."

The Major nodded. "I suppose you're right, Lizzie." He flashed a warm smile at Anna Kaufmann as she poured coffee and tea. The blue eyes and broad, ruddy face reflected assurance. The Major had hired Anna, the widow of a German farmer, as housekeeper and cook to ease some of the demands and drudgery on Lizzie. Anna had become more than maid and biscuit maker. She was a confidante and companion to Lizzie, a hearty woman with a sunny disposition. Lizzie would be in good hands. *It's a good home, a good place, with good people all around,* the Major thought as he took his seat at the heavily laden table. *That's what makes it so painful to leave . . .*

Red River Trading Post
June 1854

Emil Washburn swiped a hand across bloodshot eyes and tried to ignore the pounding in his temples as he glared at the two men across the table. The ripping hangover was as much a result of anger and twanging nerves as whiskey.

Nat Colley sipped at a bottle and passed the liquor to the big red-bearded man at his side. Hiram Oldham lifted the bottle and dropped the level by a good two inches before lowering the container with a heavy sigh.

"What's on your feeble mind, Emil? I got business to tend."

Emil Washburn glowered at his friend. "Hate to pee on your fire, Hiram, but we got to do something quick or we're both going to lose out on a big chunk of money."

Oldham frowned and reached for the bottle again. "What porcupine stuck quills in your butt, Emil?"

"That damn Neighbors got his reservation bill rammed through the legislature. Word is he's on his way to hunt a place to put his pet Injuns. That ain't good news."

Oldham took another drink and cocked an eyebrow. "Don't know why you're so riled up. We can handle this Neighbors."

Washburn snorted in disgust. "Hiram, you and that son of yours may be the best horse thieves in Texas, but you got no business sense. And you don't know Neighbors."

"I never saw a man so tough he could walk off from a Sharps slug."

"No." Washburn winced as a fresh lance of pain sliced across the back of his head. "We can't just bushwhack him. God knows I'd like to, but Neighbors throws a long shadow in this state. People around here know him and me have had words. We'd have the Army on our necks before Neighbors quit bleeding."

Hiram Oldham pulled a twist of tobacco from his pocket, gnawed off a chew and worried it into position in his cheek. "Sounds to me like that's more your worry than mine, Emil. Neighbors isn't after my butt."

Washburn leaned back in his chair and sighed. "Maybe not. But that sad-assed Caddo Albert Fox traded me some mighty interestin' news for a crock of bad whiskey. You know that chunk of land you've had your eye on? The place the Anadarkos got now?"

Oldham's eyes narrowed in a quick flash of suspicion. "What about it?"

"The damn Indians want it, Albert tells me. And if there ain't a claim filed on it, Neighbors'll likely plop his lazy redskins down smooth in the middle of it."

Oldham barked a curse. Tobacco juice dribbled onto his red beard, his face flushed. "Dammit, he can't do that—"

"The hell he can't, Hiram. Unless we beat him to it." Last night's whiskey took a fresh bite of Washburn's temple. *To hell with it,* he thought. *Maybe a little hair of the wolf will dull that damn axe in my head.*

He reached for the bottle, downed a swallow and felt his gut churn when the whiskey hit bottom.

"Quit walking around the critter, Emil. Get down to the liver and lights. What do we do?"

Washburn concentrated for a moment on keeping the whiskey down, then half-grinned at the stockman and horse thief. "First you gather up every cousin you got and every white horse thief who's workin' for you." He nodded toward his brother-in-law. "Nat and a couple of his relatives will go along with you. The lot of you will file claims on the best land on the Brazos below Belknap. If we get the claims filed first, the dirt-digger Indians won't get the good country."

Oldham's brow wrinkled in a frown. "That takes money. Hell, we got a good deal going here now."

Washburn sighed. "Look down the road a ways, Hiram. We can't count on gettin' slick and fat dealin' in stolen horses and sellin' whiskey. Land. That's the future. That's where the money is. There's a dozen pilgrims a week driftin' into the Brazos, all with money in their pockets and huntin' a place to perch. That land'll go up ten, twelve times in hard cash value over the next few years."

Understanding slowly dawned in Hiram Oldham's pale eyes. "Okay. So we get control of the best land. Then what do we do about these reservations and this Neighbors fellow? I need those Indians working for me. So do you. They can't do us any good growing beans and pumpkins."

"You leave that part of it to me, Hiram." Washburn sighed in relief. The headache seemed to be easing. He winked at the red-bearded man. "I got plans. There's ways to make sure that damn reservation idea fails. And that, my horse-stealin' friend, will take Neighbors plumb out of the picture."

Washburn picked up the bottle. It was almost empty. "By God, boys, by the time this is over we'll own the Brazos River, lock, stock and catfish."

Fort Belknap
July 1854

Major Robert Neighbors squatted at the council fire, Captain Randolph Barnes Marcy at his side, and glanced around the gathering.

Four tribes were represented, the Ionis, Anadarkos, Caddos and Wacos.

Albert Fox was there, suffering the pangs of a hangover. The Major paid little attention to the *caddi*. After the death of Charlie Two Blankets, leadership of the smaller, settled tribes had passed to the stocky Anadarko chief Jose Maria, who sat opposite the two white men. The Major was satisfied that the agrarian tribes were in good hands. On the surface, Jose Maria didn't look much like a leader and warrior. He was short, little more than five and a half feet tall, in his fifties and running a bit to paunch. His white man's clothing was worn and shiny from many washings. But if anyone proved looks were deceiving it was the pudgy Anadarko. Under the ill-fitting clothes and battered beaver hat was a fighting man to the bone. The Tonkawas and Kickapoos had found that out the hard way. The Anadarko village was an outwardly tempting target for raids, but usually not more than one by any given band. Jose Maria was a bulldog on the trail. He didn't quit until the raiders had paid the price. He usually came back with the stolen stock and goods. He seldom brought back prisoners.

Jose Maria nodded across the council fire. "The plan is good," he said. "Our people would welcome a place we could call home." He reached in his pocket for tobacco and papers and rolled a cigarette. "I have talked of this with others of my tribe at some length. We wish to have our home on the Brazos, below Fort Belknap." He plucked a twig from the fire and lit the cigarette.

Captain Marcy leaned forward. "I am curious, Jose Maria," he said, his tone polite and respectful. "Why would your people choose the lower Brazos country? The ground is less fertile there and the water is not so good as it is higher up the river on the Clear Fork."

Jose Maria squinted through the smoke and shrugged. "In the past the Plains tribes, mostly the Comanches, have robbed us of everything we had. At times the white man robs us too. But at least the white man leaves us enough to live on. He does not take *all* our food and livestock." The chief paused for a drag on the cigarette and let the smoke trickle from his nostrils. "If we must die at the hands of either Indian or white man, we prefer to enter the world beyond with something in our bellies."

Captain Marcy nodded solemnly. "I understand. If it is possible your wishes will be honored."

Jose Maria tossed the butt of his cigarette into the fire. "Give us a place to live and grow our crops in peace. This is all we ask." He rose without obvious effort to his feet, the unspoken signal that the talk had ended.

The Major and Captain Marcy stood and waited as the Indian representatives filtered away. When the last had gone Marcy turned to stare toward the west. "Well, Major," he said after a time, "it's a big country out there. Surely there's room for everybody. All we have to do is find it."

The Major's gaze also drifted west. The sun had dipped to touch the rolling hills. Its rays painted the council site a soothing gold and washed a faint salmon color into the high clouds above the horizon. *It's going to be another spectacular sunset,* the Major thought. *At least that's something all can share without bloodshed.*

Double Mountain Fork, Brazos River
August 1854

Major Robert Neighbors leaned against his saddle by the small campfire and tried to ignore the gurgling cramps in his gut. *Twenty-two days out,* he grumped inwardly, *and all we've found is rattlesnakes and bad water. And it's hard to figure how even a rattler could live out here—*

"Major?"

Neighbors turned to Captain Marcy. The officer's uniform was sweat-stained and dirty, with snags and rips from cactus and mesquite thorns. His face was pale and drawn. Bad water and short rations paid no attention to rank. "Yes?"

"Are you a Christian?"

"Duly dampened Methodist, my friend," the Major said with a slight smile. "Something on your mind?"

Marcy winced as a fresh cramp stabbed at his abdomen. "Just wondering. You think God has a sense of humor?"

The Major shrugged. "No doubt about it. Why else would He make armadillos? I've always believed He had a sense of the absurd."

"It's beginning to look like He pulled a prank of celestial proportions on mankind when He built this country," Marcy said. "From a hilltop it's beautiful. Broken hills, tall peaks, canyons, grass as far as the eye can see, rivers and creeks within a day's travel of each other." Marcy sighed. "But the Creator left out a few things—like wood and drinkable water. I'd give up my next promotion right now for a canteen of cool, clear water that doesn't give a man the green apple two-step."

The Major would have chuckled, but it was no laughing matter. The thirteen men in the survey party all suffered the intestinal outrage of bad water and short supplies. "Can't argue that, Captain," he said.

"I don't think God intended for civilized man to live out here," Marcy said. "We haven't even seen signs of Indian camps this far west."

The Major lifted his gaze toward the horizon. "We'll be seeing them soon enough, Captain. We'll be back on the headwaters of the Clear Fork in a few days. Our runners will have contacted the southern Comanche bands by now with an invitation to council."

"Think they'll come in?"

The Major sighed and shrugged. "You never know about Comanches."

SEVEN

Clear Fork of the Brazos
August 1854

Major Robert Neighbors sat cross-legged on a blanket and waited patiently as Captain Marcy neared the finish of his explanation of the reservation plan to the dark-skinned Comanche chief Sanaco seated across from him.

Several other lesser chiefs sat in a half circle behind Sanaco; in the near distance more than fifty armed warriors waited for the council to end. The Major's gaze drifted back to the one man who had chosen to stand throughout the talk. Little Elk's back was ramrod straight, chin set in defiance, and the look in the black eyes would freeze the flames of a campfire at thirty paces.

Little Elk's war shield now sported the markings of a sub-chief of the Panetekas. *Looks like Little Elk's moving up in the ranks,* the Major thought. *That's not the best possible news we've heard lately.* A half dozen scalps dangled from the edges of Little Elk's shield. Three of the war trophies appeared to be fresh; two looked to be those of white men and a third that of a woman, the Major noted. Little Elk had not spoken since the Comanche chiefs had appeared at the council site.

Sanaco listened with polite interest as Captain Marcy spoke, but the dark eyes reflected the chief's disgust.

"In summary, Chief Sanaco," Marcy said, "the United States Government will supply your people with equipment, food and any other requirements you might have until the Comanches have learned the ways of farming and ranching and become self-sufficient. In return, your people must stop all raids and attacks on both white settlers and Mexicans."

Sanaco's forehead creased in a frown. He sat in silent thought for a moment, then sighed. "I came to this talk in good faith, as asked by messengers from Agent Neighbors. Now I find that you come into the homelands of my people, pick a small patch of ground and draw a line around it. You tell us the President of the United States will make us a present of this land to live upon, when everybody knows that the whole of this country from the Red River to the Colorado is now, and has always been, ours from the beginning of time."

Silent nods of agreement rippled through the ranks of the Comanches. Sanaco shifted his gaze to the Major. "I suppose if your President tells us to confine ourselves to such a small piece of ground, we will be forced to do so whether it is our wish or not."

"Sanaco," the Major said earnestly, "we are trying our best to preserve the lives and property of both red man and white. Ketumse met with us at the place called Boggy Creek only last week. He expressed his friendship and his willingness to settle on selected lands, to learn the white man's ways. Ketumse told me he had spoken with other chiefs of the Human Beings and that they had all expressed the same willingness."

"Ketumse," Sanaco said, his tone contemptuous, "does not speak for all the Panetekas. He speaks only for himself and he says what you wish to hear. You should not take his words as the truth."

The chief abruptly rose to his feet. The sub-chiefs followed suit. "I will speak of this with my people. You shall have my answer by the Time of White Grass—the time the white man calls first frost."

"That is all we ask," the Major said. "Sanaco is wise and a powerful spokesman for the Human Beings. Think of what we say here. We wish no more blood be spilled."

Sanaco stared at the Major for several heartbeats, then turned without speaking and strode from the council site. Within twenty minutes the Paneteka chief and his lieutenants were well away from the explorers' camp, riding toward the southwest.

Captain Marcy sighed. "Major, we're likely to have trouble with that one."

"Sanaco's a tough bird. He may decide to fight rather than bring his people in." The Major stared toward the horsemen growing smaller in the distance. "In his place I'd be tempted to fight myself."

Marcy swiped his neckerchief across the sweat trickling from his hatband. "Might as well break camp, gentlemen. We're almost finished and I'm ready to get back home."

"So am I, Captain." The Major made no effort to hide the worry in his tone. "I've been away from my family too long. And it's going to increase by one in a few weeks."

Colorado River
September 1854

Little Elk sat astride his war horse before the smoldering ruins of the cabin on the Texas frontier and grunted in satisfaction.

It had been a good raid. The cabin was the fourth overrun on this campaign, and he had only one man slightly injured. His prestige would grow rapidly now. Soon others would be clamoring to join Little Elk on his forays against the Texans. By the time the grass greened again he would have many followers.

He glanced around the site of the latest raid. It was little different from the three other homesteads that had fallen to Little Elk and his band. Two mutilated bodies sprawled in front of the burning cabin. The two men were cut down as they emerged from the dwelling, riddled by arrows and rifle balls before they even knew Indians were about. Near the corner of the house the body of a small child lay, its brains bashed out against a tree stump to stop its screaming. Only the bravest children were taken as captives.

Little Elk heard the muted screams and whimpers of the mother and daughter from the half-dugout storage room behind the burning home. The woman was in her forties, the girl barely in her teens. A junior warrior emerged from the small structure, tugged his breechclout back into place, and grinned. A waiting warrior took his place.

Little Elk would not take his turn with the women. His loathing for the whites was now stronger than any lust in his loins. When the other men were finished with them the women would be killed, scalped and parts of their skins stripped away to make soft medicine pouches and tobacco sacks. It had been so in his father's time, and so it remained.

A half dozen of Little Elk's war party, young men all, gathered the scattered cattle herd. Others stood about, unsteady on legs rubbered by a gallon of fiery homemade corn whiskey from the shed, and quarreled over ownership of the dozen horses in the corral behind the house. Two braves sorted through the loot from the settlers' home. It was a substantial amount of plunder—two good

Kentucky rifles, three pistols and a shotgun, powder, lead and percussion caps, knives, steel hatchets and other utensils, clothing and foodstuffs from the kitchen. Little Elk let the braves quarrel. If the disputes became too heated, he would step in and make the decision as to ownership of the items in question. He would take little for himself. The scalp of the man he had killed would be sufficient. A real chief was measured as much by his generosity as by his leadership on the war trail.

He didn't need the plunder anyway. His success on these raids would bring many guns from the trader Washburn. The trader had spoken well; the maps he had sketched led Little Elk to these isolated farms rich in horses and weapons and lightly defended.

He waited until the spoils were sorted among the raiders and the women's screams stopped. Then he beckoned his men to gather around.

"It is enough," Little Elk said. "Our medicine has been good." *One's medicine is even stronger when one has the white man Washburn as a spy in the enemy camp*, he thought. "Now we return to the land south of Fort Belknap and rejoin Sanaco."

One of the braves snorted in disgust. "Sanaco is a squaw. He waits to move onto a small patch of land and grub in the dirt like a Tonkawa."

Little Elk raised a hand. "Hear me out. Sanaco is no woman. He will spend the time of cold winds in the warmth of his lodge with the white man's beef in his belly and his wives in his blankets. He will take the white man's presents. Sanaco will give us supplies and any men who wish to join our band. Then, when the grass greens and his ponies grow fat, he will leave the reservation and once again take to the warpath."

"And if Sanaco becomes too comfortable to wear the war paint? What of us then?"

"We leave him behind and set out on our own. When the grass is tall and green, those of us gathered here—and others eager to join —will slip past the Rangers and bluecoats and raid the whites. Our feats of war will be spoken of in stories told around Comanche campfires for generations. We will return rich men."

The warrior who had protested bunched his brows in thought for a moment, then smiled. "It is good. Little Elk's medicine is strong. I have no objection to becoming rich." He laughed aloud. "I have had my eye on taking a second wife. Already this raid has given me more than enough ponies to trade for her."

Little Elk grinned at the warrior. "Within two summers, my friend, you will be able to afford so many wives you will need a village of your own lodges to house them all." He turned his head and sniffed the air. "The time of cold winds will come early this year. It will be a fine joke on the white man to find that he has fed us through a hard winter only to have the Comanches burst forth in the spring like the flowers of the prairie and drive the pale ones from the land of our ancestors. Come. Let us go home."

Red River Trading Post

Emil Washburn chuckled to himself as he leaned against the porch post and scanned a week-old copy of the *Dallas News*. The paper carried more than a dozen reports of Indian depredations on the Texas frontier, from North Texas south to the Rio Grande.

Some of the stories were true, Washburn knew, thanks in large part to his agreement with Little Elk. Most were pure fiction, planted in letters from Washburn's friends. The false stories and rumors fed upon themselves until the people of North Texas were near hysteria. On the frontier, it didn't matter whether a story happened to be true or not. Once it spread it became gospel.

Already the public outcry had spurred the Army into action. Troops were moving toward Fort Chadbourne for a full-scale campaign against the red men. And a whole mess of Comanches from the Paneteka and Wanderer bands had settled near Chadbourne after Robert Neighbors put out the word they would be safe there. *Pretty soon,* Washburn thought, *we can fix ourselves up a genuine Indian war out here. And when the damn flea-bit redskins are wiped out to the last man, I'll be sitting on top of some of the state's most valuable land. God, it's going to be fun to be rich.*

Washburn plucked a tobacco twist from his pocket and gnawed a thumb-sized chunk free. He chuckled as he worried the chew into place. *That damn Neighbors looked like he was trying to crap a watermelon when he heard us and Hiram Oldham's kin had filed on that Brazos country he wanted for his Indians.* "That big hairy major ain't seen trouble yet," he muttered aloud. "When I get through with him he's going to be the log under the whipsaw."

San Antonio
October 1854

Major Robert Neighbors paced worriedly on the front porch of his Salado Creek home and tried not to hear Lizzie's cries and whimpers of pain from the back bedroom.

Her labor seemed more difficult this time even though the doctors said the second baby usually was easier than the first. The physician and Anna Kaufmann were with Lizzie. They had firmly escorted the Major from the birthing room. Husbands, Anna pointed out forcefully, were only in the way at such times.

He couldn't argue the point. It wouldn't have done any good, anyway. When Anna put her foot down the discussion was closed. And Robert Neighbors had never felt quite so alone.

He missed having champion beard-puller Mary Beatrice around. The girl was too young for such goings-on as the birth of a new brother or sister, so she was staying with Lizzie's folks in Seguin. Ignacio was busy in the fields, supervising the men the Major had hired to help as the farm grew. Even the mockingbird, the Major's longtime friend, was silent. There was no cheerful medley of songs from the nearby berry vines.

The Major stopped his pacing long enough to bend down and scratch the hound's ears. The dog whimpered in ecstasy. "Well, Blue," the Major said, "at least somebody around here needs me."

The Major disliked filling out reports, but at the moment he would have welcomed the diversion. His paperwork was done for now. The Indians would have their reservations soon. Captain Marcy was well along on the final survey of the lands selected. Then they needed only the final approval from Washington and the new age of the Texas Indian would begin.

He stopped scratching the hound, ignored the dog's whine of disappointment, and resumed his pacing. Despite his concern for Lizzie, the Major's thoughts kept wandering north. He was still irked that claims had been filed on the Brazos land desired by the Anadarko and Caddo tribes. The claims had been legal. The land had still belonged to the state at the time, and there was nothing the Major could do about the sudden land grab. It had cost Jose Maria and his people the superior soil of the site they had chosen and upon which they had lived for months. Now they had to pack up and move again.

It didn't take any mental giant to connect the signatures on the claim papers with Emil Washburn and his buddy Hiram Oldham. *Good thing they didn't have more relatives,* the Major grumbled to himself, *or they would own most of Texas from Gainesville west by now* . . .

At least there now was some land beyond the reach of Washburn and Oldham. Four leagues—23,040 acres—had been surveyed on the Clear Fork of the Brazos between the California Road and Fort Belknap for the Comanches. Another four leagues on the north side of the Brazos, below Belknap and near the junction of the Clear Fork and the main river, had been set aside for the settled tribes. The two reservations were separated by a good ten miles—hopefully far enough that the Comanches would cause no problems with the other bands, the Anadarkos in particular. Jose Maria's people had served the state well as trackers and guides over the years. The Comanches would never forgive that.

Agent George Hill reported from Belknap that the Ioni, Anadarko and Caddo tribes were anxious to move onto their new homeland. It was almost time for them to begin breaking ground and clearing new fields in the tough prairie sod in preparation for spring planting. Nearly a thousand southern Comanches had drifted in and were waiting to take up residence on the Clear Fork. There was no word yet from the northernmost tribes, and the Major didn't expect any. The Quahadi Comanches, Kiowas and Kiowa Apaches wouldn't even consider life on a reservation if any choice remained open. They were the best horsemen and bravest warriors of the state. They would give in to the white man's yoke only if they were crushed. The Major hoped it would never come to that. The dry, treeless plains of the Llano Estacado had nothing to offer the white man, anyway. Might as well let the Indians keep it.

The Major's pacing stopped abruptly as a thin, faint wail sounded from within the house. Moments later the physician strode onto the porch, a smile on his face as he toweled blood from his hands.

"Congratulations, Major. You have a new daughter," the doctor said.

"How's Lizzie?"

"She's weak and she lost more blood than I had hoped. But considering that it was a difficult delivery she's doing well. A few weeks' rest will restore her strength."

"The baby?"

The doctor's smile brightened. "She's small, a tiny little thing, but she seems healthy. We'll drink a toast to her later. With your whiskey. For now I'd better get back inside, Major. There's still work to do. Anna's cleaning up your new daughter." He shook his head in wonder. "Quite a woman, that Anna. If you get tired of having her around, let me know. She's a natural nurse. I could use her."

The doctor turned toward the door. "Anna will let you know when you can come in for a visit. I'll ask you to keep it brief. Lizzie needs all the rest she can get."

A quarter hour later Major Robert Neighbors sat at Lizzie's side, a small blanket-wrapped bundle in his hands. Frances Elizabeth Ritchey Neighbors still shivered and whimpered in dismay at being yanked from the dark comfort and warmth of her earlier home into a bright, cold world. The baby was scarcely bigger than the Major's two hands.

"I hope you aren't disappointed." Lizzie's voice was weak and shaky, her face the color of ashes. "I had hoped to give you a son."

"Nonsense, dear," the Major said, his tone light. "You could never disappoint me." He winked at his wife. "Besides, I happen to like girls. She's beautiful. She looks like you."

Lizzie's pale face seemed to brighten as she smiled. "She looks like I'll look in a few decades, Major—wrinkled, toothless and cranky. But you're right. She *is* beautiful." Lizzie leaned back against the headboard of the bed, pillows stuffed behind her back and shoulders. "Now, Robert Simpson Neighbors, I'll have to ask you to hand over your daughter and leave the room. It's nursing time."

The Major surrendered the small bundle and patted the back of his wife's hand. He leaned forward and kissed Lizzie gently on the forehead. "Thank you," he said.

Lizzie reached for the silk ribbon that tied her gown at the throat. "Be gone with you, Major. It's time for us girls to get better acquainted."

Fort Belknap
November 1854

Major Robert Neighbors ignored the bite of the sharp north wind
and its hint of an early and hard winter. He strode briskly across
the fort parade ground, the tension in his belly showing in the
length of his stride. Agent George Hill had to hurry to keep pace.
"Dammit, George," the Major grumbled as he walked, "the ab-
ject stupidity of the federal government never ceases to amaze me."
He jabbed a thumb over his shoulder. "Here we have a big chunk
of the Comanche nation waiting to move onto the reservation and
the Army's trying to foul up the whole project."

Major Enoch Steen, the new commander of Fort Belknap, swung
the door to his office open before the Major had time to knock.
"Come in, gentlemen. Warm yourselves by the fire while I pour
some coffee."

"We came as soon as we could, Major Steen," Neighbors said as
he settled into a chair and waited impatiently as the Army officer
poured coffee into tin campaign cups. "Is the situation here as bad
as your dispatch indicated?"

Steen handed the Major a cup and perched a hip on the edge of
his scarred desk. Steen was a veteran soldier, a quiet but competent
man. Most importantly, he knew and understood Indians and
shared the Major's empathy with them. Steen had grown up in an
orphanage. He knew how it felt not to have a place to call home.

"I'm afraid it has gotten even worse, sir," he said. "I believe I
speak for the entire population along the Brazos—white, red, civilian and military alike—when I say we're worried. It looks like we're
headed straight for a new Indian war."

Neighbors sipped at the coffee, winced and silently cursed the
man who invented tin cups. The rim of the cups always seemed to
be a hundred degrees hotter than the coffee it held. "The troop
buildup at Fort Chadbourne?"

"Precisely," Steen said, his brow furrowed. "I don't dispute the
need for a punitive military campaign against the northern tribes.
There have been raids, killings and wholesale livestock thefts all
along the frontier. I personally believe most of the outrages were
perpetrated by one or two outlaw Indian bands." The officer

sipped at his coffee. "I'm not even totally convinced the depredations were all done by Indians. But that is beside the point. The problem is that the men assigned to the Chadbourne expedition are all new to Texas. They don't know the difference between a friendly Indian and a pile of horse manure. The commanding officer not only doesn't know the difference, he doesn't care."

Steen leaned forward, his knuckles resting atop the desk. "I know the expedition commander well. Captain W. J. Newton is not going to go to the trouble of making a distinction between friendly Indians and hostile ones. He's a glory hunter. His type need battles the way drunks need liquor. I don't have to tell you what that means."

The Major shook his head in dismay. "All it takes is one mistake, one strike against the wrong tribe, and we're back to where we started," he grumbled. "Dammit, is anybody in charge in Washington?"

The Army officer winced. "It doesn't seem like it, Major. There are times I'm a bit ashamed of the uniform I wear. This could be one of those occasions."

Robert Neighbors abruptly rose. "Gentlemen, we've got to do something. I'll forward a dispatch to Governor Pease expressing our concern and asking his help. I'll also get a message to General P. F. Smith asking him to suspend any campaign that might involve friendly Indians before we can colonize them. In fact, I'll take our arguments to Washington in person. And I will point out in no uncertain terms to the Department of the Interior that it makes damn little sense for the government to hire agents to make peace and select lands for the Indians, and at the same time put soldiers in the neighborhood to make war on the friendly Indians along with the hostiles." He snorted in disgust. "No wonder the Indians don't trust us."

The Major reached for his hat and turned to Hill. "George, do what you can to calm the waters here while I'm gone. Before I head for Washington I'll tell Agent Howard to join up with the troops at Fort Chadbourne and help make sure no friendly Indians get caught in the crossfire if or when the shooting starts."

He offered a hand to Steen. "Thanks for your support, Major Steen. If the Army had more officers like you, we'd have a lot fewer headaches."

Steen's grip was firm. The Major thought he could feel the officer's outrage and disgust through his hand. "Major Neighbors,"

Steen said, "if I had a couple of battalions of troops instead of less than a full company here, I'd stop Newton on my own at the point of a saber." Steen sighed and released the Major's hand. "In the meantime, God help us."

San Antonio
December 1854

Major Robert Neighbors stood over the tiny grave on the frost-brittled grass of the hillside behind the Salado Creek farm and let the tears run unashamed down his cheeks.

Frances Elizabeth Ritchey Neighbors, age three months, lay beneath the freshly turned soil. *At least she went to her Maker without pain,* the Major thought. *She just passed on in her sleep.* He tightened the grip of his free arm around his wife's shoulders and felt the convulsions of her silent sobs of grief.

"She's with the angels now, Lizzie, a new star in the heavens. She will be happy there." The Major's voice cracked under the weight of his own inner pain. "God decided He needed Frances Elizabeth more than we did. It is not our right to question His decisions."

He led Lizzie away from the grave toward the expansive home below. *It will be springtime before grass begins to grow over that small grave.* The thought sent a new wave of hurt through his heart.

"It—it just—isn't fair," Lizzie sobbed as they walked. "She was such a good baby. Why does God take such a child from us?"

The Major squeezed his wife's shoulders. There was no answer to her question.

A half hour later Lizzie had partly regained her composure. Grief still misted her eyes and lined her face as they sat at the kitchen table. "I wasn't even home long enough to know her, Lizzie," the Major said. "I'll never forgive myself for that."

Lizzie placed a dainty hand over his forearm. "You mustn't blame yourself, dear. You had no choice. I'm sure Frances Elizabeth knows that."

"I'll build a fence around her grave. I can't abide the thought of horses and cows violating her resting place. In the spring we'll plant grass and flowers over her."

Lizzie's chin lifted and strength seemed to flow back into her eyes. "Ignacio can build the fence, Major, and I will take care of the planting. You have thousands of other souls depending upon you. Go ahead with your plans. Make the trip to Washington. The Lord put you here to serve the living, Robert Simpson Neighbors."

"But Lizzie, under the circumstances—"

"All the more important that you go on with your work," she interrupted, her tone firm. "The Indians need you. Texas needs you. Little Frances is gone and can never be brought back. But you can stop other families, red and white, from knowing such grief."

The Major patted the back of her hand and blinked against the tears that pooled in his eyes. He was silent for several moments before he cleared his throat. "You're right, Lizzie. I thank you for reminding me of my duty. I'll be leaving within the week."

EIGHT

Clear Fork of the Brazos
January 1855

Major Enoch Steen waved his ten-man patrol to a halt and squinted toward the approaching horseman. The man was pushing his mount hard.

Steen glanced back over his shoulder. The troopers waited, hands resting on carbines; two already had weapons drawn, trained on the pair of Indians bound hand and foot to their mounts. The thieves from the Waco tribe had offered no resistance. The five mules they had stolen from a settler trailed behind the patrol, their lead ropes in the hands of a veteran soldier. The Indians sat their saddles in surly dejection, heads down.

Jim Shaw rode up to Steen's side and stared for a moment at the horseman. "It is Ketumse," the Delaware scout said. "He's in a hurry. Never known that Comanche to put out much effort in a hard ride."

The patrol waited until Ketumse pulled his horse to a bouncing stop in front of Steen. "There is trouble," the Paneteka chief said by way of greeting. "Sanaco and Buffalo Hump have gathered their bands and fled."

"How did this come about, Ketumse?" Steen's face twisted in a frown. "I visited their camp only a few days ago. They seemed content then to wait for the move to the reservation."

Ketumse swung a leg over his lathered pony's back and dismounted. "Two Indians came into the camp of the Comanches," Ketumse said. "They told us that many soldiers would arrive soon from Fort Chadbourne to attack the camp from the south and kill all the chiefs and warriors. They said you were coming with a large force and would strike the camp from the north."

Steen mouthed a sharp oath. "I was afraid something like this might happen. Who spreads this story, Ketumse?"

The Paneteka shrugged. "One was the Seminole called Joe One Jug. I do not know the other by name. He was a Waco."

Steen turned the information over in his mind. Joe One Jug was Emil Washburn's pet Indian; he had earned the name because he would do anything for a jug of whiskey a day. It didn't take a great deal of deduction to figure out who was behind the stories. "All of Sanaco's and Buffalo Hump's people left?"

Ketumse nodded. "All gone. Far to the north. Maybe as far as the country of the Quahadis."

Steen fought back his growing irritation. "What of you, Ketumse? Have your people also joined the flight?"

"A few. Most stay. Major Neighbors told us there will be no killing of friendly Indians. We trust him. We wait to move onto our new land." Ketumse pulled out his battered pipe and patted the pockets of his worn shirt. "Do you have tobacco?"

Steen waved a hand at one of the troopers. The soldier produced a sack of tobacco and tossed it to Ketumse. Steen waited as the Paneteka stuffed and lighted his pipe and then tucked the tobacco into a pocket instead of returning it to the trooper.

"Will Sanaco and Buffalo Hump return, Ketumse?"

The chief exhaled a cloud of smoke and shrugged. "I do not know. They leave many lodges, many robes and much food behind in their haste. Maybe when the snows grow deep and bellies empty, they return. Maybe not."

Steen sighed in disgust. *All that work to get them to come in wasted. And if that damn Newton is on the way from Chadbourne, we could lose the rest of the friendly ones.* "Ketumse," Steen said, "I'd like to ask you to move your people closer to Fort Belknap. If the Army does come from Fort Chadbourne, my soldiers will protect you. We will set up a network of runners and keep in touch with each other every day."

Ketumse remounted. "It will be done." He started to rein the horse about, then paused. "My people have little food, no meat. The wind cuts through our blankets like the knife. Will you give us supplies?"

Steen nodded. "I will see that you receive clothing and blankets, and grain, flour and cattle for the pots."

"Whiskey?"

"You know the rules, Ketumse. No liquor."

The Paneteka half-smiled. "A man never knows until he asks." He touched heels to his mount.

Steen sat in the saddle and watched as Ketumse's figure grew small in the distance, then waved the column into motion toward Belknap. *Major Neighbors,* Steen thought, *is going to be mad to the bone over this.*

Fort Inge
February 1855

Major Robert Neighbors slammed a fist onto the top of the desk with enough force to spatter drops from the inkwell. His face was almost purple with rage; a vein throbbed in his temple as he glared at the man standing across from him.

"Dammit, Howard, you've got some explaining to do!"

Agent George Howard cringed at the outburst. "Major Neighbors, I don't know what you're so upset about," he said. His voice trembled. When the big man with all the hair got this mad, Howard knew, it was time to get nervous.

"Let me refresh your memory, Agent Howard." The Major lowered his voice but made no attempt to hide the cold rage in his tone. "Point one: I specifically instructed you to go to Chadbourne and keep Newton away from the friendly tribes. Why the hell didn't you follow my orders?"

Howard shifted his weight nervously from one foot to another. "I made inquiries, Major. There were no troops available to escort me to Fort Chadbourne."

"Escort, hell," the Major snapped. "I've ridden through half the Indian population of Texas alone. You could have put your butt in the saddle—or at least hitched a ride on a freight wagon. I'm not buying that excuse." The Major pinned an icy glare on Howard's face. "Only the grace of God and the efforts of Agent Hill and Major Enoch Steen saved a massacre. That idiot Newton scattered the Comanches from hell to breakfast and was ready to charge into the Caddos and Arapahos with sabers drawn. Steen and Hill managed to turn them back."

The Major fell silent for a couple of heartbeats to let Howard stew in his own juices. Howard glanced hopefully at a chair near the door. The Major did not ask him to sit.

"Point two," the Major said, "I left you specific instructions to prepare the Tonkawas for the move to the Brazos. Nothing was done. Now the Tonks have taken to the hills, afraid of white vigilantes, and it will take weeks to get them back. Why did you let that happen?"

"I tried, Major Neighbors. The chiefs wouldn't agree to go to the Brazos. The post commander here wouldn't help me. And there wasn't much I could do about the civilians."

The Major slowly unballed his fists as he struggled to gain control of his anger. "That's not quite the whole story, is it?"

"Well, sir, I—I haven't been well."

"That brings us to point three, Howard," the Major said coldly. "You haven't even been near the Tonk camp for almost four months. They received no rations for the entire time. Is that correct?"

Howard swallowed. "As I said, I haven't been well—"

"I heard you," the Major interrupted. "I didn't see a request for leave. You just rode off, Howard, and let things go to hell here."

Howard's face flushed. "Major Neighbors, I resent this assault on my integrity!"

"And I resent and detest incompetence, Howard! If I had known then what I know now, I would have fired you the first day we met." The Major sighed. "I misjudged you, Howard. I thought you had the makings of a good Indian agent. I was wrong. You'd rather sit on your butt and watch the Indians starve or get shot than to help them."

Howard tried and failed to hold the Major's intense gaze. "I did my best—"

"If that's the best you can do," the Major interrupted, "I sure as hell don't want to see your worst. I want your resignation on my desk in San Antonio within a week."

Howard's face flushed. "See here, Neighbors, you can't—"

"I can and I will. Resign or I'll fire you. It's your pick." The Major glared at Howard. *The man doesn't even have the backbone to admit his mistakes,* he thought. "Now get out of here before I really lose my temper."

Robert Neighbors waited until the door closed behind the departing agent, then lowered himself into the chair and dug knuckles into tired eyes. *God,* he thought, *sometimes I think it would take a dozen of me to stomp out every grass fire that flares up around this state.* The lingering rage began to slowly fade. After a few minutes he heaved himself to his feet. "Well, Major Neighbors," he muttered aloud, "you've got a little work to do. No need to sull up like a mule . . ."

Brazos Reserve
April 1855

Major Robert Neighbors pulled his mount to a stop in front of a crude half-dugout homestead on the north bank of the Brazos. A middle-aged farmer stood by the doorway, an ancient Kentucky rifle in the crook of an arm.

"Living here, mister?" the Major asked casually.

The farmer nodded. "My place."

"I'm afraid you'll have to move on. This land is part of the Indian reservation."

The farmer stiffened, his thumb moving to the hammer of the Kentucky. "The hell you say. I bought this place. You're the one's gonna have to get off."

The Major leaned forward in the saddle, forearms crossed on the horn. "Who did you buy the land from?"

"Ain't none of your business."

"That's where you're wrong, mister." Neighbors kept his tone conversational. "Looks like you've been cheated. Somebody sold you land they didn't own. This has been U.S. Government property for months. Now, who did you buy it from?"

Confusion flickered in the farmer's weathered face. "I got a paper. Signed proper by Hiram Oldham."

The Major sighed. "So the Oldhams aren't satisfied to sell land they've already stolen. They've started peddling land they don't even own. Mister, you've got a problem—"

The farmer cocked his rifle.

"—And if you point that thing at me your problem just got a damn sight bigger." The Major's voice turned sharp. "It's called staying alive." He let his hand drop to the Colt at his belt. "Ease that hammer or you'll own some land here, all right. About six foot of it."

The stooped man stared for a moment at the Major as if trying to decide whether it was worth the chance. Then he reluctantly lowered the rifle.

"All right, friend," the Major said, "I'm giving you two days to move off Indian land. At the end of that time I'll be back. I don't expect to find you here. If I do, I'll personally throw you off."

"My money—I put everything I had into this place."

"That's between you and Hiram Oldham." The Major abruptly wheeled his horse and rode away. He didn't think the farmer would shoot him in the back, but the tightly bunched muscles between his shoulder blades weren't listening to his head. Finally, out of rifle range, he relaxed in the saddle. It was the third time in a week he had been forced to evict a settler from reservation lands.

He kneed the leggy Tennessee-bred sorrel into a steady trot toward Fort Belknap.

Two hours later he sat in Agent George Hill's office in Fort Belknap, the confrontation with the farmer pushed to the back of his mind. "Everything set, George?"

Hill nodded. "As set as possible. We've got eight hundred or so Caddos, Ionis, Wacos, Tawakonos and others waiting to move onto the reservation. The Anadarkos are already here. Ketumse's Comanches are a few miles outside the fort. No sign of Yellow Wolf. I think he's gone across the Red River."

The Major nodded. "I'll call on Ketumse myself. I'd like you to start moving the others onto their lands. Get them the tools they need to start farming and begin work on the agency buildings. I've let a contract with Charles Barnard to supply beef for the Indians."

Hill grunted in satisfaction. "Barnard's a rare breed in these parts. Good cattleman and honest to boot. We won't have to worry about the Indians getting cheated on beef if Charlie Barnard's in charge." Hill cocked an eyebrow at the Major. "Emil Washburn wasn't too happy when you ordered his beef contract voided, Major."

The Major pushed back his chair and stood. "I couldn't care less about the state of satisfaction of Emil Washburn, George. I hear he's still peddling whiskey to the Indians. It's time to put a stop to that."

Major Robert Neighbors bit back a silent curse as his sorrel topped the rise overlooking Ketumse's village south of the Brazos. Below, two dozen Comanches clustered around a wagon. Jim Shaw had found the wagon tracks two miles back. The deep ruts indicated the wagon was heavily loaded.

The Major glanced at the officer riding alongside. Enoch Steen's jaw was set in tightly controlled anger. "That's one of Washburn's trade wagons," the officer said. "I warned him against coming onto reservation land."

The Major twisted in the saddle to glance over the escort detail. There were five troopers, himself, John Connor and Steen, all heavily armed. "Major Steen," he said, "let's see if we can't make the warning stick. I'll take responsibility for any civil repercussions." He touched heels to the sorrel.

A surge of anger colored the Major's cheeks as he neared the wagon. Nat Colley stood beside the off wheel, a shotgun draped in the crook of an arm. Two other men stood beside Colley, their hands on pistols at their belts. The Comanches drew back at the approach of the troops. Several of the Indians cradled crock jugs against their chests. Ketumse stood at the edge of the village, watching silently.

The Major pulled his horse to a stop before the trader. "Colley, you've been warned against selling liquor to the Indians. You know damn well it's against federal law to sell whiskey within ten miles of reservation boundaries."

"Man's got a right to earn a living," Colley said, a contemptuous sneer on his stubbled face. "The Injuns want whiskey, they're gonna get it somewhere."

"Maybe," the Major said, "but they aren't getting it from you or your brother-in-law any longer." He swung down and peered into the wagon. The bed of the conveyance was lined with assorted trade goods and twenty crock jugs.

The Major stepped away from the wagon and glanced at Steen. "Burn it," he said.

Colley cocked the shotgun, started to swing the muzzles toward the Major, and abruptly stopped as the distinct sounds of a half dozen rifle hammers eared to full cock penetrated his burst of rage. His face blanched as he looked at the big Colt Dragoon in Steen's hand. The muzzle was trained on Colley's head. "Put the weapons in the wagon, Mister Colley," Steen said. "Your friends, too. Or you won't live to see sundown."

Colley blustered. "Dammit, you soldiers ain't gonna shoot no white man—"

"Try me, Colley." Steen's voice was soft and cold.

Colley hesitated, his gaze darting from one trooper to another. His shoulders slumped as the last vestige of defiance drained from his body. He dropped the smoothbore into the wagon and turned to his companions. "Better do what the bluecoat says, boys." The other traders shucked gun belts and piled their weapons into the wagon bed.

Major Neighbors unhitched the four mules. A trooper led the animals away from the wagon. "You ain't heard the last of this, Neighbors," Colley blustered, "or you either, Steen. We got ways of dealin' with you Injun-lovers."

Steen lowered the hammer and holstered the Dragoon. "I'm scared to the bone, Colley," he said. He dismounted, rummaged in the wagon and located a can of lamp oil. He soaked the wagon contents until the can was empty, then produced a match. He cocked an eyebrow at the Major. "Care to do the honors, Major Neighbors?"

"Don't mind if I do, Major Steen." The Major struck the match against the iron rim of the wagon wheel and tossed it into the midst of the cargo. Flames flickered, then flared high. The group edged back as the heat from the growing inferno spread, fueled by the liquor and sacks of gunpowder.

Nat Colley's face twisted in renewed outrage as the flames leapt high. "Emil ain't going to take this sittin' on his butt, Neighbors. He'll come after you for sure now."

Robert Neighbors smiled pleasantly at the thin-faced man. "I won't be hard to find. You tell Washburn that." He nodded toward the north. "If you boys start walking now, you can make it to the post on the Red River before full dark."

"Walk?" The word was an outraged squawk.

"I'm confiscating your horses and saddles for violating the rules of trespass on Indian land. Start hoofing it, Colley. The walk will give you plenty of time to think."

The Major stood and watched until the three traders had grown small, already limping in the distance, then strode to Ketumse. The Paneteka had not spoken during the entire episode. "Ketumse, where are the rest of your people?"

The chief shrugged. "Many go to join Sanaco and Buffalo Hump in the Plains country." He waved a hand. "These are all that remain."

The Major surveyed the camp. There were less than two hundred people in the village. Most of the women and children looked haggard and hungry. *Probably traded the last of their food for whiskey,* the Major thought. *Maybe the men deserve to starve, but not the women and young ones.* "Gather your band, Ketumse. We will escort you to Fort Belknap."

"You will give us land of our own?"

"Eventually. For now—until more Comanches come in to the reservation—you will be assigned a place among the other tribes. You will be provided with fields to plant. We will supply your people until the crops have grown."

Ketumse's brow furrowed. "We will go. I do not think we will plant until we have our own land. But we will watch and learn how it is done."

Brazos Reserve
June 1855

Major Robert Neighbors leaned against the small corral behind the log cabin that served as the agency building and stared toward the thunderheads which towered on the western horizon. The reservation needed a good rain. The crops were showing signs of stress. *If it doesn't rain soon we'll be in trouble,* the Major thought, *but the weather's one adversary that can't be legislated, bluffed or bought. It's in the hands of the Almighty, and I sure can't fight Him.*

Agent George Hill had done his job well. There were more than seven hundred Indians settled on the Brazos reserve, from the Caddos and Anadarkos on the east side to the Wacos and Tawakonos on the west. Runners had arrived and reported that more Indians were on the way. Those already on the reservation had proved to be hard workers, with the exception of Ketumse's band. The Comanches seemed content to lounge in the shade of the postoak and mesquite trees, eat the beef supplied by the white man, and watch the other tribes labor in the fields.

Lightning flickered in the thickening storm to the west. The clouds were closer now, boiling with forces no man could understand. The wind shifted. The scent of blowing dust gave way to a gust of cooler air that smelled of rain. *Maybe it's going to be a good day after all,* the Major thought. A call from nearby broke his reverie.

"A word with you, Major?" George Hill asked as he stepped from the building which doubled as the agent's office and spartan living quarters. The Major nodded, cast one last hopeful glance toward the approaching storm, and stepped inside.

Hill poured two cups of coffee into porcelain mugs. The spout of the pot chittered against the lips of the cups. The Major studied

Hill as he sipped at the scalding coffee. The agent had lost weight. His face was pale despite the constant exposure to wind and sun. The Major had seen Hill double over at the waist as if in pain when he thought no one was watching. The Major lowered his cup.

"George, something's wrong, isn't it?"

Pain flickered in the agent's eyes. "Maybe I'm just tired, Major," he said, "but I'll be honest with you. I haven't been well of late. At times my gut feels like it's got a lance rammed into it."

"I suspected you were in pain, George. Is there anything I can do?"

Hill sipped at his coffee and winced as the brew hit his stomach. "I hate to ask, Major—there's so much to be done here—but I must request a leave of absence. I've neglected my own business affairs severely in the two years I've been at this post. This pain in the belly isn't helping my effectiveness here. And I'd like to see a doctor in Dallas—" His voice trailed away.

The Major stepped to Hill's side. "By all means, George. God knows, you've done a tremendous job here." He placed a hand on the agent's shoulder and was faintly surprised at the lack of muscle over the bone. "The main thing now is your health. Of course you can have a leave of absence. Take all the time you need. Whenever you're ready to come back, your job will be waiting for you."

Hill lifted his coffee, stared at the contents, and put the cup down without drinking. "I'm sorry, Major."

"You've nothing to apologize for, George." He dropped his hand from the agent's shoulder. "You've saved many lives here. Now it's time to look out for your own."

"But, Major, with Howard gone too, you'll be the only Indian agent in Texas. We're talking six hundred or more miles of frontier, a dozen tribes—"

"Don't worry about that," the Major interrupted. "I'll have help coming soon. The department has received several applications for agency posts. In the meantime, I have Jim Shaw, Jose Maria and Major Steen to help out until the new agents are on board. We'll make out. We'll miss you, but we'll manage. You should be on your way as soon as you can pack. I'll ask Steen to send an escort along with you."

George Hill sighed. "Thank you, Major. I'll be back as soon as I can—"

An urgent knock on the door cut the agent's comment short. "Come in," the Major called.

Jim Shaw stepped inside, his dark features twisted in disgust. "Ketumse's bunch is at it again," he said bluntly. "Mary Two Blankets came to me. The Comanches have turned their horses into the Caddo fields again. They also stole a mule and two bags of corn from the Wacos."

The Major reached for his hat. The first wind-blown drops of rain tapped against the roof. Lightning flashed and thunder rolled in the near distance.

"I'll take care of it, Major," Hill said.

"No, George. I want you to wind up your affairs here and get ready to leave as soon as possible. I'll handle Ketumse. That Comanche's getting to be a pain in the butt."

Quitaque Valley
August 1855

Sanaco stood on a low sandstone ridge and stared toward the carnage of the battlefield that had been his village. The wails of mourning women were like a lance driven through his heart.

Comanche warriors lay dead or injured among the smoldering remnants of tepees. Flames soared high above the lodge that held the band's dried meat, blankets and few bushels of grain. The hollow feeling in his belly deepened as the storehouse lodge collapsed in a shower of sparks and the stink of burned supplies.

The war was lost.

The Osage warriors had struck at dawn, the latest in a series of skirmishes against the Panetekas. The Comanches had fought well against the larger attacking force, but their ancient muskets, bows and lances were no match for the long rifles of the Osage marksmen. There would be no more buffalo for the Panetekas. The Osages stood between the Comanches and the shaggy beasts in the Plains to the north. The war had cost the lives of more than thirty of Sanaco's finest fighters. The Nakoni and Tenawa Comanches who had joined the flight from the soldiers at Fort Chadbourne had lost twenty warriors and two of their most powerful war chiefs.

Sanaco swiped a hand across the blood on his own face. A rifle ball had gouged a furrow along the side of his scalp and torn away part of an ear. But the pain of the wound was nothing compared to the ache in his heart. *I have failed my people.* The single, simple thought kept echoing through his brain. It would not go away.

The war chief's shoulders slumped in despair. He climbed from his observation point and strode through the devastated camp. Widows continued their mourning songs; many knelt beside crumpled bodies, knives or flint cutting tools in hand, and slashed their own breasts and arms until the blood flowed.

Sanaco paused before one of the tribal elders. The old man had once been a feared warrior. He bore many scars of ancient combat. He squatted beside the smoking remnants of his lodge and tried to force hands twisted by bone disease to reload the battle-scarred musket across his lap. The ancient one glanced up at Sanaco's approach.

"Raccoon," Sanaco said softly, "I must call a council. I need your wisdom to guide me. The survival of our people is at stake."

Raccoon nodded. "There is much to be decided, Sanaco. Let us bury our dead, then speak of what to do."

Sanaco stood before the assembled sub-chiefs, medicine men and warriors who had survived the Osage war. There were less than a hundred of them. Many bore fresh wounds from the battle just ended.

"The Osages have done what the white soldiers could not," Sanaco said. He made no attempt to hide the sadness in his voice. "We cannot reach the buffalo herds. Our lodges, food—all our supplies—have been destroyed. More than half our horses are gone. The Starving Time nears. Our women and children suffer greatly." Sanaco paused and glanced around the assembled tribesmen. He was telling them nothing they did not already realize.

"I have counseled with Raccoon, and we agree there is but one thing we can do. We must return to the land of the Brazos, to the place where the white man promised us a home free from hunger and want. The reservation is our only choice if our people are to survive."

"No!" The single word from Little Elk exploded over the mutters of agreement from the circle of warriors. "I will never go to lick the white man's hand like a starving dog." The young sub-chief's face was dark with fury. He stepped forward and turned to face the gathering. "Little Elk will not become a sheep in the white man's pasture. I go west to the land of the Quahadis. Other Comanche bands are there. We will plan, we will raid. We will drive the white man from the lands that belong to us."

A few of the younger warriors nodded in agreement.

"Little Elk speaks his heart," Sanaco said. "This is as it should be. It is his right and his duty. I say this not in argument with Little Elk, who has fought with much bravery against the Osages and our enemies before them. But to the south are many soldiers in blue. They grow stronger with each passing moon. Across the river the Mexican army also grows, to make war against the tribes gathered there. The Texans put their Rangers into the field. To the southwest the hated Apaches wait. We have the choice only to fight and die or go to the reservation and live."

"Then we fight," Little Elk snapped.

A mutter of voices fell silent as Raccoon rose. The old warrior stood for a moment, surrounded by the silence of respect. "Sanaco speaks true," Raccoon finally said. "We must set aside our own pride as warriors and think of the women and children." The old man drew a slow breath. "My time on this land is short. The life of one old man means nothing. But the future of the Human Beings lives on in our children. We must go to this reservation."

"No, Raccoon." Little Elk's voice was firm but controlled in respect to the elder. "The rest of you can do as you wish. Any man who wants to come with Little Elk to drive the white man from the land will be welcome."

Sanaco's spirits dropped as a dozen young men nodded in agreement. "It is your right, Little Elk, and the right of those who wish to follow you. Tomorrow I send a messenger to Fort Belknap, to ask Bear-Who-Walks-Like-Man to talk with us at the place called Council Springs."

Sanaco sighed heavily as the council ended and Little Elk strode away, followed by the warriors who had joined him. The Paneteka chief turned to the old man at his side. "My heart is heavy, Raccoon," he said. "It hurts to see the end of one's people grow near."

NINE

Red River Trading Post
September 1855

Emil Washburn shook the travel dust from his hat and stepped into his business establishment.

Nat Colley waited at the pine bar, a bottle in his hand. "How'd it go, Emil?"

Washburn chuckled. "Couldn't be better. The tame Indians on the Brazos are fat, slick and happy." He reached for the bottle and downed a hefty swallow. "Old Sanaco's come crawlin' in with his tail between his legs. There's better than two hundred Comanches on the Clear Fork reservation now. Neighbors got himself two new agents and headed for home. He'll be out of our hair in San Antonio until his wife drops that papoose she's carryin'."

Colley's brow wrinkled in confusion. "Don't see why you're so tickled over it, Emil. Sounds to me like Neighbors has got things going his way."

"Playing right into our hands, Nat." He took another slug from the bottle, massaged his saddle-numbed backside, and toed out a chair. "We sit quiet for a while, let Neighbors think he's got a tight rein on things. Then we sic the wolves on him."

Colley dug a finger into an unwashed ear. "I still don't see why we ought to be happy about it."

Washburn grinned at his brother-in-law. "Nat, we've got us a couple land outfits itchin' to get their hands on that country along the Brazos. They knew it's worth waitin' a year or two to get it. Meantime, we've got all the tools we need right here to make money and set us a bear trap for old Neighbors, all at the same time."

Colley reached for the bottle. "You mean sellin' whiskey to the reservation Indians? I don't reckon that's a good idea. Neighbors was serious about it. Hell, he's liable to bring soldiers in here and burn this place down."

Washburn shook his head in mock dismay. "Nat, you got to start thinkin' bigger. We won't sell whiskey to the reservation Indians. But we can damn sure peddle the rotgut and a bunch of guns to Little Elk and the other redskins still out on the prairie. Some of Sanaco's people are going to slip out of the reserve and spread the word."

Washburn leaned back in his chair. "Best of all, Nat, we got the man we want on the Comanche reserves now."

"That Baylor fellow?"

"One and the same. Former judge and Texas legislator John R. Baylor, duly appointed agent for the Comanche Indian nation." Washburn retrieved the nearly empty bottle and drained the last of the liquor. He cocked an eye at Nat. His brother-in-law had that slack-jawed, glassy-eyed look of a man who had put away more whiskey than his system could handle.

"Baylor's got a couple of weaknesses, Nat," Washburn said. "He's got a lot of stiff-neck pride, more than is good for a man. Best of all for us, he likes money. I hear he told his sister that he was going to make sure every Baylor from now on died with a million dollars in his sock. We're going to use that." Washburn chuckled aloud. "Won't be any big trick to turn Baylor against Neighbors and the redskins. And the fool won't even know he's been had. By the time Neighbors figures out what's going on it'll be too late for him to do anything about it. We'll have every white man on the frontier hunting Indian scalps. When the settlers wipe out the redskins, our partners move in and take the Indian land."

"How about this other agent? The new one at Belknap?" Colley's words were slurred. "We use him too?"

Washburn shook his head. "No way. Shapley Ross can't be bought and he can't be threatened." He snorted in disgust. "Lordy, how I do hate an honest man."

Brazos Reserve

Shapley Prince Ross shucked the pistol belt from his waist and hung it on a peg by the door. The way things were looking on the

Brazos reservation, he mused, a man probably didn't even need to carry a gun these days.

He shook the coffeepot. The slight slosh told him there might be a cup left. It would be thick enough to float a horseshoe by now, but it was still coffee and he wrote reports better with a warm mug in reach. He stoked the fire in the cast-iron stove, put the pot on to warm and sat behind the desk.

His report would be easy enough to write. The Brazos Reserve Indians had built fences, permanent homes and storage buildings, and the government had provided supplies and tools on time and in sufficient quantities. Now that Ketumse and his troublemakers had been moved to the Upper Reservation set aside for the Comanches on the Clear Fork, the agrarian tribes were living in harmony.

Ross couldn't help worrying about the reservation Comanches, even if they were in another agent's bailiwick. Sanaco's ragged band seemed content to settle on the land set aside for them, welcomed the white man's beef to take the wrinkles from hungry bellies and expressed eagerness for peace. Ross didn't trust Sanaco. He knew the Paneteka chief kept runners out, staying in touch with the wild bands. Agent Baylor now had almost four hundred Comanches to watch over. It was a tall order. Ross hoped Baylor could handle the job; the man didn't seem to know all that much about the wild Plains tribes.

What bothered Ross the most about Baylor wasn't his lack of knowledge about Comanches. It was the fact that the Major was scarcely out of sight on his way back to San Antonio when Baylor brought up the subject of gold and silver deposits along the Clear Fork, San Saba and Wichita rivers. Ross had paid no attention to the rumors of hidden wealth. Such stories were a staple of any frontier outpost and almost always without merit. But it sounded like Baylor intended to do a lot of prospecting during his tour with the Indian service.

Ross didn't intend to mention his concerns about Baylor in his formal reports. He would stick to his own knitting for now. At the same time, he couldn't help but fret.

Buffalo Hump's band was still at large, a matter for no small concern. The Paneteka sub-chief Little Elk had been linked to a half dozen raids of late. His band was growing, as was his stature among the Comanches. Little Elk had plenty of opportunities to recruit. Along the Red River the Nakoni, Tenawa, Tanima, Yamparika and Kotsoteka tribes of the middle and southern Comanches continued to roam free. They were small in numbers individually, but still capable of a lot of mischief.

Ross knew that come spring, when the wild Comanches' war ponies had regained their strength and fattened on new green grass, they would hit the frontier with a vengeance unless steps were taken. He had talked at length with the Major and found the supervising agent shared Ross's worries.

The Major had taken a solid step toward preventing a full-scale Indian war by requesting reinforcements from the military. And, Ross mused, the Major had certainly gotten somebody's attention in Washington this time. The Second Regiment of Cavalry was on its way to Texas.

The Second was the top regiment of the mounted arm of the Army. Its officers and men were handpicked, capable and fearless in battle. Their job here would be to protect the docile tribes and white settlers from marauding Indians and at the same time launch campaigns to harass and punish the wild Comanches. The mere presence of the horse soldiers should give any would-be war chief pause to reconsider any raiding plans.

Agent Baylor might not know Indians as well as Ross and the Major, but even Baylor openly declared it would be a damn sight cheaper to feed the Indians than to fight them.

Clear Fork Reserve
November 1855

John R. Baylor stood before the fireplace of the crude split-log agency office and living quarters and let the heat of the fire chase the chill from his bones.

His latest ride had been long and hard. And empty. There wasn't a trace of gold or silver to be found within miles of the Comanche reservation. That was the biggest disappointment, but not the only one.

The damned Comanches were impossible. Baylor hadn't heard so much whining since he had served his term in the state legislature. Ketumse was the worst of the lot. His people, Ketumse declared, would not work the field unless they were given presents. Baylor had bowed his neck on that one. The damn Indians would get presents after they earned them by working. Not a day before.

Ketumse and Sanaco both groused about the shortage of supplies and beef, but all the while their bands were handing out food and blankets to northern Comanche renegades who slipped onto the reservation in the dead of night and left again before sunrise. *Dammit,* Baylor grumbled inwardly, *there's no way one agent can stop these wild Indians from sneaking onto the reservation. Or get a bunch of lazy whiners to work.* The life of an Indian agent had turned out to be a lot less profitable and glamorous than it was supposed to be.

He lifted the coffeepot from its bed of coals in the fireplace and poured a ceramic mug two thirds full. He pulled a pint of rye from his carefully hoarded stash in the travel case beneath his bunk and poured a double shot into the steaming coffee.

His spirits lifted a bit after a couple of swallows. There was still a way to make some decent money out of this miserable job. Nobody in his right mind could expect a man to plan a future and feed his family on a miserable fifteen hundred dollars a year. There shouldn't be any objections if a man showed some initiative on his own.

He sat at the crude table and sipped at the doctored coffee as he studied the accounts ledger. Emil Washburn had been right; the only people making money off the Indians were sutler Charles Barnard and a couple other traders duly baptized by Neighbors. It would be a tricky move, but it was possible to get a Baylor thumb in that pie. The Baylors owned a piece of the trading and mercantile firm of DeWitt & Wolfe in San Antonio. *We can undercut Barnard's prices by ten percent for a few months and still make money,* Baylor thought. Then, when Barnard had been frozen out of the Indian supply trade, DeWitt & Wolfe would double its prices. It would be simple enough to claim a few extra Indians at the public feed trough on the Clear Fork. That would let DeWitt & Wolfe collect for goods never delivered, and that was a hundred percent profit any way you looked at the numbers. *I can turn in a few extra Indian expenses a month on my agency accounts, too,* Baylor thought. *As much as these savages come and go, nobody knows how many we've got.* Another hundred or so Comanches listed on the books would amount to some fair money over a year's time.

Baylor drained the last of the rye coffee, his spirits rising by the moment. He could see no reason why the switch in sutlers couldn't be pulled off. *Might as well get things started,* he thought. *Time to call on the firm of DeWitt & Wolfe. The damn Comanches do what they want anyway. No reason they can't watch out for themselves for a while . . .*

San Antonio
January 1856

Major Robert Simpson Neighbors made no attempt to hide the swelling of his chest as he sat at Lizzie's side, a small, wrinkled bundle cradled in big hands.

"Are you pleased with your new son, Major?" Lizzie's voice showed only a hint of weakness. This pregnancy and delivery had been a relatively easy one for Lizzie.

"More than pleased, dear," the Major said. "I'm so proud I could pop. He's a fine boy, healthy and strong."

Lizzie smiled and reached out as the baby whimpered. "Hand over little Robert Barnard Neighbors, Major, and leave the two of us alone," she said. "He seems to be ready for the breast."

The Major surrendered the child reluctantly, leaned over and kissed his wife on the cheek, then turned to leave.

"Major, now that the baby is here and meets with your approval, will you be heading back to Fort Belknap soon?"

The question bit into the Major's contentment. He had no wish to travel into the teeth of a frigid wind, with its hint of a full-blown blizzard to come. But something didn't feel right on the Clear Fork Reserve despite Agent Baylor's glowing reports to the contrary. Even more bothersome was the personal note from Ross; Baylor had abruptly left the reservation without notifying anyone. The Comanches there were without supervision and control, and that usually meant trouble. The Major sighed in regret. "Yes, dear. I'm afraid I must. There have been some rather disturbing developments that require my personal attention. And I should be on hand when the Second Regiment arrives. I'm sorry."

Lizzie reached for a strap of her nightgown. "Don't apologize, Major. You've been such a sweetheart to stay until the baby's birth." She stuck her tongue out at her husband, a weak but playful gesture. "Be gone with you, sir. Your presence here is no longer needed, anyway. Your son is in good hands. Godspeed and come home soon."

Brazos Reserve
March 1856

Major Robert Neighbors dropped the pen staff in disgust onto the clutter of letters and reports on Agent Ross's desk and glowered at John R. Baylor, seated across from him.

"Agent Baylor," the Major said, "I must advise you I am not at all pleased with your absence without leave during a crucial time for the Comanches under your supervision."

Baylor stiffened as if struck by a fist. His face reddened. "Sir, as I informed you by letter, my wife was ill. I returned as soon as she was out of danger."

The Major was silent for a moment, listening to the chill north wind whine around the walls of the cabin, a sharp reminder of a brutal and seemingly endless winter. Outside, patches of snow from a late season blizzard still lay in the downwind side of buildings and plants where it had drifted. *I suppose I can't be too hard on the man,* the Major grumbled silently, *since I've taken time away from my own duties to be with Lizzie.* He shrugged. "Very well, Mister Baylor. There will be no formal reprimand—at least this time." He paused for a moment and stared into Baylor's face. He saw the indignation and wounded pride in the hazel eyes, the set of the bearded jaw.

"Let's get back to business, then," the Major said. "This winter was a brute. The Comanches have suffered. They complain of inadequate rations—"

"That, sir, is an outright lie!" Baylor's retort was sharp and angry. "If they were short of food and blankets it was because they insisted on feeding their wild cousins from outside the reservation!"

"Perhaps, Agent Baylor," the Major said, his voice calm. Inwardly he was raging. *You damn fool,* he thought, *if you had been at your post you could have stopped that. Or at least made an effort to do so.* "I also have received complaints from Mister Barnard that your agency account is substantially in arrears."

He silenced Baylor's sputtered protest with a curt wave of the hand. "These matters will be reviewed in detail." The Major rose. "That will be all for now, Mister Baylor."

Baylor leapt from his chair, his ruddy face almost purple in rage.

"Dammit, sir, you cannot accuse me of everything that goes wrong around here. I won't stand for such insults!"

The Major fixed a cold glare on Baylor's face. "If you feel that strongly, Agent Baylor, you have the right to file a formal protest with the federal Commissioner of Indian Affairs. Now, as I just stated, that will be all."

Baylor snatched his hat from a peg by the door and stormed from the office. *That man's going to be trouble,* the Major thought with a heavy sigh. A few minutes later he heard a tap on the door.

Agent Shapley P. Ross stepped into the office and shrugged out of his heavy coat. "Afternoon, Major. Met Baylor out by the stable. He looked like somebody had just told him he had to stop breaking wind in public."

The Major smiled ruefully. "Something like that." He waited until Ross had a chance to warm himself by the fire. "Shapley," the Major said, "I didn't bring this point up with Baylor, but Sanaco and Ketumse both tell me they have no faith in him."

Ross nodded. "Neither of them is speaking to him at the moment. Baylor's a touch high-handed in his approach. I don't think he really cares much for Indians. Damn shame, too. The man could be a good agent if he set his mind to it." Ross turned and backed up to the stove, toasting his chilled backside. "We almost had another Fort Chadbourne runaway here, Major."

The Major lifted an inquisitive eyebrow.

"When the advance units of the Second Cavalry arrived at Camp Cooper, Sanaco and Ketumse were sure the soldiers intended to attack the reservation. They're still gun-shy where troops are concerned." Ross reached for the coffeepot and started brewing a fresh batch. "I may have overstepped my authority, but something had to be done. Jim Shaw and I went to the Upper Reserve and spent four days in council with the Comanches. We managed to persuade them they were in no danger from the soldiers."

"Have you been able to find out where Little Elk's band is wintering?"

Ross put the pot on the stove and shrugged. "Somewhere in the Red River breaks as best I can find out. Little Elk's built himself quite a band. Maybe a hundred braves."

The Major stood and began pacing the small office. "Little Elk must be stopped, Shapley, along with the rest of the wild southern Comanches. The Second Cavalry just might be the tool we need to break their war medicine for good."

Ross stared at the pot as if urging it to boil. "Everything set for the campaign, Major?"

The Major grunted an agreement. "For the first time, we have the right kind of troops in the right place at the right time, Shapley. If we sic the Second on the wild Comanches now, before they've had time to fully recover from the winter, we could force most of them to come in." The Major stopped pacing and again stared at the bleak landscape beyond the window. "Shapley, I hate to have it come to this. I hate killing. And somehow, it goes against logic that we must fight the Comanches in order to avoid a war."

Ross tapped his coffee mug impatiently with a finger. "There can't be peace as long as the wild bands are out there, Major. Now's the time to force them to come in. We've got the scouts and guides —the Caddos, Tonkawas, Tawakonos and Anadarkos in particular —to help the Second run Little Elk and others like him to the ground." Ross sighed as the coffee finally began to boil. "We've also got the support of the settlers along the Clear Fork, Major. Outside of a handful of die-hard Indian-haters and general hell-raisers the reservation approach has plenty of backing. We may never get another chance as good as this one."

Robert Neighbors nodded. "I'll get the plans firmed up as soon as the rest of the Second arrives." The cloud of disappointment lingering from the clash with Baylor seemed to lift from the Major's shoulders. At the same time the howl of wind outside the cabin dropped in pitch. "We're close, Shapley. A dream I've had for so many years may be just about to come true."

Camp Cooper
May 1856

Lieutenant Colonel Robert E. Lee stood at Major Robert Neighbors's side and watched as four companies of the Second Cavalry conducted a final check of equipment and mounts. A few yards away a dozen scouts under the leadership of the Delaware Jim Shaw slouched in the saddle and waited patiently for the white soldiers to conclude their elaborate preparations for departure.

Lee turned and offered a hand to the Major. "Well, Major Neighbors, we're ready. With the assistance of your guides and the maps you've supplied from your knowledge of the trails and camps

used by the Comanches, I foresee nothing short of full success."
Lee, his back ramrod straight, eyes alert, released the Major's
hand. "I privately admit, sir, that I am not personally convinced
that your Indian reservation experiment will succeed." The officer's smile took the sting from the voiced opinion. "But if two
Virginia gentlemen such as ourselves and a well-trained group like
the Second Cavalry cannot pull it off, no force on earth can."

The barked orders of senior noncoms set saddle leather creaking
as the soldiers mounted. A corporal stood six feet away, the reins of
Colonel Lee's gray gelding in hand.

A captain wheeled his horse about and trotted up to the two
men. "Expedition force formed and ready, sir," the officer reported with a snappy salute.

Lee returned the salute and called for his mount. He swung into
the saddle with the ease and grace of a man at home on horseback.
He lifted the reins, nodded to Robert Neighbors, raised a hand and
swept it forward. The four companies of cavalrymen fell into ranks
by the twos and passed in review, guidons fluttering in the breeze,
as Lee led them between the stone buildings of Camp Cooper
toward the rolling hills to the west.

The Major stood and watched until the troops had passed from
view, then strode to his own mount. He stepped into the saddle
and fought back the urge to join Lee and the troopers in the campaign against the Comanches responsible for the springtime outbreak of atrocities on the frontier.

To the south the scene was being repeated at Fort Chadbourne,
the Major knew. Colonel Albert Sidney Johnston would be opening
the campaign against renegade tribes on the southern frontier with
a like number of crack Second Cavalry troopers under his command.

The urge to join the hunt passed. The Major reined his horse
toward Fort Belknap a half day's ride northeast of Cooper. There,
two cavalry companies patrolled the Upper Reserve boundaries.
Their orders were to make sure no Comanches rode away from the
reservation during the campaign—and to ensure that no wild Indians slipped in to acquire arms, supplies and comfort from their
cousins.

The next few weeks held the key to the future, the Major
thought as he kneed his mount into a trot toward Belknap. He
turned in the saddle and stared for a moment toward the faint

cloud of dust on the horizon. "Good hunting, Colonel Lee," he muttered aloud.

Double Mountain

Buffalo Hump stood in a clump of juniper trees halfway up the southernmost of the twin peaks overlooking the hills and plains of the Brazos River valley and stared toward the line of horsemen in the far distance.

The Paneteka chief's shoulders slumped in despair. His medicine had failed him. He glanced down the slope toward the small group, all that remained of his once-powerful band. He had barely a dozen fit warriors left. The raid into Mexico had been a disaster. A quarter of his fighting men lay dead in the northern desert, victims of the Mexican army's big guns. Hunger, cold and sickness had taken another twenty men and three times that many women and children.

And now the damn bluecoats were everywhere. These were not regular soldiers. They knew their business. And the cursed Lipan and Tonk scouts anticipated his every move, cut his band off from the good water holes, frightened away the game. Twice he had sent out scouts to probe the bluecoat lines. Neither had returned. Perhaps the Tonks ate their flesh, as was their custom.

Buffalo Hump listened to the distant, high-pitched screech of the hunting red-tailed hawk, heard the raucous squawk of a bluejay, felt the cool breeze on his cheek, and smelled the oily tang from the junipers that studded the hills. He found no comfort in the sounds and smells that once had brought him peace.

He made his way slowly down the hillside. There was no place left to run, no warriors with which to stand and fight, no way to feed his people—except to the east, where a small patch of ground awaited those who came in defeat and shame. But at least there on the Clear Fork of the Brazos, the white man would feed the women and children.

Buffalo Hump strode into his camp and called out to his people. There was no need for a formal council. There weren't enough leaders left in the band to play the bones and sticks gambling game, let alone hold council. He waited until his people had gathered around. His heart grew even more heavy as he counted the survivors. They numbered forty-seven, mostly women and children.

"The soldiers still come," Buffalo Hump said. "We cannot outrun them. We cannot fight them. We cannot flee to the west, where the Apaches wait to take Comanche scalps." He paused for a moment, surveyed his ragged, starving band, then sighed. "We must go to the reservation. To the place where many of our cousins wait."

A mutter of protest rippled through the thin ranks of the remaining braves. Buffalo Hump raised a hand until the grumbles subsided. "We will go. The white man will feed us. We will be safe from our enemies there, safe from the soldiers. We will rest our horses, fill our bellies. We must survive until we are once again strong in numbers and in spirit." Buffalo Hump paused for dramatic effect as the circle of gaunt faces drew closer around him. "Then, when the time is right, we will leave the reservation. We will once again take the warpath and drive all our enemies before us until all that was our fathers' fathers' land is once again in its proper hands."

TEN

Belknap Road
June 1856

Little Elk sat astride his war horse and watched as his band of twenty handpicked warriors looted the two wagons bearing the Barnard and Company letters on their sides.

The wagon drivers and guards lay dead, scalped and stripped, their bodies riddled with arrows decorated in Wichita and Caddo markings. *Trader Washburn's words were good,* Little Elk thought as he watched his men slash open flour and corn sacks and dump the contents, scattering and destroying all goods that could not be packed on the stolen mules. *The tame Indians will be blamed for the killings. We have more guns, horses and scalps, all while the white soldiers chase our brothers far away. And the white man's pet dirt-digger Indians on the Brazos will get no food from this shipment.*

"Move quickly," he called to his warriors. "This white man's road has many travelers. The bluecoats may be near."

Fifteen minutes later the last of the goods that could be carried by mule were lashed in place. One warrior started to burn the wagons, but dropped his torch at a sharp word from Little Elk. "Smoke will bring the bluecoats. They are all about us. No fire. Mount up; we leave now."

The sense of urgency in Little Elk's voice jarred the others of the war party into action. They knew as well as he that the Second Cavalry still prowled the hills of Texas, that armed whites would soon discover the ambush and take up the chase. Little Elk waved a hand toward the northwest and kneed his war horse into a steady, ground-covering trot toward the hideout beyond the valley of the Comancheros in the land of the Quahadis. There they would wait until Trader Washburn sent word to the valley that the bluecoats had gone or that other easy targets had been found. *Soon,* Little Elk thought, *I wear the eagle feathers of the war chief. Those from the reserva-*

tion who are not women will join my band. One day soon I shall gather all the Human Beings to my side and drive the white man from my grandfather's land.

A Yamparika warrior moved alongside Little Elk. "Will the bluecoats go soon?"

Little Elk nodded. "The white man's government cannot do a thing long enough to do it well. They will leave. If not by the first snows, then by the second coming of spring. Then we push the white farmers back to the forests to the east from where they came."

Upper Reserve
May 1857

"Damn you, Neighbors," John Baylor shouted at the big man standing beside the desk, "you can't do this! You can't just waltz in here and fire me like a hired hand! I have friends in Washington, powerful friends—"

"You'll need them, Baylor," the Major interrupted. "In the first place, I didn't fire you. The commissioner in Washington did. In the second place, I would have fired you myself if he hadn't." The Major kept his tone calm with an effort. "You haven't done the job here, Mister Baylor, and that greatly disappoints me. I had great hopes for you when you came into the Indian service."

Baylor slammed a palm onto the desktop. "And just what the hell are the charges?"

"You know them, Baylor. Failure to keep control over the reservation Comanches. Absent from your post many times without requesting leave. Letting Buffalo Hump camp outside the reserve boundaries while his young warriors desert to the wild bands. One of your Comanches stands accused of killing a soldier at Fort Chadbourne. Two more shot at an officer in Camp Cooper. Sanaco's men have raided white settlers and stolen from the settled Indians on the lower reservation. In short, the Comanches under your control are threatening to undo everything we've gained along the frontier."

"Dammit, man, nobody can control these savages—"

"And then," the Major interrupted, his anger rising, "there's the matter of your accounts. The commissioner is freezing all reimbursements you've requested until you have justified the expenses claimed. All that, plus your attempts to get the sutler contract shifted to a firm partly owned by your family."

Baylor's face went almost purple in rage, nostrils flared in the thin nose. For a moment the Major thought Baylor was going to come across the desk after him. He hoped the agent would. Neighbors savored the thought of slamming a fist between Baylor's eyes.

Baylor stared in silent fury for several heartbeats, then slowly unclenched his fists. "By God, Neighbors, you haven't heard the last of me! I'll not stand for this—this humiliation, these unfounded smears on my character."

The Major forced his anger back under control and shrugged. "You're free to file a formal protest with the commissioner in Washington, Mister Baylor. In the meantime, you have three days to conclude your personal affairs and clear out of this office."

Robert Neighbors abruptly turned and strode from Baylor's office. Outside, he paused to breathe in the cool spring air. It carried the faint scent of wildflowers and new green grass freshly washed by gentle rains, the pleasantly acrid odor of horse droppings. A mockingbird sang from the mesquite clump nearby. A bobwhite strolled from behind a patch of spreading prickly pear, her chicks running to keep pace; the tiny birds' feet moved so fast they were only a blur to the human eye. The Major's anger slowly cooled as he swung aboard his blood-bay gelding and reined the horse toward the Brazos agency.

I'll have trouble over this, the Major thought as he rode. *I've just made another enemy. Baylor is the sort who won't go quietly.* He shook the thought away. He could deal with any problems Baylor might cause. And he had a competent man on the way. Matthew Leeper had already arrived at the Brazos Reserve. The Commissioner of Indian Affairs in Washington had handpicked Leeper for the assignment. The Major sensed the appointment was founded in politics, but Leeper seemed a decent and honorable man. *At least he's already promised to stay home and tend his knitting on the Upper Reserve,* the Major thought. *That, if nothing else, will help ease the Comanche problem.*

The Second Cavalry's campaign had punished the wild bands, but the Major knew the struggle against the Comanches was far from over. Little blood had been spilled in the Second's campaign. Less than a half dozen Comanches had been killed and only one trooper slightly injured. The Second had been unable to close with the warring bands for a pitched battle. The Comanches were simply too elusive, always a step ahead of the soldiers.

Still, the pressure had taken a toll of the wild tribes. Lee and Johnston's forces had given them no time to hunt, rest and fatten their horses. The troops had blocked war trails into Mexico and frightened away the few buffalo that remained on the Brazos side of the Staked Plains. A few Comanches had trickled onto the reservation, in family groups and small bands or as individual stragglers. Buffalo Hump's starving group, less than fifty people and most of them women and children, had been the largest band to come in. Most of the others had fled to the land of the Quahadi or across the Red River into Indian Territory where the soldiers did not follow.

Buffalo Hump had been on the reservation less than a month before his group started growing. A smattering of the Tenawa and Nakoni bands trickled in as the campaign wound down and immediately allied themselves with Buffalo Hump. And now, with most units of the Second recalled from the field and Colonel Lee transferred along with them, the wilder reservation Comanches quickly grew bored and restless. As soon as his sick were well and the band's bellies full, Buffalo Hump had started testing authority. The Major was convinced it was only a matter of time until Buffalo Hump and Sanaco both fled the reserve.

Scattered raids on settlers and traders near the Brazos Reserve had stirred ugly rumors among the whites that the peaceful agricultural tribes were to blame. The Major knew the stories were false. Agent Ross could account for the whereabouts of every reservation Indian in his jurisdiction when the attacks occurred. Most of the warriors had been afield scouting for the Second at the time of the raids.

Despite the problems, the reservation concept had been successful to the point that the Texas Legislature, in response to demands of the growing white population around the Brazos Reserve, had created the counties of Erath, Parker, Jack, Palo Pinto, Wise and Young. Most whites in the area had developed a high regard for the agrarian tribes and seemed content to have them as neighbors. Agent Ross's newly formed Brazos Indian police force had recovered a number of horses and cattle stolen by wild bands or Comanches from the Clear Fork Reserve. They had returned the stolen stock to their rightful owners.

Despite the howls of outrage from a few whites, not a single raid or theft could be tracked to the Brazos Reserve. And the Major still worried. There were too many white troublemakers around, and now they had one more gun—John Baylor. The Major couldn't shake the gut feeling that something was about to happen. And whatever happened probably wasn't going to be good.

Jacksboro
June 1857

Emil Washburn refilled John Baylor's whiskey glass in the small back room of Jacksboro's combination stage stop, post office and first hotel, and allowed himself an inward smirk of satisfaction.

The former Indian agent was already feeling the effects of the rye. Baylor's mood had grown darker and angrier by the moment. The whiskey hit him hard. Washburn had figured it would. Liquor usually kicked a man with more force when he was mad to begin with.

"Judge Baylor," Washburn said, "there isn't a thinkin' man in Jacksboro who doesn't know you've been handed the dirty end of the stick. Neighbors just decided to blame you for the fact he couldn't control his own Indians. I tell you, there's nothin' fair about it."

Baylor raised an unsteady gaze. "I told that Neighbors I'd make him pay for this," he muttered. "Blame me for everything he can't handle, insult me, humiliate me in public like this." Baylor's knuckles whitened on the water glass. "By damn, I'll fight back. I'm not one of his pet Caddos."

"I know how you feel, Judge," Washburn said as Baylor hoisted his whiskey glass and drained the contents in three swallows. "Neighbors has treated me the same way ever since he got his job back. Now, you and me have something in common—gettin' even with Neighbors—and we can serve the public while we do it."

Baylor reached for the rye bottle himself. The neck of the quart container clattered on the rim of his glass as he poured. "You've got something in mind?"

"Damn right." Washburn let the first hint of enthusiasm touch his words. He leaned forward, elbows on the table, formed a steeple of his fingers and peered across their tips at Baylor. "Now, we know who's been behind these raids here lately, don't we? Hell, I've tracked one batch of the thieves all the way back to the Brazos

Reserve myself. It's Neighbors's pet Caddos and Anadarkos that are stealin' horses and breakin' into houses. A blind man could see that. Neighbors is protectin' them. It's just a matter of time until they kill somebody."

Baylor sipped at his drink this time. "That's for damn sure, Mister Washburn. But what can we do about it? The Army won't stop it. By God, what we need are some good vigilantes."

Washburn helped himself to a shot of the rye. "We'll do that in good time, Judge Baylor. But for now, let's use the best weapon we've got."

"What weapon?"

"Public opinion." Washburn sipped at the whiskey and savored the heat it triggered in his gut.

Baylor snorted. "These damn white people around here think Neighbors hung the moon. They're getting to be as much Indian-lovers as he is."

Washburn reached in his pocket for two fresh cigars, handed one to Baylor and lit both smokes. "They just don't know the truth, Judge Baylor. And I've found a way to let them know how the jackass ate the crab apples. A newspaper."

Baylor arched an eyebrow. "Newspaper?"

"Exactly. A newspaper that's got the guts to stand up to Neighbors and his Indians. We'll call it *The White Man.*"

"We?"

Washburn flashed a confident grin. "I'll put most of the money into it, Judge. But I'll let you call the shots as to what gets printed." He paused for a moment to let Baylor chew on the idea as well as the cigar in his mouth. "I've got a man lined up who hates Indians with a passion. He'll edit the thing, but the stories will be the ones *we* want printed—the truth."

Understanding dawned slowly in Baylor's eyes. "By God, it might work!" He thumped the table with his free hand. "When do we start?"

Emil Washburn sipped at his drink and sighed inwardly. *He took the bait. Emil, you are one sly fox.* "Soon, Judge Baylor. I've got a feelin' there'll be a lot of Indian trouble around here this fall. After the locals get stirred up over losin' some stock and maybe some scalps, the first issue of *The White Man* will come off the press. In the meantime, you've got more friends here than you think. If you start spreadin' the word that Neighbors's pet Indians are up to no good, people will listen to you. After all, you were there on the reservation. You know what's going on."

Baylor stared into his drink for a few heartbeats, then glanced up. "How do you know there's going to be raids, Emil?"

"I've got sources of information in every tribe, wild or tame, in North Texas, Judge. And in the Texas Rangers, too. There'll be Indians crawlin' out of every hole soon."

Excitement danced in Baylor's expressive hazel eyes. "That would stir up a hornet's nest, sure enough. And by the time we're through, by God, there won't be a reservation Indian left in Texas." He stuck a hand across the table. "You've got yourself a partner, Emil."

Washburn returned the handshake. "It might be best for now if we kept this deal a secret, Judge," he said. "Since I trade with a lot of the wild Indians up north and west, I have to watch my step. You spread the truth about those murderin' reservation Indians for now. When the time's right, we'll bring out the first issue of *The White Man.*"

"Agreed." Baylor lifted the bottle and topped off both glasses. He raised his own in a mock toast. "Here's to Major Robert Simpson Neighbors and his beloved flock," Baylor said with a smirk, "and may they all roast in hell when we're done."

Baylor pushed back his chair and strode, his steps a bit unsteady, toward the door. Emil Washburn watched the former agent leave, a satisfied smile on his face. "The fool doesn't know he's being had," Washburn muttered aloud. He finished his drink, then rose. It was time to send out Joe One Jug and a few other runners.

North Texas, Washburn thought as he stepped into the busy thoroughfare that was the main street of the booming town of Jacksboro, is going to be up to its butts in Indians before first snow.

ELEVEN

Palo Pinto County
August 1857

Angus McGowan stood at the edge of the cornfield and wiped a callused hand across the back of his sunburned neck as he lifted the burlap-covered water jug.

Cicadas burred their raucous mating calls from the mesquite bordering the fields of corn, melons, late season squash and beans. *At least they aren't crop-eating locusts,* McGowan thought as he drank. *We've had no grasshoppers to speak of, the rains came on time, and this year we'll make a fine crop.* The sound of his wife and three children laughing and singing as they worked in the field brought a warmth to Angus's heart that had nothing to do with the still and stifling summer air. *Aye, but the hard work is worth it,* McGowan thought. Hiram Oldham's price for the half section had been high, but the soil was as fertile as the water was sweet. And with this crop Angus would be able to pay off the last hundred dollars he owed on the note Oldham held. *A happy, healthy family, a good farm soon to be paid for free and clear,* Angus reminded himself in contentment, *this is a thing that could never have happened in the old country.*

McGowan started at the sudden approach of the five horsemen through the mesquite. He reached for his rifle and almost called out a warning to his wife before he recognized the lead rider. Harris Oldham, Hiram's son, had paid a few calls on the McGowan clan over the past eighteen months.

Angus relaxed. There had been Indian raids since the Comanche bands of Sanaco and Buffalo Hump had fled the Clear Fork Reserve two months ago, but a visit from a known white man was no cause for alarm. He lowered his rifle and lifted a hand to the horsemen as they stopped twenty feet away. "Greetings and a good morning to you, Mister Oldham," Angus called. "It is good to see you again. How is your father and the family?"

Harris Oldham smiled cordially and nodded. "Doing well, thank you." His smile faded. "Angus, have you seen any Indians pass this way? Some mules were stolen yesterday from the Garrison place a few miles north."

Angus noticed for the first time that Oldham and his men were heavily armed. Oldham carried a shotgun across his saddle. Angus did not recognize the other four men in the party. New arrivals, perhaps, or volunteers from Jacksboro searching for the stolen mules. One of the riders held a feathered war lance. It looked strange in a white man's hand, Angus thought. He shook his head. "Haven't seen an Indian in weeks. I've heard reports of Indian trouble, but there has been none around here."

Harris Oldham grinned. A light seemed to flare in the cold, pale eyes. "There is now, Angus."

The last thing Angus McGowan saw was the twin bores of the shotgun in Harris Oldham's hand swing toward him. The double charge of buckshot took him full in the chest.

"Let's go get the rest of them, boys," Harris said. "You all know what to do."

Texas Ranger Captain Thomas C. Frost knelt beside the mutilated bodies in the cornfield and swallowed hard against the taste of bile in the back of his throat.

The three youngsters, the eldest maybe twelve and the youngest perhaps six, had been gutted and scalped. A war lance fluttered above the body of the woman. It had been driven all the way through her body and pinned her to the ground. It was obvious she had been raped.

Frost swore bitterly as he stood and brushed the dirt from his knees. He glanced around the grim circle of faces that made up his twenty-man patrol. "Dammit," Frost snapped, "somebody cover her up. And pull that lance out of her, for God's sake." One of the Rangers tugged at the shaft of the lance; he had to put his boot on the dead woman's chest and yank hard to pull it free. The iron spearpoint came loose with a sickening pop.

Captain Frost turned aside, rage adding to the nausea in his gut. "A couple of you boys get a shovel and bury them," he said over his shoulder. "The rest of you follow me. We've got some Indians to track."

Brazos Reserve

Agent Shapley P. Ross stood before the reservation headquarters building, turned the bloody lance shaft in his hands and studied the distinctive markings. He glanced up at the scowling group of Texas Rangers before him.

"It's Anadarko, all right," Ross said. "That doesn't mean reservation Indians killed that poor family."

"The hell it doesn't," Captain Frost snarled. "The tracks led straight here. You got some murdering red animals on this reservation, Ross." Frost started to turn his mount. "Come on, boys," he said. "Let's go find them."

"Hold it!" Ross's voice was sharp and hard. "There hasn't been an Anadarko off this reservation in three weeks, let alone three days. I'll not stand by and let you people ride in here and shoot up an innocent village."

Frost glared at the agent for several heartbeats. "And what are we supposed to do, Ross? Ride off and let the scalp-crazy savages rape and murder more whites?"

Ross's hand dropped to the butt of the big Colt Dragoon at his belt. "I expect you to ride off, all right," he said. "If the Anadarkos were behind the killings, I'll find the guilty ones and hand them over to the authorities."

"Bull!" Rage flared anew in Frost's eyes. "You're standing in the way of Texas Rangers now, Ross. This isn't some bunch of town boys you're talking to."

Ross pulled the pistol. "I said I'd investigate, Captain. And I'll shoot the first man who tries to ride past me, Ranger or not."

Frost held Ross's glare for a tense moment. "I'm half a mind to call your bluff, Ross."

"So call it or get off reservation grounds, Captain." Ross cocked the Dragoon.

The Ranger captain finally dropped his gaze. "By God, Ross, the governor's going to hear about this!"

"I don't doubt that, Frost," Ross said calmly. "You file your reports. I'll take the matter up with Major Neighbors and Jose Maria. If there are Indians on this reservation guilty of murder, we'll find them. Move on."

Frost yanked his horse's head around and drove spurs into the animal's ribs. Ross waited until the Rangers had passed from view around a bend in the river, then lowered the Dragoon hammer and sheathed the pistol. He turned the bloody lance in his hands. "Dammit," Ross muttered softly, "it's started again." He sighed and went to find Jose Maria.

Austin
January 1858

Major Robert Neighbors folded Agent Ross's latest field report and returned it to the courier's pouch. The McGowan family massacre was still unsolved, but both Ross and the Major were convinced the killers had not been from the Anadarko tribe. The lance had been stolen from outside a lodge a week before the massacre. A thorough investigation accounted for the whereabouts of every Brazos Reserve Indian at the time of the attack.

The McGowan slayings had not been the only ones.

On the western frontier in the last few weeks, two mustang hunters had been ambushed and slain, a teenage boy hunting a stray milk cow had been found scalped and a pair of teamsters were found dead, the bodies mutilated. Within ten miles of Fort Belknap a mail carrier was killed, his body riddled with arrows. Thousands of dollars worth of horses, mules and supplies had fallen to Comanche raiders who swept down from the north and blazed a trail of death and destruction along the frontier.

Sometimes the tracks of the raiders led toward the Brazos or Comanche reservations. On most occasions the marauders fled beyond the Red River. Only a handful of Second Cavalry troopers remained to protect the settlers, and the commander of the remaining forces, Captain George Stoneman, refused to cross the Red into Indian Territory in pursuit of the raiders. The frontier was, for all practical purposes, now without federal troop protection.

The bands led by Sanaco and Buffalo Hump had not returned to the reservation. In fact, when Agent Leeper submitted his initial report, he had found less than two hundred Comanches on the Clear Fork Reserve. Baylor's last report and supply requisitions had claimed there were seven hundred Indians on the Comanche lands. Now there were only seventy warriors left on the upper reservation.

The Major rose from his chair and strode to the window overlooking the seat of Texas government. The gruesome slaughter of the McGowans was the incident that fanned dormant flames of hate along the Brazos. McGowan, his wife and children had been popular people, hard-working, honest and God-fearing. The atrocity triggered a howl of outrage that still echoed, even beyond Texas borders.

Robert Neighbors snorted in disgust. The real killers probably would never be caught. Ranger Captain Frost had botched his end of the investigation like an overturned inkwell. He had *thought* the killers' trail led to the reservation; there were Indians on the reservation; therefore, reservation Indians had done the deed. Frost had not been shy about letting his opinions be known across the state. The Ranger captain had even attacked the Major personally in his reports and in public. He had a goodly number of settlers convinced that the Brazos Reserve tribes were about to start an extended war against the whites.

It seemed that every theft of horse, mule or shovel had been blamed on the tribes at the Brazos Reserve. The first ripples of fear had spread through both camps, red and white. The Lipans and Tonks had finally agreed to move to the Brazos Reserve, swelling the ranks by two hundred warriors. The anti-Indian faction used the new arrivals as a tool, clamoring that the southwestern tribes were sent to build up the fighting forces on the reserve for a general attack on the white settlers in North Texas.

The Brazos area was a powder keg.

It didn't help matters one whit that the new Indian agency on the Arkansas River in Indian Territory freely made gifts of guns, powder and lead to the northern Comanches and also fed the rebel tribes through the winter months. The Arkansas agency either didn't know or didn't care that those same guns were being used against white settlers and civilized Indians across the river in Texas. *The river may be a barrier as far as the white man's concerned*, the Major groused inwardly, *but it never stopped a Comanche.*

The Major abruptly turned from the window, scooped up the dispatch case and strode from his room. *This time, by God*, the Major fumed, *our new governor's going to hear me out. I'll get into Hardin Runnels's office if I have to break in at gunpoint.*

He didn't need a weapon after all.

Runnels's secretary kept the Major waiting only a half hour. Just long enough to let him know that the governor was a busy and powerful man.

Runnels greeted the Major with a firm handshake and a gesture toward a comfortable chair across from an expensive mahogany desk. "I've been hoping to see you, Major," Runnels said. "I welcome a chance to talk with you in person about the Indian problems on our frontier." The governor eased his stocky frame into the high-backed chair behind the desk and reached for a folded sheaf of papers.

"I thought you should see this right away," the governor said solemnly. "It's the latest report from Captain Frost. Look it over. I'd like to hear your reaction to what he has to say."

The Major skimmed the report and felt the flush of anger rise anew in his neck. After a few moments he grimaced in disgust and placed the papers back on the desk. "Captain Frost is not only an incompetent, Governor Runnels," the Major said bitterly, "he's a liar as well. Every charge he's made in this report is absolutely false in every particular."

The governor cocked an eyebrow. "Strong words, Major Neighbors. But then I did ask for your opinion. I suppose I got it." He half-smiled, the practiced grin of the professional politician. "I assume you wish to refute his charges?"

"Yes, sir." The Major struggled to contain his growing fury. "First of all, he says these raids and killings are the work of Indians from the reservations, primarily from the Brazos Reserve. That, governor, is a pile of horse apples. My agents have investigated each one of these incidents thoroughly. There is nothing to link the reserve Indians with these raids."

Runnels leaned back in his chair. The leather creaked. "And of his charges against you, Major? That when the settlers appealed to you for help that you cursed and threatened those who complained?"

"A flat-out lie, Governor Runnels." The Major gripped the arms of the chair hard enough to turn his knuckles white. "My office never refused to cooperate with any settler or officer, including Frost. We stopped him from killing some innocent Indians, that's all. I admit I felt like laying a few choice words on the captain, but I did not, sir." The Major forced his muscles to relax. "If Captain Frost had spent half the energy chasing the raiders that he spent in writing and circulating these falsehoods he probably would have caught the real culprits and brought them to justice."

Governor Runnels plucked a cigar from a rosewood box on his desk, fired the smoke and gazed across the desk at the Indian agent for a moment. "Major Neighbors, you should know that I do not agree with your plan for the Indians. It is my belief that only extermination or removal will solve the problem." He puffed at the cigar. "Apparently the voters of our great state feel as I do, or I would never have beaten Sam Houston in the last election. The vote proves, I believe, the prevailing notion that savages can never be turned into farmers. I intend to take steps to solve the problem."

"Governor," the Major said, "all we have ever asked is that the Indians be given a chance to prove they can live in peace with the white man on their own lands. We've made a lot of progress to that end. It's the outlaw bands—and, frankly, a handful of white men— who are standing between us and that success."

Runnels blew a smoke ring and watched the gray doughnut drift toward the ceiling. "Major," Runnels said at length, "it has also been brought to my attention that Captain Stoneman and you have had some rather strong differences of opinion?"

"Yes, sir. Since Colonel Lee was transferred from Camp Cooper, Captain Stoneman has spent most of his time agitating against the reservation Indians. He claims they are in connivance with their wild cousins. Our field investigations show that an overwhelming majority of the atrocities Stoneman attributes to the Brazos Reservation farming tribes are in fact the work of the Kickapoos, Kiowas, a few renegade Comanches and white outlaws."

Runnels tongued the cigar to the other side of his mouth. "Regardless of which tribe is at fault, Major," he said, "these raids and murders must be stopped. I'm calling out several companies of Texas Rangers to run the red predators to earth. So far we Texans have only fought sporadic skirmishes. I now intend to field a Ranger force capable of conducting an all-out war on the wild Indians."

Runnels tapped ashes from the cigar. "Now, sir, if you will excuse me, I have many matters of state to attend."

Jacksboro
February 1858

John R. Baylor drew himself to his full six-foot-two height and surveyed the gathering of men in the small church that served a dual role as place of worship and community hall at the end of Jacksboro's main street.

A blue haze of tobacco smoke had begun to build near the ceiling of the sanctuary. Baylor stepped behind the chapel lectern and waited as low conversations died to an expectant hush. A score of faces turned toward the pulpit. Almost a quarter of the men were business partners of Emil Washburn, John R. Baylor or Peter Garland of Erath County. The others were hotheads, Indian-haters to the bone. *The perfect audience,* Baylor thought.

"Gentlemen, I think we all know why we're here." Baylor's rich baritone carried well in the small room. "This business of outlaw Indians has to stop."

He paused until the mutter of agreement died away. "I know from personal experience that these damned reservation Indians are feeding and sheltering their wild kinsmen from the Plains. Some of these pet Indians are directly responsible for the deaths of our friends and neighbors, the wanton theft of livestock. If the U.S. Army isn't going to stop the thieving redskins, it's up to us to do it ourselves for the sake of our families and our property!"

The former agent heard a couple of "amens" muttered from the group. "We must organize a volunteer force to protect the settlements along the Brazos. How many more outrages like the butchery of the McGowan family will we tolerate?"

"None, by God!" The voice from the back of the room trembled in rage. "Enough is enough!"

Baylor stroked his beard as if in deep thought. "Let's look at the facts as we know them," he said. "The *real* problem we have here is the Indian agents, and Major Robert Neighbors in particular. You all know Neighbors is wiping the backsides of his pet Indians." He pulled a thick stack of papers from beneath his coat. "I have here letters, reports, sworn statements and other documents from U.S. Army officers at Camp Cooper, from many of our own white settlers, even from Texas Ranger Captain Thomas C. Frost, *all* stating that the raids and depredations have been traced to reservation Indians, the Comanches on the Clear Fork or the farming tribes on the Brazos Reserve."

Baylor dropped the reports back onto the lectern. "And finally, gentlemen, Ketumse himself told me that renegades from the Comanche reserve are involved in many of the most atrocious raids." The lie fell easily from Baylor's tongue. Only one man in the crowd knew that Ketumse had stopped speaking to Baylor months before the agent had been fired, and Hiram Oldham had too much at stake to say anything. "My friends," Baylor raised his voice for emphasis, "that many Indian experts can't be wrong!"

Baylor waited until the grumbles of agreement subsided. "It appears to me that the easiest way to get rid of the Indians is to get rid of the agents—to put our own people in charge of the heathens. We must petition the government to remove Neighbors. Let everyone from here to Washington know that Neighbors and his clan are living high off the hog on government money while his red pets are killing our people and stealing our stock."

"Damn straight," a man seated on a front pew said. "It's our money that fills the savages' bellies and gives 'em horses and rifles so they can kill our own kind!"

"That is correct, sir," Baylor said. "I know from my own experience that is precisely what happens. We've got to put a stop to that. You all know how many times Neighbors has been told what's going on. And what does he do? He insults us, denies everything, blocks every attempt we make to bring justice to the frontier." Baylor paused for dramatic effect. "Neighbors and his agent cronies have to go, gentlemen. We might as well start now. My name will be the first on a petition to have them removed, and I have authorization to add a dozen names—good, honest people who dared not leave their families unprotected to attend this meeting—to just such a document."

"I'm game," Peter Garland said. "How many of you boys are with me?"

An hour later John R. Baylor chuckled inwardly as the group filed from the church sanctuary. It had been even easier than he had hoped. He had his petition. It didn't matter that he had forged many of the names and signed others without permission. And he had a scorching letter directed to Agent Leeper charging that Indians holding passes to leave the reservation to hunt took advantage of the opportunity to steal cattle and horses and raid farms. The letter repeated a paragraph from the petition: "Henceforth, any Indians found off the reservation without a white man or a Delaware accompanying them are to be killed forthwith; and further, that if a white man should be killed along the Clear Fork, a civilian force will be raised to break up the reserve."

The letter and petition represented the first steps in getting Neighbors kicked out of his comfortable little job as God on the Indian reservations. Similar petitions were being drafted by Baylor's friends in Lampasas and Williamson counties. Within days, messengers would carry the word across the entire state.

Baylor tucked the petition into his pocket. *When the first edition of* The White Man *comes out next week, Neighbors is going to be holding the dirty end of the public opinion stick. And public opinion can carry more firepower than a battalion of cavalry troops.*

The former Indian agent strode to the door, winced at the sudden contrast of brisk, still air to the smoke and stuffy heat of the sanctuary and glanced toward the northwest. Out there somewhere the Comanche Little Elk would be splitting his band into small raiding parties. The white settlers wouldn't expect any widespread raids before the spring grass came. They were about to get a surprise. Little Elk was no ordinary Comanche, especially with Emil Washburn planting ideas in his head.

Any day now the raids would start. Little Elk had the guns. His horses were fit and fattened on grain and forage supplied by Washburn, and his band of followers had grown to nearly two hundred fighting men. *If Emil's done his job right,* Baylor thought, *we've got the table set to take over all the Brazos Valley . . .*

Brazos Reserve
March 1858

Major Robert Neighbors stood at the edge of the council grounds and studied the two Comanche captives who waited stoically as a tribunal of Brazos Reserve chiefs debated the prisoners' fates a few yards away.

At the far edge of the council grounds an aging Comanche woman knelt, her body rocking as she covered her face with weathered hands. She was the mother of one of the captives.

The Comanches had made quite a haul of horses along the

Brazos. They had also made one serious mistake. They had taken the scalp of an aging Waco from the Brazos Reserve on the way north and relieved the hunter of his horse and gun. Agent Ross had a party of the Brazos Reserve's Indian police on their trail within hours. A party led by the Delaware scout Jim Shaw caught up with the raiders at the headwaters of the Red and Arkansas rivers. The two captives were all that remained of the raiding party. Eighty horses recovered after the Brazos force's slashing dawn attack grazed nearby, loosely herded by young Caddo riders. The Major recognized a few of the brands. He had already sent messengers to notify the owners that their stock had been recovered.

Under Shaw's interrogation the captives confessed to raiding stock farms and killing the Waco. They denied slaying any whites, but had no explanation for the two fresh scalps recovered from their campsite. The raiders told Shaw they were members of Little Elk's band, an admission that wasn't likely to help their chances with the tribunal. There wasn't a warrior on the Brazos Reserve who wouldn't have traded his best wife and finest horses for the renegade Comanche's scalp.

"Looks like the verdict's about to come in," Agent Shapley P. Ross said at the Major's side.

The ten tribal chiefs and elders strode toward the captives, a Waco chief in the lead. The Waco stood for a moment and glared at the prisoners. "The council is in agreement," he said. "The punishment for theft and murder is death."

A sudden shriek from the old Comanche woman pierced the mild spring air. The two captives' expressions remained impassive.

"The prisoners will be taken off the reservation and be shot," the Waco said. "The council has spoken." The old woman's shrieks faded to a wailing chant of grief.

The Major watched as the Comanches were bound and boosted aboard horses. The Brazos Reserve head men mounted to follow, rifles in hand.

"Want me to go along, Major?" Ross asked.

The Major shook his head. "The Indians will take care of it. Ask him to give the old woman permission to take the bodies home."

Ross nodded and strode toward the execution party. He returned a few moments later, his own bearded face as impassive as any Indian's. "Let's get back to the office, Major," Ross said. "I could use a cup of coffee."

The two walked in silence for several strides. "Any word from Jose Maria?" the Major finally asked.

"No. He and a dozen reserve police scouts are still out prowling the river breaks. If there are any wild Indians out there, that old Anadarko will find them. I'm glad he's on our side." Ross's untrimmed beard ruffled in the slight breeze. "I'd better send out Albert Fox and some Caddo police to make sure the Comanches don't try to retaliate for the executions."

The Major grunted his approval. Albert Fox had crawled from the bottle a year ago, had been sober ever since and now was one of the rising leaders among the Brazos Reserve tribes. There was even talk of elevating Albert Fox from *caddi* to *xinesi* in recognition of his leadership. *Give a man a reason to straighten out his life and the chance to do so and he'll come through most of the time,* the Major thought. *Albert Fox finally realized he has a home.*

"Shapley," the Major said, "my compliments on the efficiency of your reserve police force. They've done a fine job."

Ross nodded his acceptance of the compliment. "The more reasonable whites hereabouts have been impressed too, Major. Seeing the Indians punish transgressors has helped take a little of the edge off the anti-Indian faction's damned lies. It's a shame Leeper hasn't had the same success on the Clear Fork Reserve as I've had here."

The Major shrugged. "He's got a different breed of Indian to work with, Shapley. His Comanches have too many blood ties with the renegades to field an effective police force."

The two men stopped before the agency building. A small slip of paper tacked to the door fluttered in the wind. Ross plucked the note from the door, frowned and handed it without speaking to the Major. The note was addressed to the Major. He glanced at the crude block lettering. The message was simple and to the point: *You're a dead man, Neighbors.* The Major crumpled the paper in his fist.

"How many does that make now, Major?"

"Four so far, not counting the verbal threats. I'm not the most popular man on the Brazos at the moment."

Ross sighed as he pushed the door open. "You're not alone, Major. The buzzards are circling all of us. I'm thinking we'd best take the threats seriously."

"That," the Major said as he stepped inside and swept off his hat, "is one reason I don't go anywhere without a pair of good Colts. I've even started wearing them indoors." He plopped his hat onto a peg. "I take it seriously enough, Shapley, that I've updated my last will and testament. What aggravates me most, I think, is that Lizzie's frightened and worried half to death whenever I'm out of her sight."

Ross shucked his coat and busied himself at the stove. "In times like these, anything could happen. Have a seat, Major. Coffee will be ready in a few minutes."

Robert Neighbors settled into a chair and pondered the tense atmosphere that had grown along the Brazos. The cry had gone up for the Major's scalp even before the latest atrocity barely two weeks ago. In the Lost Valley of Jack County a band of Little Elk's renegade Comanches had hit two adjoining farms in one sweeping raid. Seven people, including three children, were dead. The Lost Valley massacre came a day after a similar strike in Erath County that left a settler dead and two of his children taken captive. The settler's wife was alive, if it could be called that—she was now totally insane from the horrors she had endured. There had been other raids, other deaths, but the sheer brutality at Lost Valley had been the spark that rekindled the firestorm of outrage sweeping the Brazos River country.

The flames of hatred were fueled by rumor and outright lies reported as fact by the new publication called *The White Man*. The newspaper had no regard for the truth in its tirades against the Indians and their agents. And a story need only appear in print for the public to believe it, the Major thought in disgust.

The arrival of the mail courier interrupted his worries. There were two letters addressed to him, one from the War Department and another from the Commissioner of Indian Affairs. He opened the packets, scanned the contents and tossed them in disgust onto Ross's desk.

"More trouble, Major?"

The tempting aroma of boiling coffee seemed to sour in the Major's nostrils. "More complaints filed in Washington, against me personally and the reservation Indians in general. And still no action on my request for a formal hearing into these damned lies and allegations." The Major sat in Ross's chair behind the desk and reached for pen and paper. Absurd as they were, the charges had to be answered.

"At least you've still got friends out here, and not just among the Indians," Ross said. He lifted the coffeepot lid, sloshed in a bit of cold water to settle the grounds and reached for mugs on a nearby shelf. "Several men have already denied in public that they authorized Baylor to sign their names to his damned petitions. The biggest problem we've got in fighting this thing is that we have so many new settlers in the area."

Ross poured the coffee and handed a steaming mug to the Major. "The old-timers aren't buying the lies about us and our Indians —at least, not most of them. But the new people don't understand what's going on here. Just having Indians in the area's enough to spook them."

Ross plopped down in the chair across the desk. "That newspaper out of Jacksboro's getting to be a pain in the butt. I'd burn the place down if it was up to me."

The Major sipped at his coffee and found it more than satisfactory. He sighed. "I'd like nothing better myself, Shapley. But we can't. It would just give them more ammunition to fire at us."

"Damned if we do, damned if we don't," Ross said in disgust. "I went to see the man who edits that paper. He's a scrawny little runt about a hundred years old who hates Indians worse than the pox. He wouldn't publish my rebuttals to the lies he prints." Ross hoisted his cup, took a sip and stared toward the ceiling. "Leeper's taken it upon himself to fight *The White Man*. His stories never get printed in that propaganda sheet, but he's getting letters and reports published in Dallas, Austin, Gainesville and other newspapers across the state."

The Major nodded without a reply. He would have preferred that Agent Leeper stay out of the mess. Still, he welcomed Leeper's public support and hoped the man's words reached the right ears.

Ross reached for his pipe. "I'd sure like to know where the money behind *The White Man* is coming from. That old bonebag of an editor doesn't have a dime of his own as near as I could tell."

"I've got my own ideas about that, Shapley," the Major said with a frown. "I can't prove it, but I expect John Baylor's behind it somehow." He sighed heavily. "Maybe I made a mistake. Baylor may manage to kill us all off from the outside. At least while he was agent, I could keep some control over him."

Ross lit his pipe, rose and began pacing the small office. "You did the right thing in asking that he be removed. He would have wrecked the whole reservation concept from the inside anyway." Ross paused at the window to gaze out at his Brazos Reserve domain. "Major, there's only one sure way to stop the lies. We've got to run down those renegade Comanches and their allies. It's going to take one hell of a good campaign to bring peace to the Brazos."

"The governor agrees with you, Shapley. And as much as I dislike the idea, I suppose Runnels is right. Rip Ford's on the way to take control of the whole frontier Ranger force. He can get the job done."

Ross turned from the window and smiled. "I took the liberty of sending for reinforcements myself, Major," he said. "My son Sul should be getting here any day now."

The cloud on the Major's spirit brightened a bit. "That's good news, Shapley. I wish we had a couple of battalions like him."

The Major wasn't just blowing smoke for the sake of Shapley Ross's feelings. Lawrence Sullivan Ross, known as "Sul" to friend and foe alike, would be a good man to have around. Sul Ross looked like a teenaged kid, gangly, thin to the point of being bony, with overly large ears that stuck out from his head and eyes that looked to be half-asleep most of the time. The looks were deceptive. Sul Ross was one of the toughest men around and one of the best Indian fighters in the country.

Ross strode to the tin washtub by the stove, rinsed his cup and reached for his hat. "If you'll excuse me, Major, I've got to check up on my Indians. It's been a while since our last disbursement of supplies. I want to make sure they don't need anything."

The Major watched as the burly agent strode to the door. He noticed that Ross also wore two pistols and carried a rifle and Bowie knife and wondered how many death threats Ross had received. Ross hadn't mentioned any, but he wasn't the type of man who would.

Robert Neighbors dipped the pen point in the inkwell. It would take hours to put his reply to the complaints from Washington into words. The Major's main concern was not for his own reputation, or even that of his agents.

His concern was to save a dream. A dream for the Indians of Texas.

TWELVE

Brazos Reserve
March 1858

Major Robert Neighbors strode toward the agency, Rip Ford along-side, the Ranger company settled in for the night on the reserva-tion council grounds.

"Rip, I'm glad they sent you," the Major said. "I was afraid the governor would overlook the best man for a tough job and send someone like Frost to handle this campaign."

Ford grinned and waved a hand. "Wouldn't have missed this one, Major," he said. "Might be the last time I get to do any real Indian chasing for a spell—at least if I do it right. Be for damn sure the last if I do it wrong. I'd hate to see my hair hanging from a Comanche's lance."

The Major led Ford into the office and waved toward a chair. "Any problems on the trip up?"

Ford shook his head. "Not a one. I decided to make a sweep of the area south on the way in. Split up my force. Didn't see a single fresh Indian sign along the way."

"How many men are under your command?"

"Five companies. About three hundred all told. Better than half of them—the ones already in the field that I inherited—are scat-tered from hell to breakfast. Most of them are good men. I'll weed out the other kind in a hurry."

The Major rustled up two clean mugs and poured coffee. "This stuff may be ranker than a Tonkawa blanket, Rip," he said. "If it takes the kinks out of your mustache I'll make a fresh pot."

Ford took a swallow of the heavy brew and nodded his approval. "Just right, Major. A little too thin to plow but not too thick to drink."

Robert Neighbors chuckled aloud for the first time in weeks. The two men spent a few minutes catching up on news of friends and families before the Major brought up the Indian campaign question.

"My plans are pretty simple on the surface, Major," Ford said. "The instructions from the governor said we were to follow any and all trails of hostile or suspected hostile Indians we find, overtake them and, as he phrased it, 'chastise them.' Makes it sound pretty simple, doesn't he?"

The Major half-smiled. "I guess it is simple from where he sits," he said. "The governor's not the one who'll be getting saddle sores and ducking arrows and rifle balls."

Ford shrugged. "That's what we're paid these grand sums to do, Major. Dollar and a half a day and supply our own horses and guns."

The Major cocked a quizzical eyebrow. "I don't suppose you thought about turning down the job and staying in San Antonio?"

Ford's eyebrows shot up in mock surprise. "What? And miss all the glamour and excitement in the life of a frontier Texas Ranger? Now, my friend, why don't you pry another lump of that pine tar out of the pot and tell me what's *really* going on around here."

The Major reached for the coffee. "Might as well make yourself comfortable," he said. "This may take a while."

The sun had dropped toward the western horizon before the conference ended. Both men were satisfied with the overall plan for the campaign. Ford didn't seem concerned that most of the federal troops had been transferred from the area, leaving only a few companies at scattered outposts. "Doesn't matter that much," Ford said with a shrug. "One good Texas Ranger's worth a dozen blue uniforms in an Indian campaign. I could have used some help from the Second, though. Best cavalry outfit in the Army. Guess the generals decided they were needed more in Idaho."

Finally, Ford stood. "I'd best get my men settled in for the night, Major." He reached for his battered and sweat-stained felt hat. He paused at the door. "Major, I'll tell you this straight up, friend to friend. I want no part of the spat between you and Baylor, and I'm telling my officers not to take sides. From what I've heard the reservation Indians are involved—one way or another—in a lot of the raids here of late. Maybe they are and maybe they aren't. I don't know. Maybe where there's that much smoke there's some fire. If I find out there are Indians from either reservation involved, I'll kick their red asses and kick them hard. Then I'll shut down the reservations."

The Major sighed. "All I can ask, Rip, is that you be fair about it, and I know you will be. This thing is in your hands now. We don't have a prayer of any lasting peace until the wild Indians are brought to heel. Tomorrow I'll show you around the Brazos Reserve, let you meet some of our people. Later we'll call a council and see how many guides, trackers and fighting men our Indians here will supply. Recruiting won't be hard. The Brazos Indians don't care much for Comanches."

He escorted Ford to the door. "Care to come along with us, Major?" Ford asked.

The Major sighed. "I'd like to. God knows I would. But while you're out ripping and tearing all over the frontier, I'm going to be stuck in Washington."

"Washington? What the hell you want to waste your time and talent in that pile of political cow patties for?"

Robert Neighbors felt his jaws clench as the anger and frustration returned. "It's the only way I'm going to get this business with Baylor and his faction settled, Rip. I'm going to force a showdown. It will be a tough fight, but it's something I have to do if the Indians are ever going to have a home of their own. I've never ducked a scrap in my life and I'm too set in my ways to start now. I'll have my board of inquiry if I have to grab some bureaucrats by the scruff of the neck and slam them down into a chair."

Ford's chuckle was soft in the stillness of the early evening air. "I reckon you just might do that, too. Going to stop by San Antone on the way?"

"I plan to. Haven't seen my wife in weeks," the Major said. "I'm beginning to wonder if maybe Lizzie hasn't left me for a better man."

Ford cuffed the Major playfully on the shoulder. "Hell, Major, there ain't but one better man around than you. That's me and I'm here. And Lizzie doesn't approve of my language anyway."

The Major chuckled. "She's only heard you when you were on your best behavior, Rip. See you in the morning."

Rip Ford sat on his bedroll beside the fire and glanced around the circle of Ranger officers. The session he had called was not much different than the war councils held by the Comanches. Each man who had an opinion was free to say what was on his mind.

"Well, gentlemen, that's it," Ford said. "I expect every one of you to keep all that's been said here in strictest confidence. We don't want every Indian and settler on the frontier knowing where we're

going, what we're up to and when we're going to take a leak. Any
questions or comments?"

Lieutenant W. A. Pitts lifted an eyebrow. "Captain, are you sure
the reservation Comanches are behind the killings?"

"That's what I plan to find out, Pitts," Ford said. "That's why
we're sending out scouts to keep an eye on them. If we catch any
Comanches off the reservation and raising hell, we'll have proof
enough to break up their reserve."

Pitts frowned. "Only way we can prove that is to catch them in
the act. Or follow a trail from a raid back to the reserve."

"That can be managed," Lieutenant Allison Nelson said. "A trail
like that can be made."

Ford stabbed a hard glare toward Nelson. "By God, Nelson, that
is something I won't do—and no man in my command will lay any
false trails." Ford heard the sharp edge on his words. "Nelson, I
don't like Comanches a damn bit better than you do. But I'll not
stand by and watch evidence created. I'm not here to prove them
guilty—I'm here to find out if they *are* guilty. I'll punish the Comanches hard if they step out of line, but I damn sure won't do so
on the basis of any false, improper or unjust acts. Is that absolutely
clear?"

Nelson's face flushed at the rebuke. "Clear enough."

"Very well, Nelson," Ford said, "I want you to take out a scouting
party. Circle the Comanche reserve and look for any signs that the
Indians there are tied in with or helping the wild bunch. Meet us
back here in a week." Ford held Nelson's stare until the younger
officer dropped his gaze. "And, Nelson," he added, "if you bring in
evidence the reserve Indians are involved, make damn sure it's
accurate."

The Ranger captain shifted his gaze from the lieutenant. "If no
one else has any question or comment, men, let's turn in. When
Nelson gets back we'll see Major Neighbors off and then take to the
field in force."

Brazos Reserve
April 1858

Captain Rip Ford stood at the edge of his gathering of men and
watched the figure of the lone horseman fade to a speck in the

distance. Ford was already beginning to miss Major Robert Neighbors.

He hoped it wasn't the last time he'd see him.

Ford had tried to talk the Major into taking two or three Rangers along as an escort, but the bull-headed bear of a man wouldn't hear of it. "You need every Ranger you have here, Rip," the Major had said. "Don't waste any manpower nursemaiding me. I've ridden this country alone more often than with someone."

"Yeah," Ford replied, "but you didn't have little men with big guns threatening to put holes in your hide then."

Robert Neighbors merely shrugged. "If they want me bad enough they'll get me anyway." He shoved his Sharps carbine into the saddle boot, tied down his bedroll and possibles sack and kneed the bay into motion. He hadn't looked back.

Ford heard the men gathering behind him, the creak of saddle leather as they mounted, the snort of horses feeling frisky in the fresh morning air, the murmur of quiet conversations among the ranks.

Lieutenant Allison Nelson had ridden back in a few days ago, his scout complete, and reported the patrol had found no sign of wrongdoing on the part of the reservation Indians. In fact, Nelson added, most of the white settlers in the area did not fear the reserve Indians and did not want the reservations broken up.

Ford was satisfied. Nelson might have bad feelings toward Indians, but the man had enough integrity to report the truth. And, Ford thought, the fact that Nelson had found nothing carried more weight than any other officer's word would have. Nelson would have looked harder than most for any bad signs. It was why Ford had sent him on the scouting patrol in the first place.

Agent Shapley P. Ross stood beside Ford. A few yards away Ross's son Sul, not much bigger than the rifle in his saddle scabbard, sat his horse in front of a hundred Brazos Reserve warriors. The Major had been right, Ford mused; asking a Caddo, Delaware, Tawakono, Waco, Tonkawa, Anadarko or any man from the smaller tribes to hunt Comanches was like asking a kid if he wanted a licorice stick. He had doubled his main fighting force without spending a dime of the governor's precious money.

The Ranger senior captain had already dispatched his reports to the governor. Ford was impressed by what he had seen on the Brazos Reserve. More than eleven hundred Indians lived and worked there. Most had adapted well to the white man's ways. As far as he could tell, they were honest and honorable people. *If there's nobody among them who hasn't killed a white man or stolen a horse or mule,* Ford thought, *then they're a damn sight better than the same number of white people.*

Lieutenant Edward Burleson, Jr., waited with the balance of the Ranger force at a site selected as home camp at the mouth of Hubbard's Creek. The place had good grass, adequate fresh water and plenty of timber for fuel.

The only problem left was finding a few thousand Comanches, Kiowas, Kickapoos and various other renegades in a chunk of country bigger than a lot of foreign nations. No big deal, Ford thought wryly. He mounted and reined his horse about to face his troops. "All right, men," he said. "Day's half-gone and not a lick of work done yet. Let's go find us some wild Indians."

Indian Territory
April 1858

Captain Rip Ford knelt beside the travois tracks on the hoof-scarred earth and grunted in satisfaction. The Brazos Indian guides had found the trail of the Comanche band.

The outlaws were nearby. The tracks were fresh. A man didn't have to be Indian to read sign this plain. The Comanches that fled Texas had found buffalo on the Plains north of the Red River. The travois tracks were deep, heavy with meat. *Probably figured they were safe on this side of the river,* Ford thought. *The soldiers never followed them this far.*

He rose to his feet and surveyed his hunting party. He had just over two hundred men, half of them Indian scouts under the command of young Sul Ross. The attack force was ready. All that remained now was the return of the tracker sent to pinpoint the enemy camp.

Ford figured he probably would catch hell from the U.S. Government for crossing out of Texas and driving this deep into territory set aside for the Indians. He didn't worry much about that. There were Indians to deal with now. He'd handle the hollering from Washington later.

A horseman appeared on the horizon, his mount moving in a steady lope.

"Looks like Jim Crowfoot found our Indians," Sul Ross said at Ford's side.

The Keechi tracker pulled his lathered gray mustang to a skidding stop before the two men. He waved a hand toward the valley beyond the rising slope of grass and jabbered something in a tongue Ford couldn't quite make out.

"Jim says they're in the valley up ahead, about three miles from here," Ross said. "They don't seem to have any idea they're being followed. No pickets out. What's your pleasure, Captain?"

Ford glanced at the young man with the prominent ears. "We'll slip up close tonight. Hit them at dawn tomorrow. Comanches don't fight as hard when they're jolted out of their blankets."

Ross nodded. "A favor, Captain?"

"Name it."

"Our Tonkawa and Caddo warriors have asked to lead the attack. They want the first Comanche scalps and horses for those on foot."

"Fine by me," Ford said. "They've walked all this way. If anybody's earned a horse they have. We'll work out the signals later. Right now, I'd like to get as close as we can to the Comanches before dawn." He nodded toward the Keechi tracker. "Does Jim here have any idea who we're following?"

Ross and the Keechi jabbered for a few moments, then Ross turned back to the Ranger captain. "He's pretty sure he saw Iron Jacket. Wears an old coat of chain mail he got somewhere. Big medicine. It's supposed to stop all arrows and bullets." Sul reached into a pocket, pulled out a twist of tobacco and gnawed off a chunk. The bulge in the cheek looked a little out of place in a face that seemed to belong in a schoolroom, not heading into a fight with three hundred Comanche warriors, Ford thought.

"Tell our friend Jim he has my compliments. Good tracking job."

Ross grinned. "No need. He speaks perfect English. He just likes to aggravate a white man once in a while."

Ford grinned in spite of himself. "Well, Mister Ross, let's go make some good Comanches out of some bad ones."

The lip of the sun was a thin crescent on the eastern horizon when the battle cry of the Caddos, Tonks and Arapahos sounded over the valley. Ford held his own men back, his Colt Dragoon cocked and raised overhead, as the Brazos Indians charged the camp on foot.

Comanches stumbled from lodges, weapons in hand. But eyes still groggy from sleep, full bladders and a hefty jolt of pure terror threw their aim off. Ford waited until the Brazos braves had driven halfway through the Comanche camp, rifles blasting and lances bloodied, then swept his hand forward.

The Texas war yell rose in a roar from the ranks. Men put spurs to their mounts and charged. Ford heard the whack of lead against flesh. One of his Rangers grunted in pain and surprise. Then the skirmish line slammed into the long row of Comanche lodges. The combat swirled at close quarters, powder smoke and dust thickening the air.

One Comanche leveled his rifle toward Ford; the Ranger slapped a shot, felt the slam of the pistol butt against his palm and saw the Comanche tumble backward. The roar of pistols and shotguns became an almost continuous thunder over the valley, punctuated by the clang of steel on steel as individual battles closed to one-on-one combat.

Ford kneed his horse to the side, ducked a lance point and fired at arm's length into a Comanche's chest. He whirled his mount as a knife point flashed near his knee and slammed the heavy barrel of the pistol into a warrior's forehead. The man went down without a sound. Ford caught a glimpse of young Sul Ross, calmly aiming and firing his Colt in the midst of the raging combat.

Then Ford and thirty other horsemen, most of them Brazos Indians now mounted on Comanche ponies, broke through the first ring of lodges; the second row was a hundred yards upstream. Ford drove spurs to his horse. A rifle ball buzzed by his ear, another plucked at his sleeve. Ahead, he saw a broad-chested, bow-legged Comanche wearing a coat of ancient chain mail aim down the barrel of a musket. A rifle cracked, then another. The Comanche chief Iron Jacket staggered and sank to one knee. He struggled to lift his rifle. A Caddo a few yards in front of Ford yanked his horse to a stop, leapt to the ground, aimed and fired. Iron Jacket's head snapped back and the chief's body thumped into the dirt, spread-eagled.

Ford lost track of the individual battles that raged up and down the valley. He emptied his Colt, jammed it into his holster and pulled a second pistol from beneath his belt. The Comanches were trying to regroup, to form a rear guard at the end of the lodge row. Six Anadarkos charged the rear guard; three Comanches went down in a barrage of pistol and shotgun fire. Two others sprinted for the cover of brush and rocks alongside the river. An Anadarko yanked his horse toward the men, ran one through with his lance and dove from his mount to send the second man tumbling with a shoulder. The Anadarko's knife was in the Comanche's throat before the two hit the ground.

In the near distance Ford saw about fifty Comanche warriors scramble onto horses and lay quirts to the animals, all thought of fight forgotten as they fled the field of battle. Ford lost track of time in the swirl of dust and powder smoke, the din of war whoops and screams of wounded men as the fight strung out over a three-mile front. The running battle lasted until the sun was overhead. The fight ended when the attackers' horses gave out and stood trembling, sides heaving and nostrils flared.

Ford's own horse was bleeding from an arrow wound in the neck when the Ranger captain finally signaled a halt to the attack. He dismounted, saw that the horse's wound was not serious, and led the animal back down-valley through some of the worst carnage he had seen in his years of fighting Indians.

Dead Comanches lay sprawled over more than three miles of the Washita Valley. Here and there a woman or child lay dead, caught in the crossfire or run down by charging horses. Victory cries of almost a dozen Brazos tribes sounded amid the dust and smoke and echoed from the low hills that bracketed the valley.

Ford was almost an hour finding Sul Ross and the other officers in his command. By then the valley was bathed in a pall of smoke as the Brazos hunters set fire to piles of captured weapons and lodges.

"Sul," Ford yelled, "you all right?"

The young man sat on his lathered horse and replied with a calm smile, "Never better." *That,* Ford thought in silent admiration, *is one tough hombre.*

The inventory of losses and gains took the rest of the day. By nightfall the totals were known. The Texan force had two killed, a Ranger from LaGrange and a Waco warrior. Two of the attackers had suffered minor wounds.

Ford tallied seventy-six dead Comanches, eighteen captives—mostly women and children—and a captured horse herd of more than three hundred head. The Texans and their Indian allies had badly bloodied a Comanche force of some three hundred fighting men.

Jim Crowfoot strode to Ford's side. "More Comanches a dozen miles away." He waved a bloody scalping knife toward the northeast. "Buffalo Hump's band."

"They heading toward us?"

"Going the other way. We chase them?"

Ford shook his head. "Our horses are worn out and our men are just as tired. I think we've delivered the message from Texas. We'll start back to headquarters first thing tomorrow. Gather the Brazos Indian leaders for me, Jim, while I assemble our own troops. I want to tell every one of them how proud they've made me—and Texas —today."

Washington
June 1858

Major Robert Neighbors sat at the end of the conference table in the Secretary of the Interior's office and waited patiently for the decision that was soon to come from the four men seated in a haze of pipe and cigar smoke.

The Major had presented his arguments, answered their questions and lodged his protests over the petitions and falsified reports filed by Baylor and his bunch. Now the matter was in the hands of the unofficial joint committee on Indian affairs.

Rip Ford's report on the success of the Washita battle could not have come at a better time. Ford's report showered compliments on the Brazos Reserve Indians for their part in the campaign. It further stated that no proof had been found of reservation Indians being involved in frontier atrocities. And Ford's campaign had sent a distinct message to the wild bands—they no longer could hide beyond the Red River between raids into Texas. That one had caused some sputtering and snorting among the duly anointed in Washington, the Major thought, but in the end they came to agree that pursuit and punishment was necessary.

The only bothersome thing about Ford's report was that while he was leading his men on the Washita campaign, Comanche raiders had struck hard at isolated farms and stock ranches along the upper reaches of the Brazos. Four white settlers had been killed, two children taken captive and scores of horses and mules stolen. The raids behind the Ranger lines had taken some of the luster from Ford's victory in the Washita. The more vocal Texans were still yammering for Indian scalps by the wagonload.

"Major Neighbors," the Secretary of the Interior said around a thick cigar clenched in a square and stubbled jaw, "we have reached a conclusion. You shall have your court of inquiry, a public examination of the charges against you, your agents and the conduct of the reservation Indians."

"Thank you, sir," the Major said. "All I hope to do is lay the truth before the people of Texas and the nation."

The secretary worried the cigar for a moment. The Major could hardly make out the man's features behind the cloud of blue-gray smoke. "We will appoint an investigator to look into the situation on the Brazos and determine the place and time for a full and complete public hearing. We would appreciate your cooperation with the investigator."

The Major nodded solemnly. "He will have it, sir."

The secretary flicked the ash from his cigar into a stone tray. "Regarding your suggestion that a major military campaign be mounted against the Comanche raiders, Major Neighbors, we have received similar requests from your Captain Ford, Governor Runnels and the Army's Texas commanding general D. E. Twiggs. We in Washington are in agreement that such action should be taken. We are recalling units of the Second Cavalry from Idaho. They will be reassigned to Fort Belknap with orders to kill or capture any Indians guilty of depredations on the frontier."

The Major leaned back in his chair and sighed. "As much as I dislike the spilling of any blood, Mister Secretary, I welcome the news. It's the only way peace can be brought to the Texas frontier and the only way our Indian allies will have their own homes."

The secretary waved his stub of cigar. "If you have no other questions or comments, Major?"

The Major recognized the query as a polite signal of dismissal. He rose, shook hands around the table and reached for his hat. Outside he paused for a few deep breaths of the springtime air. The trip had been a greater success than he had hoped, the Major mused. It seemed that a heavy weight had lifted from his shoulders.

It was good to be going home.

THIRTEEN

Fort Belknap
November 1858

Major Robert Neighbors strode along the dusty supply road that had become the main street of the new City of Belknap, a booming center of commerce whose boosters proclaimed soon would surpass Gainesville and possibly even Dallas as the crown city of North Texas.

A stage line now ran from Belknap to Dallas and on to San Antonio. Belknap had been chosen as the seat of government for Young County and now had its own county commissioners, a sheriff, a courthouse and even a jail. Business ventures were opening by the day. New residents arrived on horseback, by wagon and on foot, while the more affluent came to town in comfortable four-horse coaches.

What the boosters failed to take into account, the Major knew, was that the primary fuel feeding the flames of prosperity was Fort Belknap itself. The post was now official headquarters of the Second Cavalry, recalled for the campaign against the northern Comanches. When the troubles ended and the soldiers left, the town would wither and die along with the post.

The Major could only wish the public uproar against the reservation Indians and the agents would die an equally peaceful death. The official public inquiry was now a matter of public record; not one shred of evidence of wrongdoing by agents or Indians had been uncovered by the special investigator. Only three men had appeared to testify against the Major, and they produced no concrete evidence—only remarks about the horse-stealing nature of Indians in general. The three did bear a petition asking the removal of Robert Neighbors and Matthew Leeper and the appointment of John Baylor and Rip Ford in their places.

The move to put Ford in charge rankled the Major. He didn't

think Rip would go behind his back to try to get the post, but he would find out when he got back to Austin, where Ford was now stationed after being recalled from the frontier expedition when the Second arrived. It would be a simple matter. He'd ask Rip.

Baylor hadn't showed for the hearing, nor had Peter Garland, Baylor's newest partner in trouble. And all who had formally complained to the government had been notified by letter or by messenger. Still, the hearing had done little to quell the public outcry against the agents and the reservation Indians. The ranks of troublemakers seemed to grow by the day. The ravings of Baylor and Garland found fertile ground among new residents uneasy over living near Indians and willing to believe the worst.

The Major idly wondered why he never saw Baylor in person. Several times he had tried to find Baylor for a face-to-face showdown, but it seemed Baylor was always elsewhere when the Major was around. It was as if the former agent carefully avoided any direct meeting. In a way the Major was relieved. He knew he would kill Baylor if he had the chance, or at least beat him within an inch of his life, and neither action would help matters much on the frontier. The lies, rumors and insults continued to pour from the press of *The White Man*. The hate sheet had carried not one line of news about the findings of the official inquiry. Every issue new horror stories appeared on its pages. Hardly a sunset came that some new depredation, real or imagined, was not laid at the feet of the reservation Indians.

The Brazos Reserve Indians in particular were bewildered by the surge of hatred against those of copper skin. They had lived among the whites in peace, taking up arms only to defend themselves against predator Indian tribes or outlaw white men, or to fight alongside the Rangers and soldiers as equals against the wild Comanches.

Despite the turmoil in Belknap, progress still was being made on the reserves. When the last fall crop was harvested, the Brazos Indians would have full granaries. They now grew enough food and raised sufficient livestock to sustain themselves. The federal government's outlay of funds for the settled tribes dwindled by the month.

On the Clear Fork Reserve a school opened for Comanche children had been a better than expected success to date. The youngsters were learning the white man's tongue; already most of them could read, spell and even compose simple sentences in English.

New Indians came almost daily to the Comanche reserve, their fear of the soldiers and Texas Rangers greater than their inbred yearning for freedom.

The campaign to punish the wild northern Comanches and their allies had to be considered a success. Major Earl Van Dorn had taken up where Rip Ford left off. Van Dorn and a company of Second Cavalry, along with a hundred Brazos Reserve warriors led by Sul Ross, had hit the Comanches hard along the Wichita River in Indian Territory. The attackers lost five men. They had killed fifty-six Comanche warriors and recovered two hundred stolen horses along with three white captives. The Comanches were from the bands led by Buffalo Hump and Sanaco.

The Major stopped outside a mercantile store, planning to buy presents for Lizzie and the children in an admittedly feeble attempt to atone for being away so often and for such long stretches. Now, with the Second Cavalry back in action and agents Ross and Leeper with their reserve Indian police forces holding a firm hand on the reservations, the Major figured he would be able to spend at least part of the Christmas holiday at home.

His hand was on the door when he heard the call:

"Hey, squaw man!"

The Major glanced to the side. A stocky red-haired man in teamster's clothing stood an arm's length from the mercantile door, feet spread in a cocky, challenging stance.

"Are you talking to me, mister?" The Major kept his tone casual despite the flare of anger in his belly.

"Damn right I am, *Major* Neighbors." The stocky man's tone made the title an epithet. Hate sparkled in the pale eyes. The Major returned the teamster's stare. The man was a stranger, yet somehow familiar. After a few seconds the Major made the connection—the red hair, square jaw, thick chest and arms bore the stamp of the Oldham family. Another cousin or brother, the Major concluded. If he was an Oldham that made him part of the Baylor faction.

"Then you've mistaken me for someone else, mister." The Major tried to keep his tone calm, even conversational. He shrugged and started to pull the door open.

"I reckon I'd deny it too, Neighbors." The red-haired man's voice dripped venom. "Anybody who'd bed a Lipan squaw would damn sure be smart enough to lie about it."

The Major dropped his hand from the door and turned to face

the teamster. He felt his face flush in growing rage. "Mister," the Major said, "I don't know who you are or where you get your information, but I'm getting a little tired of listening to all these lies going around."

"You calling me a liar?"

"I'm calling you sorely misinformed," the Major said, his tone cold. "Take it however you wish."

"You damn Injun-lover! Nobody calls me a liar." The red-haired man slapped a hand against the haft of a knife at his belt.

The Major's right fist hammered deep into the man's gut, a short but powerful blow with better than two hundred pounds of muscle behind it. The teamster's breath whooshed out and the knife fell from his hand. The Major calmly measured the distance and drove his left fist into the bridge of the man's nose. He felt the satisfying crunch as cartilage crumpled. The teamster staggered backward and fell against the wall of the store. The Major hammered him again in the gut, then stepped to the side and cracked a solid left fist into the man's temple.

The teamster was unconscious before he hit the dirt of the street. The Major stood for a moment, stared at the downed man and shook his bruised left fist. There were raw scrapes across his knuckles.

A bystander knelt beside the red-haired man, muttered a curse and glanced up at the Major. "You damn near killed him, Neighbors," the bystander said. "By God, the sheriff will hear about this."

The Major glared at the bystander until the man dropped his defiant gaze. "Fine," the Major said. "Just be damned sure you tell him *exactly* what happened. If the sheriff or your friend wants me, I'll not be hard to find. I won't be leaving Belknap for a few days. And while you're at it, tell Baylor and Garland I'll be happy to treat them to some of the same."

Erath County
December 1858

Peter Garland mounted his palomino and turned to face the band of twenty men gathered in a grassy valley a mile west of the small settlement of Golconda. An angry mutter rippled through the band of heavily armed men.

"All right, men," Garland called, "we've put up with these damn redskins long enough! The Bible says we take an eye for an eye, and the red heathens owe us more than that now!" Garland raised a hand to quiet the mutters of agreement from the crowd. "Now, gentlemen, you all heard what John Baylor had to say. You know he's right. The murdering red savages hide out on the reservations and laugh at us while they're tanning the scalps of our women." He paused to let his words fuel the hate among the men.

"There isn't a man among us hasn't lost friends or relatives to the red savages," Garland continued. "You've read the newspapers. Five families—*five*—raided around here just in the last two weeks. The damn government won't help us white men protect our families and our livestock." He shifted his chew to the other cheek and spat to emphasize his disgust. "So, by God, we'll do it ourselves! Let's go make some good Indians!"

Garland reined his horse about. The time for an attack couldn't be better, he knew. Major Robert Neighbors had gone back home to spend Christmas in San Antonio, the Rangers had been recalled and most of the Second Cavalry was still afield in the campaign against the northern Comanches. Agents Ross and Leeper had their hands full on the reservations. It was a perfect time for the white man to make a statement—in blood.

Keechi Creek

Julia Small Foot edged closer to the fire and let the warmth of the flames ease the chill in her old and aching bones. It had been a good hunt. The Great Father had led several fat deer and two antelope within range of the guns of the Brazos Reserve band.

She glanced around the still-sleeping camp in the cold half light of early dawn. Twenty-six other Indians, half of them women and children, huddled in blankets and buffalo robes against the chill. It was a good camp, Julia Small Foot thought with a contented sigh. Her brother-in-law Choctaw Tom had chosen well. There was food, shelter, good water, grass for the hunters' horses, and in the daytime the laughter of the women and children as they worked and played brightened the spirits of all.

Julia would miss this place. For a brief time it had been like the old days, and she felt young and pretty again, even to the point of flirting with some of the unmarried men. But this time would end tomorrow. Choctaw Tom and his nephew would return with a wagon to carry the meat and camp equipment back to the reservation. *It is good,* she told herself, *that the Great Father lets me live the few years I have left in such peace and contentment.*

The rustle of dried leaves and crack of a twig sounded at Julia's back. She rose to her feet, the creak and pop of her joints audible in the still morning air, and turned toward the sound.

A white man stood at the edge of the clearing in the stand of cottonwood trees, a shotgun in his hands. Julia Small Foot did not recognize the man, but still smiled and raised a hand in greeting. Choctaw Tom had many friends among the whites, had ridden with them for many years, and the band had a pass signed by Agent Ross permitting them to hunt off the reservation lands. There was nothing to fear.

Fire blossomed from the muzzle of the shotgun. A heavy fist hammered into Julia Small Foot's breast. She fell backward across the fire. She did not feel any pain from the coals.

San Antonio
January 1859

Major Robert Neighbors stared in stunned disbelief at the message delivered by courier from Agent Ross. *This can't be,* he thought, his mind still unwilling to accept what the message reported. It seemed that a gaping hole had opened where his stomach had been.

"What is it, dear?"

Lizzie's question didn't register with the Major for a few heartbeats. Then he turned to her. "Some white men attacked a harmless band of Indians, a hunting party from the reservation. Choctaw Tom's group. Seven Indians dead, executed in cold blood while they slept."

Lizzie clapped a hand to her mouth in dismay. "Oh, how horrible," she murmured. Her face went ash white. She came into his arms and buried her face in his shoulder.

"Three women were among the dead and several children were wounded," the Major said. The first embers of rage began to fill the void in his gut. "Agent Ross says he has the names of several of the men responsible. Peter Garland was the leader."

Lizzie finally drew away. "You must do something, Major."

The Major swallowed and nodded his head. "Yes, Lizzie. If I don't, there could be a full-scale war. Agent Ross reports the Brazos Indians are clamoring for retaliation. So far Jose Maria has been able to keep them from reaching for the war paint."

The Major strode to the window and stared for a moment across the frost-crisped tall grass, the skeletons of trees stripped bare of leaves by the winter winds. The stark landscape reflected the thought that had been building in the back of his mind for months. *I'm losing the battle. The dream is fading . . .*

"There's even more to it than that, Lizzie," he said as he turned to face her. "Governor Runnels is in a rage over the constant Comanche raids. He's calling back Rip Ford's Rangers to protect the outlying settlements. A second Ranger force is on its way to help the Army pursue the renegades. My agents report there's talk of a mob gathering to storm the reservations and slaughter the Indians there."

"Then you must go to them," Lizzie said, her lips now set in a determined line. "Someone must put a stop to this. You are that someone."

"I'm not sure I can, Lizzie."

"Can you afford not to try?"

The Major fell silent for a moment, the call to duty wrestling with the powerful ties to home, hearth and pregnant wife. "No, I can't. Not as long as there's a chance—" His voice trailed away as his brows bunched in thought. "That bunch of murderers has to be brought to justice before the whole frontier catches fire. If we let them get away with it the Indians will never trust white man's justice again. I'll have to find a judge to issue warrants for the arrest of those men, then make sure they stand trial for murder. I must meet with the governor and try to get him calmed down, convince him to provide protection for the reservation Indians against any raids by Baylor's gang."

"Then of course you must go." Lizzie's tone was one of finality.

The Major leaned down and kissed his wife on the forehead. "I'll be back soon, Lizzie. I want to be here for the birth of our child."

Camp Leon

Texas Ranger Captain Rip Ford tamped powder and ball into the sixth chamber of his Colt, capped the weapon and tucked it into his belt holster, then turned to the big man at his side.

"Rip, you can't be serious!" Major Robert Neighbors's fingers trembled in anger and disbelief. The stack of arrest warrants fluttered in his big hand.

"Yes, Major, I am," Ford said, his jaw set and firm. "I will not serve those warrants. I have no civil authority here."

"Dammit, Rip"—the Major waved the legal paper almost under Ford's nose—"the men named in these writs killed innocent Indian women and children in cold blood. You're an officer of the state. I expect—no, by God, I demand—that you do your duty and bring them in!"

A couple of Rangers standing nearby exchanged glances and quietly moved away, embarrassed at being privy to a private quarrel.

Rip Ford's gaze was calm as he returned the Major's stare. "And I told you that I have no civil authority. My orders from Governor Runnels are specific—to protect the outlying farms and settlements from Indian raids. This is a *military* operation, Major. If you'll find a sheriff or any other official with the authority to serve those warrants, I'll help him serve them." Ford turned away to tighten the cinch on his sorrel gelding.

The Major's anger boiled over. He reached out, grabbed Ford's shoulder and spun the Ranger captain about. "Damn it all, Rip," the Major all but shouted, "we're talking about cold-blooded murder here! You can't spit in the eye of justice like this!"

The first glimmer of aggravation flickered in Ford's eyes. "Take your hand off me, Major," he said.

The Major loosened his grip on Ford's coat. "I can't believe what I'm hearing here, Rip. We've been friends for a long time—"

"And we still are, Major," Ford said calmly. "We've ridden many a trail together. I'm not fighting you on this. As I said, get a civil authority to serve the papers and I'll help bring those men in, face down across a saddle if need be. But I'll not put other lives in danger to run any errands for you, friend or no. Now, leave me alone. I've got a patrol to lead."

The Major's jaw ached as he tried to control the anger and hurt that clamped a heavy hand on his chest. Ford swung into the saddle. "Dammit, Rip," the Major snarled, "you sure as hell never balked at killing Indians or looking for some to arrest. Then you try to undermine my powers as supervising Indian agent—"

"I told you I never asked for that job, Major," Ford interrupted. "Somebody put my name up without my knowledge. I have no idea who it was."

The Major's fist closed around the warrants, crumpling the papers. "And now you're backing a bunch of white killers who deserve to hang for what they did. I guess I've seen your true colors now, Captain Ford. I just couldn't believe that you hate all Indians so much."

Rip Ford shifted his weight in the saddle and stared at the Major. "I never said I liked Indians, Major. I'd as soon see them all moved out of Texas, or dead, as not. But don't be so quick to judge me without looking inside yourself. You're so damn worried about your Indians you've lost sight of everything else. I've got better things to do than sit here and waste the day arguing about it."

Ford touched the spurs to his sorrel and moved out at a brisk trot. The other Rangers followed. The Major stood and watched, unable to check the confusion, anger and dark sense of betrayal that boiled in his gut. Then, with a bitter curse, the Major strode back to his own horse.

FOURTEEN

San Antonio
May 1859

Major Robert Neighbors thumbed through the stack of reports that had filtered in over the past few days, trying to find something there that would lift his spirits.

There was nothing.

Nothing to ease the aching sense of failure that gnawed at his gut or the urgency that squeezed his chest harder with each day. The men who ambushed Choctaw Tom's party remained at large. The Major had been unable to find anyone with enough nerve to serve the arrest warrants, and his appeals for help from the governor's office had been ignored. The prevailing attitude seemed to be that it was just a bunch of Indians. No big loss. Not something to risk spitting in the face of public opinion and losing a political career or chance retaliation from the killers.

And now, Agent Ross's letter brought by special courier. John Baylor was assembling a large band of armed men with the avowed purpose of lifting Indian scalps along the Brazos. Albert Fox, the Caddo who had climbed from the bottle to lead his people, was dead—shot, mutilated and scalped while returning from Fort Arbuckle with horses stolen from the Brazos Agency. The Indians of both reserves were nervous and jittery, fearing attack at any moment from the Baylor and Garland faction.

The only path left open to avoid massive bloodshed was to abandon the reservations. Give up on the dream and move the Indians to safety beyond the Red River.

Baylor had won.

Washington had approved the Major's proposal to move the Indians from the reservations. The government had also, in its usual state of competence, neglected to appropriate funds for the removal. It would be autumn, possibly next spring, before the move could be made. In the meantime the reservation Indians were bait for any white coyote with an appetite for scalps.

"More bad news, dear?" Lizzie waddled into the room, heavy with the baby, her face pale. She had always been frail, but never so much as now, the Major thought.

He sighed heavily. "I've failed them, Lizzie. The Indians trusted me, befriended me, looked to me to give them permanent homes and a life of peace and contentment. I couldn't do it."

Lizzie squeezed his shoulder in reassurance. "You didn't fail, Robert Neighbors." Her voice was soft, her tone sincere. "The rest of the world failed you." He felt her slight shudder. "That Baylor— such an awful man." She fell silent for a moment. The Major saw the glint of tears in the lids of her eyes. Then she squared her shoulders and stepped away from his chair. "You must return to the Brazos, Major. You are the only man in Texas strong enough to stop a wholesale massacre or a full-fledged war now."

"There's something else, Lizzie. Something I haven't told you before. Agent Leeper says that Baylor or one of his friends has put a price on my head. I understand the price is five hundred dollars."

Lizzie did not reply for a long time. The steady tick of the mantel clock seemed to keep time with the Major's heartbeat. Finally Lizzie cleared her throat.

"Major, your life has been threatened many times before. But no one has ever had the courage to make the attempt." She forced a wan smile. "You've always been on good speaking terms with the Almighty, haven't you?"

"He hasn't mentioned anything to me in person, dear, but I'm sure He has been listening and watching over us."

"Then there you have it," Elizabeth Ann Neighbors said with a tone of finality. "The Lord directs each life on this earth, Robert Neighbors. Some men are special, above all others in their destiny. You're one of those special men, my husband." Lizzie's voice was firm, her tone reflecting the inner strength of conviction that often amazed the Major. "The Almighty has chosen you to lead the native red people of our state from danger and death. You must go to them. It is your duty."

"Lizzie, I—" The Major's voice caught in his throat. "I can't leave you. Not now, not like this. You haven't been well. I must stay until the baby is born. Just a few more weeks—"

Lizzie reached up and placed a finger on his lips. "No, Major.

You must go now. Don't worry about me. God will watch over your wife and your unborn child. The fate of an entire race of people is in your hands. Perhaps this is a test of our faith."

Robert Neighbors pulled his wife to him and kissed her gently. He swallowed around the sudden, painful lump in his throat. "Lizzie," he said tenderly, "I don't deserve you."

Jacksboro

John R. Baylor stood at the front of the combination saloon and billiard parlor, Peter Garland at his side, and glared through the swirls of tobacco smoke at the standing-room-only crowd. *By God, I've got them right where I want them now,* Baylor silently congratulated himself.

"Men," Baylor shouted above the murmur of angry voices, "it's high time we wiped out these red vermin—to the last man, the last squaw and the last papoose! We've stood aside too damn long and let the thieving redskins have their way. They've stolen their last horse and killed their last settler, by God! Now we're going to settle accounts. This is one group of white men who aren't going to stand for it any longer!"

A chorus of "amens" rippled through the crowd.

"I got a question for you, Baylor," a burly farmer in the front rank said. He held a copy of a Dallas newspaper in a ham-sized fist. "It says here that the Injuns are goin' to be moved out of Texas. Ain't that gonna solve our problems for us?"

Peter Garland snorted in derision. "You know damn well what that Neighbors is trying to do. He's stalling. He knows this whole country's about to blow up and his pet Indians are sitting on the powder keg. He's trying to keep us from getting our justice while his thieving animals steal our horses and kill our families. By all that's holy, we won't stand for it. Me and my boys showed everybody the only way to handle Indians down on Keechi Creek. Only thing we did wrong there was quit the job too soon."

Baylor raised a hand to quiet the whoops of agreement. "You all know what the Bible says," Baylor called out. "An eye for an eye, a tooth for a tooth. Vengeance is mine, sayeth the Lord!"

The whoops and yells of response were louder than before. After a moment, the yells died away to mutters, then stopped completely.

Two women strode into the room. "Gentlemen," one of them said, her voice shrill with excitement, "the ladies of Jacksboro are pleased to present you with your own flag to fly in your glorious campaign." She held a bundle aloft. The second woman helped unfurl the cloth. The hand-stitched banner was emblazoned, "Necessity Knows No Law."

The sight of the banner touched off a fresh round of cheers. Baylor and Garland took the cloth from the women and held it overhead for all to see. Then Baylor bowed to the women. "Thank you, ladies, for your expression of support. This flag will fly high and proudly in our quest."

The Reverend Noah T. Byars stepped forward, helped fold the banner as if it were a revered flag, then placed both hands atop the cloth. "The Lord blesses this symbol of our venture as a just crusade in the name of righteousness," he boomed in his best pulpit voice. "Blessed be the warriors of the Almighty against the heathen hordes!"

A roar of approval practically shook the rafters of the saloon. One of the women raised a hand until the tumult subsided. "It is a small thing we do, gentlemen, a small thing to show that the women of the frontier are tired of sorrow and suffering. A small thing to remind you that our hearts ride with you." She curtsied to the crowd. "We shall take our leave now, and let our men plan this crusade against the red offspring of Satan."

Every man present removed his hat, stood and applauded as the two women passed through the gathering and strode through the door, heads held high. *A nice touch,* Baylor thought. *Peter Garland knows how to use a woman's hand; every man here will feel like one of the knights of old, following the handkerchief of femininity into battle.*

A half hour later the final plans were made. A group of fifty men would feint an attack on the Comanche reserve to freeze the troops in place there. That would leave the Brazos Reserve protected by only a handful of dirt-digger Indians. It would be a swift, punishing strike, with no quarter given.

"Let's hit the saddle, men!" Baylor called. "We've got some scores to settle!"

The heavily armed crowd, the throb of the lynch mob surging through its collective veins, shoved through the doors to the horses that waited outside. Baylor allowed himself a smug smile. From a purely tactical standpoint, now was the perfect time to hit the lower reservation, Baylor knew. Robert Neighbors was home, safe and sound and snuggled up to his pregnant wife in San Antonio—and, therefore, out of the way. The best fighting men of the Brazos Reserve were miles away, on scout with either Van Dorn's soldiers or Rip Ford's Rangers. Shapley Ross had left the Brazos Agency for a couple of days, trying to arrange transportation for the Indians' move from Texas.

Nothing stood in the way but a handful of dirt-digger Indians. The white avengers would hit the Caddo camp first, then sweep through the other villages on the Brazos. *By the time we're finished there won't be a live Indian for miles,* Baylor thought in satisfaction. *And when Neighbors comes running back to wring his hands and whimper, I'll have his hair, too.* Baylor swung aboard his long-legged roan and waved his men toward the Caddo village on the Brazos.

Brazos Reserve

Mary Two Blankets leaned against her hoe handle and swiped a sleeve across the beads of sweat on her forehead. The sun was hot for a spring morning, but the heat helped ease the pain in her swollen knuckles. The Army doctor said there was nothing to be done for the pain in her hands or her hip—arthritis, he called it— but the warmth of the sun and the smell of earth and growing plants seemed to help.

Even if it had made the pain worse, Mary would still be in the fields. Working the earth was her life, even though it meant nothing since the fields would be abandoned soon. But here, with the sun on her shoulders and the gentle spring breeze in her hair, was her church, her reason for being. It had always been so.

Today there were but two Caddos tending the crops, Mary and an old man whose love of the soil was as deep as her own. Jose Maria had gathered all the available Brazos Reserve warriors in the village almost a half mile from the field, the men armed and waiting for the attack that was rumored to come. The fear that had made other women captives in their own lodges was not as strong in Mary's heart. A life of fear and dread was worse than no life.

From a thicket a few yards away at the end of the corn rows a bobwhite called from its home along the timbered creek. The quail's *too-wheet* cry was sweet and clear in the morning air. The sound brought a smile of contentment to Mary's face. The covey had become known throughout the tribes as "Mary Two Blankets's quail," and even when times were hard and bellies empty the small birds were left alone. No hunter dared touch them for fear of Mary's wrath. It was, she thought, as it should be. As long as there were birds and animals and sky and trees and clouds and sun the Mother Earth would survive. Man might appear and scar the soil before vanishing one day, but the earth and its wild creatures lived on.

Mary's smile faded as a dust cloud rose from the far side of the tree-lined creek. A jay squawked in indignation and fluttered from limb to limb in a pecan tree. Mary heard the burring beat of small wings as the quail covey flushed. A moment later the thud of hoof-beats shattered the peace of the morning. A line of horsemen burst from the trees, yelling as they put spurs to their mounts. Mary's heart skipped a beat. Guns bristled from the line of riders like the quills of a porcupine.

The quick surge of fear drained from Mary's muscles. There was no escape, no place to hide or run. Mary stood her ground and watched as the old Caddo man tried to dodge the riders. A rope flicked out, settled about his neck and shoulders and yanked him from his feet. His body bounced from the hills of corn as the man holding the rope spurred his horse into a run. The old man's cries faded; corn stalks severed by the taut rope fell in quarter circles as the rider reined his horse first one way, then the other.

The horsemen were almost upon her now. Mary still leaned on her hoe, her face without expression as the horses thundered toward her. For a few heartbeats her breast swelled with the pride of the Caddo who stared death in the face and did not blink. Then smoke belched from a pistol barrel. Something struck Mary's chest a heavy blow. She staggered, but remained on her feet. A second ball, then a third, tore into her body. Her knees buckled, the last of her strength faded and she fell forward on her face. A horse's hoof cracked against her skull as the riders sped past. The last thing Mary Two Blankets saw was a small spotted ladybug scurrying along a downed corn stalk. The bug seemed to be in a terrible hurry, she thought as the darkness fell.

John Baylor heard the whoops of triumph from the line of riders as the raiding party swept through the cornfield. The Caddo village was only a hundred yards away now—his heart jumped in his chest as a rifle ball hummed past his hat. A split second later he heard the solid thump of lead against flesh and one of the riders at his left cried out. *Dammit, it wasn't supposed to happen like this,* Baylor thought as a surge of fear pushed against his bladder.

Smoke billowed from the edge of the Indian village. The sharp crack of rifles and the whir of arrows filled the air. Baylor yanked his horse around, almost running down a man slumped over the horn of his saddle. He heard the thud of an arrow into flesh, a man's gasp of pain and shock. Then Baylor's horse fought its way clear of the milling riders. He drove the spurs home.

The white mob's attack shattered in the first wave of fire from the Indian camp. Yells of triumph became curses of surprise and alarm as the line of horsemen wheeled their mounts and followed Baylor's flight from the hail of lead and arrows.

Baylor glanced back after a half mile run and barked a sharp oath. Mounted warriors poured from the village, the war cries of a half dozen tribes sounding above the hoofbeats of running horses. Baylor recognized the lead Indian at a glance—the Anadarko chief Jose Maria.

One of the raiders went down hard as his horse fell. Another toppled from the saddle, an arrow between his shoulder blades. The surviving attackers leaned low over the necks of their mounts and spurred for their lives.

The battle swept on horseback for eight miles. A rear guard of white men twice tried to make a stand, only to be forced back before the charging warriors.

Desperation gripped Baylor as his exhausted horse stumbled and almost fell. Then hope surged through his gut as his horse topped a ridge. The flight had led them to a farm home. The farmer stood by the doorway, rifle in hand, eyes wide as the fleeing horsemen bore down on the house. The farmer dropped his weapon and fled to the cover of a nearby stand of trees.

Baylor swung from the saddle and barked orders. The raiders ignored his commands, tried to jam their way through the narrow front door to the safety behind the heavy logs of the farmhouse walls. Others spurred exhausted mounts toward the barn and corrals.

Baylor ducked and pushed his way through the door as a lead ball spatted against wood only inches from his ear. Inside, a woman and several children cowered in a back corner of the front room.

"Get some rifles at those windows," Baylor yelled. He glanced around at the raiders gathered in the room. Their faces were pale. The lark of a raid against a bunch of tame Indians had turned into a deadly game. A rifle thundered at one of the windows. Baylor glanced at Hiram Oldham as the red-haired man muttered a curse and dropped away from the window to reload.

Peter Garland fumbled a ball into the barrel of his rifle, tamped the load home and glared at Baylor. "Damn your soul to hell, Baylor," Garland snarled, "if the Indians don't get you I've half a mind to put a slug in you myself. You lead us into a damned ambush and then you turn tail and run like a rabbit." Garland stowed the ramrod and capped the weapon.

Baylor returned the stare for a moment. "I noticed you weren't far behind me yourself when the shooting started, Garland. Don't go calling me a coward when you're a little shy in the guts department yourself. Those savages weren't supposed to be able to fight back."

Baylor turned away from Garland and took a quick count of his losses. So far he had three men dead, two hit hard, and several others with lesser wounds. Nat Colley crouched in a corner as Emil Washburn tended a bullet hole in his brother-in-law's shoulder. Washburn didn't look especially pleased as he glanced at Baylor.

One of the raiders eased his way to a window, stuck the rifle barrel out, fired without aiming and then dropped back below the portal.

"Pick your targets, dammit," Baylor yelled. "Most of our ammunition's on the horses and they've scattered from hell to breakfast. Don't waste a shot."

Outside, Jose Maria raised a hand high. "Don't shoot at the house," he shouted to his warriors. "The people who live here are our friends! We do not wish the woman and children to come to harm!" The firing from the Indians stopped immediately.

Jose Maria studied his position with care. They could not rush the house. It would cost too many lives. There was no way to burn out the white men without endangering the woman and children. The white raiders had stumbled into a fort. Most of the men who had taken refuge in the barn or corrals already had been shot or had escaped into the trees beyond. It was a standoff. If Baylor's men decided to use the woman and children as a shield, the battle could cost innocent lives. It was a chance he did not want to take.

"What do we do now, Jose Maria?" an Anadarko crouching nearby asked.

Jose Maria's brows knitted in thought, then he shook his head.

"We must return to the reserve. If there are other such bands of white men about, our lodges will be unprotected. We will leave."

John Baylor watched in astonishment from a window as the Indian force withdrew. *The damn fools had us dead to rights and now they're backing off,* he thought. *The next time we'll do this a little different.* He turned to the room crowded with would-be raiders. "We can still get the red sons, men. Somebody catch some horses—"

"You want 'em that bad, Baylor, you go get 'em yourself." Hiram Oldham's face was flushed in disgust and anger. "I don't reckon I'll be riding with you anymore."

"Me neither," another voice chipped in. A general murmur of agreement swept the room. It had become stifling hot and smelly from the scent of sweaty bodies and coppery scent of blood.

"All right, have it your way," Baylor said. "Anyone who wants to ride with me, let's go. We're not done yet, not by a long shot." *Let the other lace-drawers boys go,* he grumbled inwardly. *I can always get more men.*

Brazos Agency

Major Robert Neighbors slammed a fist into the desktop and somehow managed to bite back the string of oaths that swirled in his mind. Cursing never solved a problem, but there were times when it was an opiate to a raging soul. This was one of them.

He had read all available reports of Baylor's raid on the agency, and each one fueled the fires of his rage. *By God, if I'd gotten here in time I would have shot that damn fool myself,* he fumed inwardly. Three Indians dead, seven of Baylor's men killed and the number of wounded on each side still unknown. Baylor's bunch had scattered, but the Major sensed the core of the Indian-haters were still out there somewhere.

At least now the reservations were as secure as could be expected. Two companies of cavalry and one infantry company patrolled the Brazos Reserve perimeter in addition to Jose Maria's capable scouting and police force.

The Comanches on the Upper Reserve were convinced they would be the next target of the white gang. The warriors were armed and ready to fight. Agent Leeper's Comanche police force and other tribesmen prowled the reservation boundaries. The Army was sending more troops to protect the Clear Fork Reserve.

The Major glanced up as Agent Ross stepped through the doorway. Ross carried a brace of pistols and a Bowie knife at his belt and held a carbine in his oversized hand. Ross hung the rifle on pegs by the doorway and turned to the Major.

"No luck, Shapley?"

Ross shook his head. "Not a sign of Baylor or his men anywhere. I was hoping we could put a quick end to this. I'd like to string that fool to the nearest tree."

"You're not the only one, Shapley," the Major said with a grimace of disgust. "I rode out to his ranch myself yesterday. I guess it's a good thing for both of us Baylor wasn't there. I'd have shot him on the spot." The Major rose and paced to a window. "It's a hell of a note, Shapley. We can protect the white settlers from the Indians, but we can't protect the red men from the white savages." He suddenly spun to face Ross. "Shapley, if that bunch comes back, throw everything we've got at them. Wipe them out to the last man."

Ross nodded solemnly. "Precisely what I had in mind, Major." He slapped his hat onto a peg and headed for the coffeepot. "So what do we do now?"

The Major's shoulders slumped. "Wait. That's about all we can do. I've filed reports with Austin and with Washington. I've written every newspaper of consequence in the state, trying to set straight what happened here." He turned from the window and took the coffee mug Ross held out to him. The Major scrubbed the knuckles of his free hand across eyes reddened by lack of sleep, wind and more than a little worry. "I plan to prosecute Baylor to the full extent of the law, Shapley. I've drawn up a partial list of charges, from murder to horse theft, and forwarded it to the United States district attorney in Austin."

"I doubt anything will ever come of it, Major," Ross said. "Governor Runnels isn't going to let anybody take action when it might cost him votes in the Indian-hater crowd."

The Major took a swig of his coffee and grimaced. "To hell with Runnels," he grumbled. "At least I tried. Now we have to keep as many people alive as possible until we can get the Indians moved across the Red River."

Ross was silent for a moment. He swirled the contents of his coffee cup idly in one hand. Finally, he sighed. "I'm sorry, Major—

sorry to see it end this way. You and I may be in the minority, but by all that's holy I thought the reservation plan really would work. I hate to see that dream end. I know how much it hurts you."

The Major turned back to the window, staring out at what appeared to be a peaceful and pastoral scene. "My feelings don't matter, Shapley. The dream was for the Indians. They're the ones who have suffered. And their pain hasn't stopped yet. It won't be stopped until they're out of Texas, out of reach of the Baylors and the Peter Garlands and their ilk."

Ross cleared his throat. "Major, I hope I haven't stepped into your authority. I've already met with the chiefs on both reservations. They're disappointed at having to give up their homes once again, but at the same time anxious to see their children have a chance to grow up."

The Major placed his coffee cup on the desk and clamped a hand on Ross's shoulder. "You did the right thing. I thank you for taking that step. Now, let's see how many people we can keep alive until the government gets off its backside and lets us move. It would be nice if we can keep ourselves alive in the process."

Shapley P. Ross flashed a wry grin. "That could take some doing, what with a price on both our heads."

The Major squeezed the agent's shoulder. "If it comes to that, Shapley, we'll make them pay their own price."

FIFTEEN

Brazos Agency
July 1859

Shapley P. Ross swung open the door of the agency office and stopped in his tracks.

Major Robert Neighbors sat behind the desk, a wide grin on his broad face and a twinkle in his eyes that Ross had not seen in months.

"Major, you look happy as a possum in a tree full of ripe persimmons," Ross said. "Good news for a change?"

"Better than good, Shapley. You are now looking at the father of a fat, healthy and happy baby boy."

Ross was at the desk in two strides, hand extended. "Congratulations, Major. How's Elizabeth?"

"Doing very well, thank you. She's still weak, of course, but should recover quickly." The Major released Ross's hand. "I was just about to write to her. I'm glad to share such news with a good friend."

"I'm delighted to hear it, Major. I know how much you've worried about her over the past few weeks." He started to remove his hat, then paused. "I just remembered something. I have the best bottle of champagne in North Texas in the well house. I've been saving it for a special occasion. This seems to be that time."

The Major chuckled. "Shapley, you are a thoughtful and generous man. A toast to young Ross Simpson Neighbors, newly arrived in San Antonio, Texas, seems to be in order."

Ross's eyebrows lifted in surprise. "Ross?"

"Man has a right to name his son for one of his best friends and a good man, Shapley."

"Well, I'll be—I'm honored, Major." A wide grin spread over Shapley Ross's bearded face. "A double reason to pop the cork on that champagne."

A couple of hours later, with the champagne and Shapley Ross both gone, the Major scanned his letter to Lizzie:

> Permit me, my sweet wife, to congratulate you and to express a hope that the pleasure the Almighty may afford you after life may nicely compensate you for all the pain He has cost you, and to hope that you will soon recover and enjoy better health than ever heretofore. I have been through many trials—but none that has given me more pain than my separation from you during your own trials. Our difficulties here are gradually assuming a manageable state and I hope soon to report them over and that I shall soon be able to pay respects to the small stranger . . . Give my love to all. Kiss our three children and remember me to all our friends . . . I cannot yet say when I will be home. I am extremely anxious to make this my last visit to the frontier on Indian matters.
> Your very true and devoted husband
> R. S. Neighbors

The Major puffed the last few lines of ink dry, addressed the letter and placed it in the dispatch case. He hadn't told Lizzie the whole story; the situation with the Indians was far from over. But now he had the official approval of the federal government to move the tribes from Texas, out of reach of the likes of John Baylor. All that remained were the details of moving a couple of thousand Indians from two reservations to their new homes in Indian Territory—and keep them alive in the process.

Jacksboro

Major Robert Neighbors squatted beside the sprawling wagon yard and swiped a hand at the sweat that trickled down his cheek. At his side sutler Charles Barnard whittled idly at a chunk of cottonwood.

"That's it, Charlie," the Major said. "Everything is finally organized to move the Indians. I've never seen so much paperwork in my life. The only problem left is that the government sort of forgot to vote money to do it with."

Barnard shrugged. "Your word's good enough for me, Major. I know I'll eventually get paid if you say so. I'll handle the beef supply end of the deal. The Indians won't go hungry on this trip."

The Major heaved himself to his feet. "Thanks, Charlie. I knew I could count on you."

"No problem." Barnard folded his pocket knife, dropped the whittling wood and stood. "We've got a scorcher today," the sutler said. "Hot enough to fry a lizard in the shade out here. Want to pop into the cantina for a beer?"

"No, thanks," the Major said. "It's tempting, but I've still got a lot of work to do. I'd best get back to the Brazos."

The Major started to turn away, then stopped as a familiar figure on horseback moved toward the two men on the dusty street. "Looks like the Rangers are back home," Barnard said.

Rip Ford pulled his horse to a stop, swung from the saddle and extended a hand to the Major.

The Major ignored it.

Ford's face flushed at the obvious snub as he dropped his hand. "They told me at the agency I'd find you here, Major. I just wanted to let you know my company's been recalled to Austin. We didn't cut any fresh tracks, either Indian or white raiding parties. Looks like the trouble's about over here anyway."

The Major tried to fight back the simmering anger that churned behind his belt buckle. "No thanks to you, Captain Ford." The Major heard the hard edge on his own voice. "If you had done your job there wouldn't have been a need for this."

Rip Ford tensed. "What in the blue-eyed hell are you talking about, Major?"

"In the first place, I know now that you planned to break up the reserves all along," the Major said. "Well, you sure as hell got that done. And if you'd arrested Garland and Baylor like you should have, we wouldn't have had innocent people killed here."

Ford's eyes glittered in anger. "Dammit, Major, we've whipped this horse before. I told you I'd help any sheriff or constable arrest Garland—"

"You ducked your responsibility, Captain Ford," the Major interrupted. "You didn't *want* to arrest those men and you know it."

Rip Ford glared into the Major's eyes for several heartbeats. Then he shrugged. "I've said all I'm going to say about it, Major. I did what I thought was right and proper. I did my duty as I saw it under the law. As far as breaking up the reservations is concerned, yes—I thought about it at first. I made a mistake listening to Allison Nelson. I didn't know he was one of Baylor's outlaws at the time."

"Excuses are a weak man's whiskey, Captain Ford. You've hated

Indians all your life. And you took advantage of the situation here
to punish them."

Ford's face flushed anew. "Dammit, Major, don't push me! We've
been friends for too long. But I won't stand here and take talk like
that from any man!"

The Major balled his fist. "Then let's settle it here and now,
Captain Ford."

Charles Barnard shouldered his way between the two men. "Listen, you damn fools," the sutler said, "it's too hot for any street
brawls today. Neither of you is listening to what the other has to
say. I personally don't give a stomped toad's butt who's right, but
I'm not going to let two old friends get into a fistfight just because
their long johns are in a wad over a difference of opinion. If you
two want to fight, by God you can start with me!"

For a long moment Rip Ford and the Major glared at each other
over Barnard's broad shoulders. Then the tension slowly faded.
Finally, Ford shrugged. "The hell with it," he said. He turned
away, mounted his horse and rode off at a steady trot. He didn't
look back.

Barnard turned to the Major. "Dammit, man, you made a mistake here just now. Blame it on the heat, blame it on the pressure
you've been under, blame it on me if you like. But for Christ's sake,
don't blame it on Rip Ford. We both know he had no hand in the
mess around here."

The Major's fury began to fade. He sighed and cast one last
glance toward the retreating Ranger captain. "Maybe you're right,
Charlie. Maybe I was out of line. I guess I just needed to hit something and Rip Ford happened to be handy. I'll apologize to him as
soon as I get back home to San Antonio."

North Bank of the Red River
August 1859

Major Robert Neighbors sat astride his big bay gelding and
watched, an empty feeling in his chest, as the last of the long caval-
cade from the Brazos reservations filed past.

The chiefs and warriors among the more than a thousand Indians from the Brazos Reserve rode or walked with heads held high
and proud, but the inner pain showed through the dark eyes.

Many of the women wept openly and frequently turned to gaze back at the land that had been their homes. Young children clung to their mother's skirts or gripped their father's hands, eyes wide in fear and confusion. The older youths walked stoically with the warriors or ran and played in excitement, depending on their ages.

Two companies of the Second Cavalry flanked the line of Indians. Junior officers and warriors of the Brazos police scouted far afield in search of potential danger. An infantry company from the First Regiment marched in close support at shoulder arms, alert for attack from the rear. Rumors had persisted for weeks that lawless bands planned hit-and-run raids on the Indians as they left Texas for the last time.

The Comanches, ever scornful of Indians who dug in the dirt, rode or walked in a group apart from the others, under the watchful eye of Agent Leeper and the cavalry troopers. The Major caught the eye of Jose Maria, mounted on a small gray mustang at the head of the Anadarko band. The chief reined his mount about and trotted to the Major's side. Both men sat for a moment in silence, each with his own emotions and thoughts.

"It is a sad day, Agent Neighbors," Jose Maria finally said. "A sad day for both our peoples."

The Major swallowed against the lump in his throat. "Yes. It is as a lance through my heart to see my friends driven from their homes."

Jose Maria shrugged. "It is not the first time our people have been made to leave their lands. It is my hope this will be the last. The sadness will pass, in time. Perhaps in this new land we will have peace and our women and children will no longer know fear." The Anadarko's gaze drifted over the long line of supply wagons, Indians and soldiers. He sighed. "The sun will remain, the rains will fall and birds will still sing when you and I are no longer able to hear them, my friend. I am old and grow tired of fighting and bloodshed. If this new land brings laughter back to my people, it will have been a fair trade."

The Major turned to face his old friend and blinked against the sudden sting in his eyes. "No, Jose Maria, it is not a fair trade. My Indian friends deserved better. And the deepest wound of all is that I have failed you and your people."

Jose Maria's weathered face creased in a slight smile. "You did not fail us, Major Neighbors. You fought well and bravely on many fronts. You fought the traitors among the white men, the traitors among the Indians. You fought the Great Father in Washington and the chief of the Texans. You fought as long and as hard as any warrior ever fought in battle. No man can do more."

The Anadarko stared for a moment toward the north. "Perhaps this Red River is to the Indian what the River Jordan of the white man's religion is to him. My people have crossed over."

Jose Maria rode away without further comment. The reference to the River Jordan lingered in the Major's mind. He slowly became aware that he was watching what could be a reenactment of another chapter from the Good Book.

It was the Exodus replayed.

Major Robert Neighbors leaned closer to the flickering light of the campfire, a stub of pencil in hand, muscles aching from the strenuous exertion of the river crossing.

The caravan had made the crossing without loss of life. The river had claimed only a handful of supplies. The full significance of the crossing had hit him only after all were safely on the north shore: The Indians of Texas were no more.

The "River Jordan" comment by Jose Maria clung to the Major's mind. There was no more apt description, no better way to put his own feelings of loss and despair into words. He again touched the pencil to the letter to Lizzie.

> If you want to hear a full description of our Exodus out of Texas read the Bible where the children of Israel crossed the Red Sea.
>
> Our enemies did not follow. If they had, the Indians would have in all probability sent them back without the interposition of Divine Providence . . .
>
> I am still in excellent health and hope that when I do get home that you will yet be satisfied with your old husband in place of taking the chances for a new one.
>
> I will be with you as soon as I can. Give my love and kisses to the children. I am as ever your truly affectionate
> Husband
> R. S. Neighbors.

Washita River, Indian Territory
September 1859

Major Robert Neighbors leaned over the makeshift table in the canvas tent that would serve as temporary agency headquarters for the Indians from Texas and signed the papers transferring his charges to the resident agent. His duties were at an end.

At least, he thought as he handed over the list of names of the relocated Indians and the possessions of each family, the transplanted tribes seemed pleased with their new home. The water and grass on the Washita was good, the soil almost as fertile as that they had left behind. There was plenty of timber for permanent homes. An adequate supply of game still roamed the forested hills.

The soldiers had left four days ago at the end of their escort duty, leaving behind only the teamsters, the Texas agents and civilian employees. Today they would be gone. A new piece of land would belong to the Indians. *Until,* the Major thought with a touch of disgust, *another group of white men decides it wants the same land.*

The Major shook hands with the new agent, stepped from the tent into the mild September sunlight and stopped short at the sight that greeted him.

Almost a thousand warriors—Caddo, Waco, Tawakono, Anadarko, Keechi and others from the Brazos Agency, along with a smattering of Comanches from the Clear Fork—stood in line from the tent to the Major's camp two hundred yards away.

Jose Maria stood alone at the front of the line. Tears glistened at the corners of the Anadarko's black eyes as he reached out to embrace his old friend.

The Major felt the tightness build in his own chest as he hugged the Anadarko to him. "Ride safely home, old friend," Jose Maria said softly in the Major's ear. "Our hearts go with you."

"My own heart is empty at parting," the Major said, a catch in his voice, "yet it is full, that I have had such friends."

Jose Maria abruptly released his bear hug on the Major and stepped aside. A Tonkawa chief, tears streaming unashamed down his face, offered a handshake of farewell.

The Major worked his way slowly down the line, exchanging embraces or handshakes with each of the Indians. He found himself struggling to hold back his own tears by the time he reached the end of the line. The Comanche chief Sanaco was last in line, his body held erect and proud. The Major wondered if Sanaco planned to shake his hand or stab that big butcher knife into his gut.

Sanaco did neither.

He reached into a pocket and produced a small leather pouch. He opened the drawstring to show the contents: a braided strand of hair from a horse's tail, an Indian scalp, two bear's teeth, a perfectly formed flint arrowhead and a feather from the wing of an eagle. They were the most powerful symbols of the Comanche tribe. Sanaco solemnly drew the string shut, reached out and placed the medicine bag around the Major's neck, then stepped back.

"We were once enemies, Bear-Who-Walks-Like-Man," Sanaco said, "yet we share the same spirit. From this day onward forever, we are brothers."

The Major had to blink to keep his eyes from showing his emotions. "You do me great honor, Sanaco. I am proud to be brother to the great Comanche chief." He offered a hand and inclined his head as Sanaco accepted the handshake. Then the Major turned and strode toward the group of men awaiting his arrival at the campsite.

At his back he heard a rawhide drum begin to beat a slow cadence. The chant began in the Caddo tongue, a single voice raised from far back in the ranks of Indians. Another voice took up the chant in the Anadarko language, until finally almost a thousand voices were raised.

To anyone else it would have sounded like nothing more than a babble of conflicting tongues. To the Major it was the highest tribute ever paid him.

The Indian chant spoke of a bear who became a white man, a great warrior and hunter of much bravery, a man who spoke only the truth, who rode as friend and brother to all tribes, and who one day rode from their lodges into the lowering sun but whose spirit remained to guard the red men.

The Major swiped a thumb across the moisture on his cheeks. He had outwardly regained his composure when he reached the camp.

"What was all that about?" one of the teamsters asked.

The Major smiled. "Nothing much," he said. "Come on, men. Let's go home."

SIXTEEN

Belknap Road
September 1859

Shapley Ross squatted at Major Robert Neighbors's side as the big man sliced bacon into a skillet for the noon meal a day's ride from Belknap.

"I don't like the looks of this, Major," Ross said, his hand on the receiver of the carbine in his lap. "Leeper said he saw something move on that ridge to the west. I'm getting that itch on my scalp that says trouble's close by."

The Major let his gaze drift around the horizon. The nooning site was bracketed on the west by a rocky ridge and on the east by a steep, timbered ravine. There were twenty men in the homeward-bound party, most of them top hands with firearms. The Major shrugged. "Shapley, you're getting to be an old maid. Fretting all the way back from Indian Territory."

"Yeah," Ross said, "because there's Kickapoos in this area who don't like you much, a few wild Comanches who don't like anybody, plus Baylor's so-called 'minute men' and a few assorted horse thieves and killers who wouldn't mind seeing both of us lose our hair from unnatural causes. And every mother's son of them knows we've a price on our heads."

The Major turned his attention back to the skillet. Shapley Ross wasn't a man who spooked at shadows. "Have the men check their weapons and stay alert, just in case."

Ross nodded. "Already told them. Major, I wish you wouldn't go into Belknap. That place is crawling with Baylor men and others who would give up their *cojones* for a shot at you. Or me, for that matter."

The major half-smiled. "Shapley, nothing's going to happen in Belknap. The Indians are gone from Texas now. And it's the shortest route to San Antonio. I'm sort of in a hurry to get home to

Lizzie and the children, now that the Indians are in someone else's hands."

Ross nodded glumly. "I know better than to argue with an old badger like you, Major." The agent stood and strode toward a wagon a few yards away.

The Major checked his own rifle, both handguns and tested the edge of the big Bowie knife at his belt, then relaxed. The heartache he had felt at the parting with the Indians had faded a bit with the passing miles. Now he could feel the stirrings of a deep sense of relief. *For the first time in years,* he thought, *I can go home and stay there, meet little Ross Simpson, get to know Lizzie and the children again. No more couriers banging on the door in the middle of the night, no more riding in blizzards and rainstorms, no more political games to play. No more birthdays or Thanksgivings passing while I'm in the middle of nowhere.*

He almost burned the first few slices of bacon before he pulled his attention back to the present. He glanced around at his companions.

Shapley Ross stood by the wagon, rifle in hand, his gaze flicking constantly around the campsite. Ross's son Sul and Matthew Leeper also stood watch. They were good men and could handle themselves if anything happened. The Major wasn't sure how capable the others, most of them teamsters and other civilians, might be if it came to a fight. Three of the men stood guard over the horses picketed nearby.

"Major." Shapley Ross's soft call carried easily through the warm, unusually still air.

"What is it, Shapley?"

"That brown mule of mine's got his ears up again. I think he smells something."

The Major edged his Sharps carbine closer to his side. The brown mule was a better watchdog than any mongrel; he could smell an Indian a hundred yards away. If Leeper and Shapley Ross got a bit twitchy, that was one thing. When the mule got nervous it was time for some serious worry.

"Keep a sharp lookout—" The Major's call to Shapley ended abruptly as a dozen Indians boiled from the ravine, whooping and yelling. Rifles cracked from the lip of the gully. A ball whizzed past the Major's ear. He scooped up his rifle and threw himself to the side as another ball cracked into the skillet.

The Major heard the crack of Shapley Ross's carbine and the flatter boom of Leeper's shotgun. Then the first of the Indians reached the edge of the camp. The Major's breath caught as he found himself staring into the face of the Comanche Little Elk less than twenty yards away. Little Elk's rifle barrel came up; the Major rolled again as smoke billowed from the Indian's weapon. The ball kicked gravel and dust at the Major's elbow. The Major leveled the Sharps and pulled the trigger. The heavy ball slammed into the Comanche's chest and tumbled him backward into the tall grass. The Major dropped the Sharps and pulled his Colt.

The rattle of gunfire was almost constant for a few seconds. Over the crack of rifles and bark of pistols the Major heard Leeper cry out in shock and pain. The Major fired almost point-blank into the face of one Comanche, slapped a shot at a second and missed. He dove behind the scant cover of his saddle, steadied his aim and shot an Indian who had crept up behind the wagons. Shapley Ross calmly knelt and fired his revolver, his shots aimed and deadly. At the corner of his vision the Major saw gunsmoke bloom from the edge of the ravine; two Indians went down in that volley. Sul Ross and a half dozen teamsters had flanked the attackers. They poured a heavy fire into the Indian ranks.

The ambush ended moments later in a clatter of hooves as the Comanches gave up the fight and fled for their lives. The Major lay still for a moment, breathing hard and his heart pounding in the sudden quiet, until he was sure there would be no other attack.

The Major scrambled to his feet and made a quick survey of the site. Three Comanches lay dead inside the camp itself. Agent Leeper had been hit hard. He lay by one of the wagons, moaning in pain from gunshot wounds to the abdomen, leg and wrist. One of the teamsters had a minor wound, little more than a scratch. Sul Ross's group filtered back to the camp, none of them injured.

Shapley Ross knelt beside Leeper, doing what he could to stop the bleeding. The Major snorted the acrid scent of dust, powder smoke and blood from his nostrils and strode to the spot where Little Elk had gone down.

The Comanche lay on his back, sightless eyes opened wide to the bright sky. The heavy Sharps ball had slammed into his breastbone. The Major didn't bother to turn the dead man over. He knew what a fifty-caliber ball did to a man's body when fired at close range. He walked back to where Leeper lay half-conscious and in growing agony.

"How bad is it, Shapley?" he asked.

Shapley shook his head. "Bad enough, Major. We've got to get him to a surgeon quick or he won't make it."

The Major barked a series of orders. Moments later the mules were hitched and horses saddled. Three of the party's mounts were gone, stolen during the fight. One of the teamsters started to pick up the skillet and coffeepot.

"Leave the equipment," the Major said. "We have to get Leeper into Belknap in a hurry." He swung aboard his horse and moved out at a brisk trot.

Near the top of a hill a quarter mile away, Emil Washburn lowered his spyglass and spat a stream of tobacco juice. "The damn Injun didn't get the job done," he groused.

"Neighbors got away?"

"Free, clear, big and ugly, Nat," Washburn said. He shrugged. "But at least he done us one favor. He shut Little Elk up for us. That Comanche knew too much for his own good." Washburn flashed a quick grin. "Besides, I've got a little surprise set up for Neighbors at Belknap. Always have another trap ready, Nat, and you don't get et up by a bear."

Belknap

Major Robert Neighbors sat at a borrowed desk in the office of District Clerk William Burkett's office and finished his report of the fight on the Belknap Road.

"How's Agent Leeper doing?" Burkett asked.

"Holding his own. The surgeons say if there's no infection he'll live," the Major said. He leaned back in the chair and sighed. "Mister Burkett, I've seen enough of death and treachery for two men's lifetimes. Now I'm free from all responsibility to my government, free to return to my wife and children. I've a son I've never seen, and I'm looking forward to making his acquaintance. I don't plan to leave my family again until my time on this earth ends."

He pushed the chair back, flexed his shoulders and stood. "I thought about writing Lizzie, but with any luck at all I'll beat the letter home. I'm going to check on Agent Leeper. Would you care to come along?"

The clerk shook his head. "I've work to finish up here, Major, but give him my wishes for a speedy and complete recovery. Will you be leaving soon, sir?"

"Within the day, God willing." He offered a hand to the clerk. "Thank you for your hospitality, Mister Burkett. And for your support during my stay on the Brazos."

The Major strode from the door, nodded to an acquaintance lounging against the wall and stepped into the street for the short walk to the hospital two blocks away. The day held the first hint of coming autumn, a fresh brisk feel to the air. Autumn was his favorite time of year along Salado Creek, when the sumac turned scarlet and the cottonwoods and oaks were swathed in reds and golds. *God, it's going to be good to get home,* he thought as he strode past a narrow alley.

"Robert Neighbors!"

The call snapped the Major's musings. He stopped and stared for a moment at the man before him. The man held a pistol in his right hand.

"Are you speaking to me, sir?"

"I am, Neighbors. My name is Patrick Murphy. I hear you've been calling me a horse thief and a liar."

The Major dropped his own hand to the butt of the Colt in his pistol belt. "No, sir, I never did."

The Major heard a slight rustle behind him and started to turn. A massive fist suddenly slammed into his back, hammered him forward into the dirt of the street. He heard the muffled whump of the shotgun blast, the sound of footsteps running away. The sounds were near, yet somehow seemed distant. He tried to push himself onto his elbows, to lift his cheek from the dirt of the street. He did not have the strength. It was as if only his mind still moved. *God, not now,* he thought. *Please, not now!* He heard the sound of someone running toward him.

Sheriff Ed Wolfforth knelt at the Major's side, slid a callused hand under the Major's cheek and lifted his head from the dust. "Who shot you, Major Neighbors?"

Robert Simpson Neighbors did not reply. His broad shoulders shuddered once and were still.

Ed Wolfforth removed his hat, slipped it beneath the Major's bearded cheek and lowered his head gently. The Major's light jacket was scorched and still smoldered from the shotgun blast.

The sheriff glanced around the faces of the gathering crowd. "Did anyone see who did this?"

One man stepped forward. "Yes, sir. It was Patrick Murphy's brother-in-law. Ed Cornett. The Major here was talking to Murphy. Cornett stepped up behind him, shoved a double-barrel shotgun against his back and pulled both triggers."

Sheriff Wolfforth stood and stared for a moment at the big man lying dead in the street. *Dammit all to hell,* the sheriff fumed inwardly, *why is it always the good men who get killed?* The sheriff glanced at the man who had identified the gunman. "Get a judge and a warrant. Mister Burkett, stay with the body until the inquest. The rest of you come with me. We're going after that damn backshooter!"

District Clerk William Burkett knelt beside the big body in the street and swallowed against the knot in his throat. *After all he went through, it came to this,* Burkett thought. *It wasn't enough to take one dream away from the Major. They had to take this one too. All he had wanted to do now was go home.*

EPILOGUE

Major Robert Simpson Neighbors was buried in the civilian cemetery at Fort Belknap near the reservation land his Indians had been forced to abandon. A Texas State Historical Marker now stands near his grave.

Elizabeth Mays Neighbors continued to make her home in San Antonio, as best the author can determine.

Shapley Prince Ross returned to his home in Waco, Texas, where he lived until his death on September 17, 1889. He was buried in Waco.

Lawrence Sullivan "Sul" Ross was later appointed a captain of the Texas Rangers and is most frequently remembered as the leader of the Ranger force that attacked the Comanche village of Peta Nacona on the Pease River, a strike which resulted in the recapture of the legendary captive Cynthia Ann Parker. Sul later enlisted as a private in the Confederate Army and rose to the rank of brigadier general. In 1880 he was elected to the Texas Senate and took office as governor in 1887. He was a major force in the development of the public education system in Texas. He died January 3, 1898, after becoming ill on a hunting trip along the Navasota River, and was buried in Waco. Sul Ross University is named in his honor.

John R. Baylor never faced charges for his part in the white uprising along the Brazos River. After the Indians were removed from the state he made his home on a ranch near Weatherford and took little part in public life until the outbreak of the Civil War, when he joined the Confederacy and became lieutenant colonel of the Second Regiment of Texas Mounted Rifles. After the war he lived for a time in San Antonio and finally settled at Montell, Texas, where he died February 6, 1894.

John S. "Rip" Ford continued in the service of the Texas Rangers and commanded operations in the Cortinas War on the Rio Grande. He served as colonel in the Second Texas Cavalry in the Rio Grande during the Civil War, and in later life became a publisher, scholar and author. He died in San Antonio on November 3, 1897.

Ed Cornett, the slayer of Major Neighbors, was "killed while attempting to escape" by a posse soon after the Major's death. The motive for the killing was never solidly established.

The fate of Peter Garland is unknown to the author.

The characters of Hiram and Harris Oldham, Emil Washburn and the Comanche Little Elk are strictly fictional, composites of various factions who conspired against the Texas Indian reservation concept. No similarity to any persons, living or dead, is intended in these characters.

About the Author

Gene Shelton is a lifelong Texas resident, raised on a ranch in the Panhandle. As a youth he worked as a ranch hand and horse trainer, and rode the amateur rodeo circuit as a bull rider and calf roper.

He is the author of *Last Gun, Captain Jack, Rawhider* and *Tascosa Gun,* also in the *Texas Legends* series, as well as two other acclaimed Western novels, *Track of the Snake* and *Day of the Scorpion.* He has been an active member of the Western Writers of America, Inc., since 1981.

A newspaperman by trade, he has been a reporter for the *Amarillo News* and *Globe-Times* and the *Dallas Times Herald.* His most recent assignments were as managing editor of the *Sulphur Springs News-Telegram* and as copy editor for the *Tyler Courier-Times.* He has also written numerous magazine articles for *The Quarter Horse Journal, The Ranchman,* and *Black Belt Magazine.*

He has taught fiction-writing classes at several colleges and universities in the East Texas area.